PRAISE FOR RUTH DUGDALL
AND *THE WOMAN BEFORE ME*

'Authentic…diverting.'
Daily Mail

'Hypnotic…gripping and powerful.'
Shotsmag

'Dark, disturbing and authentic.'
Crime Writers' Association

'Impressive in its unflinching realism,
this is a dark and haunting psychological thriller
that possesses both depth and sensitivity.'
Crime Time

Ruth Dugdall is a British crime writer. She worked for almost a decade in the criminal justice system as a probation officer, specialising in the most extreme crimes when she was seconded to a high security prison. *The Woman Before Me* is her first novel to feature Cate Austin.

RUTH DUGDALL

THE WOMAN BEFORE ME

TEXT PUBLISHING MELBOURNE AUSTRALIA

textpublishing.com.au

The Text Publishing Company
Swann House
22 William Street
Melbourne Victoria 3000
Australia

This edition published by The Text Publishing Company in 2012
First published by Legend Press in 2010

Cover design by W.H. Chong

Printed in Australia by Griffin Press, an Accredited ISO AS/NZS 14001:2004 Environmental Management System printer

National Library of Australia Cataloguing-in-Publication entry (pbk)
Author: Dugdall, R. E.
Title: The woman before me / Ruth Dugdall.
ISBN: 9781921922893 (pbk.)
ISBN: 9781921961168 (ebook.)
Subjects: Bereavement—Fiction.
Infants—Death—Fiction.
Obsessive-compulsive disorder—Fiction.
Adultery—Fiction.
Psychological fiction.
Epistolary fiction.
Dewey Number: 823.92

This book is printed on paper certified against the Forest Stewardship Council® Standards. Griffin Press holds FSC chain-of-custody certification SGS-COC-005088. FSC promotes environmentally responsible, socially beneficial and economically viable management of the world's forests.

For Margaret Dugdall, my mum.

Who tells stories like other people breathe and taught me that even the most painful of happenings can be beautifully told.

With love and thanks.

BEFORE

1

Creeping across the threshold, I listen to the silence of the sleeping house. These middle hours, between three and four in the morning when deepest sleep can be reached, make the kitchen seem larger and emptier than in daylight. Different. Although the difference is me. This time I'm saying goodbye.

The fragrance of Emma is everywhere, the delicate tang of her green apple perfume. That small wooden box, holding an assortment of tea bags, on the shelf – I'll never again see her bend over it, her hair falling like a veil, sweeping it away as she dithers over her selection. And Luke. She told me I'll never see him again.

There's a large picture on the wall, a print of the Eiffel Tower, a place she visited on her first honeymoon. On the work surface are unwashed plates, remains of their last meal encrusted on the cutlery. I thought she was so neat, but then I never really knew her. Not like you did.

Through the kitchen into the large dining room, I move slowly. I don't want to miss a thing. I want to capture the memory of it. That is where we've sat, Emma and I, cradling hot cups of tea. I notice the red paint on the walls, the white pine of the window seat. On the table is a packet of Silk Cut cigarettes, a box of matches. She's supposed to have given up, but today has been a hard day.

I see myself, reflected in a small mirror above the seat. I'm shocked by what my face reveals: there are flushed, red patches on my cheeks and forehead, my eyes are black. Curious, I look closer and see my pupils are fully dilated. I look excited, aroused even.

Momentarily, my heart palpitates; my hands are clammy with sweat. This must be the nervous thrill that burglars feel. But I won't steal anything. Emma was the thief, not me. I've only ever taken one thing from this house: the back door key. Secretly copied, and then returned to its hook.

I climb quietly up the stairs, avoiding places I know would groan under my weight. Night-lights illuminate the hall, making me blink. Emma's door is ajar and I can see into the bedroom. Her curtains are open and the moon is full.

Emma sleeps facing the window, the duvet pulled high on her face. Next to her is the bulk of a man, hidden under the bedding. Dominic. Entering their bedroom, I creep up to her foetal shape, studying her perfect ear, her cheek, her blonde hair turned ashen in the half-light, and wonder if I could touch her without her waking. Only inches separate me from her sleeping body.

She turns and my muscles tense. Then I realise that she's moving to the rhythm of troubled dreams. She now lies half facing me and I can see the crease on her brow, the tightness of her mouth. Have I caused that, or are you to blame?

Leaving Emma I walk further along the hall to the nursery, snaking behind the half-closed door. Inside the small room is the beautiful baby boy, asleep in his cot. Luke is surrendered on his back, hands fisted against the blanket, face peacefully fallen, soft skin and round fat cheeks. Usually I just watch him sleep, but tonight that isn't enough.

He's familiar with my touch and smell. He stirs when I lift him and I think I hear a voice in the next room. I pause but hear nothing. His weight is natural to me, I cradle him expertly, one arm along his body, my hand on his thigh. Luke is so peaceful in my arms, head nestled to my chest.

I love him, love him fiercely.

I hear something in the next room; I freeze, waiting, and the noise becomes louder. Low whispers and then moaning. The repetitive sound of the bed banging against the wall. Careful not to wake Luke, I place him back in his cot and make my way from his room, passing the bedroom where Emma's moans are getting louder. "Yes, yes, yes, yes, yes."

2

I'm still asleep when I hear loud knocking at the front door. I think it's you, hope it is, but it's the police. They've come for me. We know you were in the house, they say. There was a fire, they say. Then they tell me that Luke is dead and the air goes from my lungs. They want me to help them with their enquiries and I say I will.

I'm led down stairs and locked into a police cell: grey painted walls and a bench fixed to the wall. No fresh air. The door is unlocked and a man enters. He's going bald and wears a short-sleeved shirt, his arms are sunburnt and peeling. "I'm Mike Hogg, duty solicitor."

He doesn't sit or look directly at me, but scribbles on a jotter. He asks nothing that matters, just if I'm suicidal, if I'm hungry. I ask him if it's true, if Luke is really dead. He says yes, but that we had better not talk about that.

Next I'm taken by a uniformed police officer to an interview room. It is small and dim with high windows and a wooden desk, like you'd find in a school. Sat behind the desk, a different police officer – in a suit, not a uniform – unwraps a black disc, slides it into the recorder. He chats to Mr Hogg, who sits next to me. They ask after each other's wives. This must be normal for them, something they do every day, so they don't notice that I'm shaking. Mr Hogg tells the police officer about his holiday in Greece, how his son learned to swim in the sea.

I feel closed in, lost. How can they chat about holidays when a baby has died? It takes all my energy to sit in the chair and not collapse. I'm tired and heavy and dull, as though my brain has been switched off. All I can think about is Luke.

Finally, ready to begin, the police officer leans back. He takes a cigarette packet from his inside pocket, showing the gold box first to Mr Hogg, and then offers it to me. "It's hard, this smoking ban. But you can take one for later, if you like?"

"No, thank you."

"No? But then you don't smoke B & H, do you, Rose? Silk Cut is your brand, isn't it?"

Somewhere in the distance my brain registers what he's implying.

He presses the record button and a red light comes on. He speaks slowly and deliberately. "This is Sergeant West. Also in the room are…"

"Mike Hogg. Duty Solicitor."

West points at me and I say, "Rose Wilks."

"I have read Miss Wilks her rights. This interview is commenced on Sunday 6th June at 11.26 a.m. Now, Miss Wilks. Can you tell me when you last visited the house of Emma and Dominic Hatcher?"

"Yesterday."

"For the benefit of the tape, yesterday was Saturday June 5th. And what were you doing there?"

"I was babysitting Luke." His name catches in my throat. I grip the chair to keep my hands from shaking.

"And what was your relationship with the Hatchers?"

"We're friends. Luke is – was – like a son. I babysat for him a lot. Emma is my friend."

"I see. And what time did you leave the Hatchers' home on Saturday?"

"When they got back from their trip to Southwold. They were back earlier than they said they would be. It was about four in the afternoon."

"And did you return at any point that evening?" he asks.

"No."

"No? Can you speak clearly for the benefit of the recording, please?"

"No, I did not return that evening."

"You are absolutely certain about that? You didn't go back into the house? You need to think about what you are saying; anything you fail to disclose now but tell us later will be used against you."

"I returned early this morning. Around three."

Sergeant West's jaw loosens. He hadn't expected me to admit this and a smile ghosts his lips then fades away.

Mr Hogg shifts in his seat. "I want to stop this interview and speak to Rose alone, before the interview goes any further."

West shoots him a look of contempt, betraying their earlier friendly chat. But I don't want to speak to Mr Hogg alone. I want to tell the truth. I'm intent on the recorder trapping my voice, trapping my words in that plastic casing forever.

"I went back to see Luke at three this morning."

"Rose, I really think you should…" interrupts Mr Hogg.

Sergeant West ignores him. "How did you get in?"

I feel the warm metal on a necklace around my neck. My precious key.

"The back door was unlocked. Emma is careless about things like that."

"And did you go to Luke's room?"

"Yes."

"Did you light a cigarette?"

"No! I would never smoke around him."

"Did you drop a cigarette as you left, starting a fire in the house?"

"No!"

"I will ask you again: did you light a cigarette in the Hatchers' home?"

"No. I did not."

"A cigarette started that fire and you admit to being there, in the early hours of the morning."

"But Emma smokes! It would have been hers. She was awake when I left. She was having sex with her husband."

Sergeant West looks at me with undisguised contempt. "Mrs Hatcher was alone last night. Her husband was sleeping elsewhere. She was alone and asleep and you were in her home, holding their son who shortly after died in a fire. How can you explain that?"

I close my eyes, hot tears behind my eyelids.

"Rose Wilks, did you start a fire in Luke Hatcher's bedroom?" Sergeant West says the words slowly, giving each one weight. Mr Hogg shifts beside me.

I summon all my strength and lean forward, whispering into the speaker as if my words are only for its benefit. I speak low, my mouth touching the plastic. "No." And then I can't stop myself, because I'm tired and Luke is dead and I can't bear any of it. "No, no, no, no, no."

3

It's Monday. I spent last night in a police cell and this morning the magistrates refused bail, so I've been remanded into custody. I'm led into a white van and a guard shackles me into a tiny booth. A few years ago protesters blocked the Felixstowe docks, worried about how animals destined for slaughter were transported. No-one protests about prisoners, though.

I feel sick. I never travel well, and I'm facing the side, my back to the window. I can only see out if I twist my neck. Someone's in the next booth, but I can only see the top of a head, brown hair, thick and wavy. No-one's told me where we're going.

It's a long journey and the sickness doesn't ease. There's no drink, no toilet break. I'm exhausted, I haven't slept for two nights. I want Luke, I ache for him.

After an hour the van slows and gates are opened for us to drive through. When we stop I hear women's voices, some with an Essex accent. The prisoner next to me is removed, the door is slammed shut and we are on our way again.

The guard in the back of the van sleeps and I listen to the sound of his snoring, the sound of the engine. I watch the service stations and motorway cafes flash by. I'm so tired that I doze off, waking to find the van has stopped and the guard is opening the door.

A voice shouts, "Just the one?" and then a burly female

officer pulls me from the back of the van. She has a clipboard, like a holiday rep, but she isn't smiling. "Wilks?"

"Yes."

She ticks her sheet and unshackles me. My wrists are sore and I rub them, breathing in the rancid smell of rotting waste.

"Welcome to Holloway," she says.

I'm marched past hospital-style green screens where a woman dressed only in her underwear is having her hair inspected by an officer. I see her place a watch and jewellery into a plastic tray. I can't give up my key. It's the only thing I have left, now Luke is gone. The only thing that links him to me.

"Please? I need to use the loo."

"Through there. But leave the door open."

The officer is moving around the corridor, chatting to someone. Quickly, I remove the key from my neck and undo my jeans, squatting on the toilet seat.

I can't give up. Luke wouldn't want me to. The officer stops talking, turns and walks my way. I slide the key inside my vagina, wincing as it catches. I hitch up my jeans and the officer is standing in front of me.

"Hurry up, Wilks. Some of us have work to do."

I follow the officer back to where the hospital screens are.

"Take off your clothes and put them on the chair. Jewellery in the tray."

I lift off my top, unbuckle my jeans and step out of them, feeling the cold air on my skin. I remove my earrings and watch.

"Undies as well," she says. "Come on, I haven't got all day."

I unhook my bra and slide it off. My breasts are large with milk, the veins blue and prominent. I can feel her looking at them. I bend over and slide off my knickers, folding them in half. I haven't had a change of underwear for two days, or a shower. I feel dirty.

She grabs my knickers and opens them up, running a finger along the seam. She picks up my bra and feels the cups, then inspects my other clothes. She puts on gloves and sharply tugs at my hair, looking and pulling. I'm taller than her, so I have to bend over until my back aches.

"I haven't got nits."

"Not nits I'm looking for."

"Open." Her gloved finger circles my mouth, making me gag.

"Do you feel suicidal?"

"No."

She looks me up and down. I clench my legs together, hoping the ordeal is over. Please don't search inside me. She glances at the clock on the wall.

"Okay, get dressed. It's bang-up time."

I follow her through gates and corridors. A cell door is opened and I see two narrow metal beds, a sink to one side. To the right is a silver toilet, only partly screened. There's another woman in the cell, lying on a bed, drawing with wax crayons. She has a wide smile and a dozy, sleepy look. The officer throws a threadbare towel and a sheet on the unused bed. "I'll get you some nosh. You'll have to make do with whatever's left." She bangs the door behind her and locks me in.

I stand in the small cell, my hands shaking. The other woman stares at me, wide-eyed. She has mousy hair and grey eyes. On her lap is a drawing of a stick person and a house.

"Hello," she says, "would you like a sweet?" She opens her palm, revealing a squashed tube of Rolos.

"No thanks."

I sit on my bed, my fingers scratching the rough wool of the blanket.

"Are you okay?"

"No."

"You'll get used to it," she says, sucking chocolate off her fingers. "I've been in and out of prison since I was fifteen. They all know me here. They put me with the new ones so I can help them – sometimes they can't cope at first." She parrots the question I've been asked before. "You're not suicidal, are you?"

"No."

"You'll be alright," she says, with confidence. "Some of the new ones shake like kittens."

I hold my hands behind my back, glad she hasn't noticed that I am.

"What's your name?"

"Rose."

"That's a pretty name. I'm Jane." She smiles trustingly. "But friends call me Janie."

"I need to use the loo," I say.

"You don't need my permission." She points at the silver loo behind the half-screen.

"Would you mind not looking?"

She stares at me like I'm mad, then shrugs and rolls onto her side, so her back's to me. Behind the screen I slide my hand down my trousers, into my knickers. After a few moments I sigh, releasing the uncomfortable pressure I've been carrying for over an hour.

I pull the key into the light, rubbing it on the fabric of my jeans. My precious key. The only thing I have left.

4

I have waited nine months for the trial. The time a baby takes, though all that grows inside me is fear. Ipswich Crown Court isn't what I expected, not like the courtrooms I've seen in films. It's smaller, and darker, people whispering so you never know what's going on.

I've been brought up from the court cells to the dock. Makes me think of boats in a harbour, although I'm not sure if the barrier is to keep me safe, or to keep the people in the courtroom safe from me. My handcuffs are removed but either side of me sits a guard: a man and a woman, in identical grey and white uniforms. They're too close, and I can smell the vinegary tang of the man's body odour. Even if I could jump the railing and run, I'd never get past the mass of reporters outside. Seeing them was a shock. It makes no sense that they're interested in me. Just an ordinary woman caught up in a sad story about a boy who died.

I can hear voices in the public gallery, so I twist round and look up but what I see scares me. All those men and women leaning over, trying to get a good look, writing things about me in their notebooks.

At the front of the courtroom, behind a long desk, is a massive wooden chair with a gold crest above it and some Latin inscription. It's like a throne. Lower down, behind a smaller desk, sits a woman. Small and perfect, she has a glossy bob and a neat black suit and she's flicking through a thick file.

She must be reading about me, the lies people have told about me over the last nine months while I've been on remand.

I'm relieved when I see someone I know coming towards me. My barrister, Mr Thomas, is fat and rosy; he's wearing a black cloak over a pinstripe suite. He comes to the front of the dock, at least a foot below me, and I can see he's beginning to lose his hair.

"Right, show's on the road. The judge will be through any minute. Remember to stand when he comes in, and bow your head." He looks me over. "I like the suit, but undo a couple of buttons at the neck. Your hair would be better in a ponytail, make you look younger. And put some makeup on tomorrow. Not too much, you don't want to look like you're too confident, but it doesn't hurt to look pretty."

I rub my lips, knowing I'll never be pretty. I've not worn lipstick, or any other makeup, the whole time I've been on remand. My hair hasn't been cut either and it hangs like a dark veil.

"I'll have to ask Jason to bring me some makeup," I say, looking around for him.

"He's outside in the corridor. Like all the witnesses, he can't come into the court until after his testimony, which won't be for several days." He's told me the trial will last for two weeks.

A loud buzz makes everyone freeze and the room falls silent. Mr Thomas hastily takes his place on the front table and pulls on a wig. My guards stand, pulling me to my feet, just as the wooden door behind the throne opens.

It's the judge. He's terrifying in his red gown and white wig. He's got a long face with narrow slits for eyes. He reminds me of a wizard. The court is his home, and he takes his time, looking around and positioning his papers before taking his seat so everyone else can sit too.

"Madam Clerk?" he says, his voice loud and firm. "Have the jury been sworn in?"

The smart woman with the shiny bob turns round. "Yes, Your Honour."

I look over at the cluster of men and women for the first time and study them closely: those twelve people will decide my future. They look so ordinary, like people you'd see in a supermarket. One or two wear jackets, one man has a tie, but most just look like they're off to town. A woman in the front row is wearing a pretty floral dress, like this is an occasion for her. She's nervous, looking around and touching her dangly earrings. *Believe me*, I silently beg.

The clerk swivels to face me. "Rise please, and state your name."

"Rosemary Ann Wilks." I hope no-one can hear the tremor in my voice.

"Rosemary Wilks, you are charged with the murder of Luke Hatcher. How do you plead?"

"Not guilty," I say, as firmly as I'm able.

She scribbles something on the file. "In relation to the alternative charge of manslaughter, how do you plead?"

I look at Mr Thomas, who nods. "Not guilty."

"May the defendant be seated?"

The judge looks bored. "Sit. Prosecution may begin."

Almost immediately a dwarfish man in a black gown and a white wig jumps up. He walks over to the jury and studies each face then opens his arms wide and shouts, "Sometimes, things are not as they seem. And sometimes our closest friends can be the enemy. Take a moment to look at Rosemary Wilks. An average-looking woman, mid-twenties. Someone you might invite to your home for a cup of tea?"

He pauses, turns to me. They all stare like I'm a circus freak.

"That was what Emma Hatcher thought, when she let Rosemary Wilks into her home, never guessing what evil intentions lurked behind that ordinary face."

He moves slowly to the centre of the room, an actor taking centre stage.

"This woman systematically stalked Emma Hatcher, prowling her home in the night as Emma slept, destroying personal possessions and, worst of all, pretending to others that Emma's son, Luke, was her son. She even went so far as to breastfeed him."

The woman in pink draws a sharp breath.

"And when Emma discovered this, and told the defendant that she could no longer see her or her son, what did she do? She went into their home at night, and started a fire. Luke Hatcher died of smoke inhalation, his tiny body charred by fire. This woman, this average woman who could be anybody's friend, anybody's mother, murdered Luke Hatcher. And over the course of this trial, ladies and gentlemen, I shall prove it."

As he takes his seat it scrapes the wooden floor, making me shudder.

Mr Thomas lets the murmuring quieten before speaking. His voice is even and without theatrics.

"I too would ask you to look at Rose Wilks. I too would ask you to consider that she looks average. The kind of woman you would invite home, the kind of woman who could be your friend. And I will show you, ladies and gentlemen of the jury, that Rose Wilks looks like this because that is exactly what she is. An average woman, who is not to blame for the tragic death of Luke Hatcher – a boy whom Rose loved. It is unjust that this woman has been charged with murder and remanded in prison for nine months. Let us stop the injustice now, ladies and gentlemen. Let me persuade you that Rose Wilks is as she appears. She is innocent."

On the second day of the trial Emma takes the stand. I haven't seen her since the day Luke died, and I would have walked past her in the street without recognising her. Grief has eaten into her, taken her angel face and made it sharp. She was a small woman anyway, a petite ballerina compared to me, but now she's like a starved child. She sits in the witness box like

15

a shadow. The clerk has to ask her to speak up twice, and the usher fetches tissues and water.

I want her to look at me, want to meet her eyes. Once we were best friends and we both loved Luke. Now we are both grieving. Seeing her across the room, her head bowed, her thin body, my heart aches. Even her hair, which she was so proud of, looks lank and uncared for. *Oh Emma, please look at me.*

She's asked, delicately and then more directly, about my 'unnatural relationship' with Luke. She talks in monotone, mumbling one-word answers, and the prosecution barrister looks peeved. He gives up and the questioning is handed over to Mr Thomas.

"Mrs Hatcher, when you left your son with Rose Wilks, did you trust her with him?"

"Yes."

"Did you have any reason to believe that she might want to harm your son?"

"No."

"Did you ever see her behave in any way that caused you concern?"

"When Nurse Hall told me that…"

"Did you *see* anything, Mrs Hatcher?"

"No. I didn't."

"One further question, if I may. Do you smoke?"

Emma looks ashen. "I did. Only when I was stressed."

"You were stressed the night of the fire, weren't you, Mrs Hatcher?"

"Yes."

"Do you mind me asking why that was?"

The silence drags out until she finally says, "I had an argument with my husband."

"Did you smoke that evening?"

I have to lean forward to hear her answer: "No. I didn't have any cigarettes in the house."

"No further questions, Your Honour."

Emma is helped from the witness stand. Not once did she look my way.

Dominic Hatcher stares at me the whole time. His look tells me that if he had a gun, he would shoot me dead. He's flushed, black-eyed and very angry. The prosecution tries to calm him down, but every answer he gives is louder than the one before. I shrink back into the wood.

He says I was always at their house. He says he never trusted me.

Mr Thomas softens his voice, as if to show his self-control next to Dominic's aggression. "Mr Hatcher, you say you always mistrusted Rosemary Wilks. Is that right?"

"Yes. I never liked her."

It stings to hear it, even though I always knew he hated me. He was jealous of my friendship with Emma, of how close we were.

"I wonder if you can explain to the jury how it was that this woman whom you never trusted, never liked, was left to care for your son while you enjoyed a day out at the races?"

"I didn't like her. She gave me the creeps. But I never thought she was a murdering bitch."

"Objection, Your Honour."

"Sustained. Mr Hatcher, please restrain yourself," says the judge.

Mr Thomas continues, "One more question, if I may. Were you at home the night your son died?"

"No. I was sleeping at the boarding school. I work there as a head teacher and when –"

"You were away from the house, is that correct?"

"Yes."

"Why was that, Mr Hatcher?"

He sighs, breathing out slowly. "Because Emma and I had an argument. About that bitch."

Dominic glares across at me as he leaves the stand.

It is four days since the trial began, and Nurse Hall is called forward. My favourite nurse from the hospital, she doesn't look comfortable in the courtroom. She speaks softly, touches her mouth often. Mr Thomas goes up to the witness box first.

"Thank you for coming today, Miss Hall. It can't be easy getting time off from a children's ward. I imagine it is a heartrending job?"

"It can be, yes."

"You say you met Rose Wilks in the hospital when she was in labour with her son?"

"That's right. Her son Joel was in intensive care. I took special note of Rose, as I knew it was so hard for her, him being so poorly. But it was still a shock when he died."

I clench my stomach.

"And how did Miss Wilks react to her son's death?"

"She was devastated. And so was her partner. They were just in pieces."

"Not the behaviour of someone capable of murder?"

"Objection!" shouts the prosecution. "Nurse Hall is a nurse, not a psychologist."

"Sustained," the Judge says, "please rephrase, Mr Thomas."

"Miss Hall, did you ever doubt that Rose loved her son Joel?"

"Never." Her voice is louder than before.

"And when you saw her in the cafe with Luke did she show him anything other than care and affection?"

"She was very attentive."

I catch the eye of the woman on the jury, the one in pink, to make sure she's heard.

"So, although she may have been overly involved with Luke, perhaps as a result of losing her own son, there were no signs that she wanted to harm him?"

"Not harm, no." Miss Hall pauses. "But when I saw she was breastfeeding him I thought that was odd."

Mr Thomas is prepared for this. "Odd, maybe. But not harmful?"

"I suppose not."

"In fact, in other cultures it is quite common for babies to be nursed by women who are not their mothers. In this country it was not so long ago that wealthy women would employ wet nurses."

"I believe so." She sounds uncertain.

"Thank you. No further questions."

I feel warmth flood my heart for Nurse Hall. I want to call over to the woman in pink, *See, I loved Luke. I would never hurt him!*

Mr Thomas waits until Nurse Hall has left the witness stand before turning to the audience.

"Ladies and gentleman of the jury, it is for you to decide. Does the woman before you seem capable of murder? Or does she seem a normal woman, a woman who loved her son Joel, who bore the terrible loss of his death, and was then caught up in a tragic set of circumstances? Could we not look at this sorry woman who has been accused and admit that 'There, but for the grace of God, go I?'

"Rose admits to being in Luke's bedroom on the night he died. She should not have been there, she admits it. She should not have given in to her love and breastfed the boy. But she was grieving for her own son and depressed.

"She is adamant that she did not smoke in the Hatchers' house. By Mrs Hatcher's own admission she too is a smoker. Mrs Hatcher had argued with her husband that night and was unhappy; the cigarette that started the fire may have been hers. Whatever the case, however the tragic accident occurred, one thing is certain: Rose Wilks did not deliberately start the fire that killed Luke Hatcher.

"I put it to you that the proper verdict is that Rose Wilks is not guilty of murder. She is not guilty of manslaughter."

NOW

5

"Hurry up, Amelia. We'll be late!"

Cate was pouring milk over Amelia's Rice Krispies. She had already buttered a piece of burnt toast for her own breakfast. Hearing no sign that her daughter was on her way down, she took the stairs two at a time, and found Amelia on her bed amid a heap of dolls and teddies, still in vest and knickers.

"Why aren't you dressed?"

"I'm tired." Amelia flopped onto the bed. "I want to stay here."

Cate retrieved the pink dress she had laid out from the floor. "Arms up," she commanded, pulling it over her daughter's blonde hair. This was Tim's fault; he'd returned her late the night before even though Cate had asked him not to. Amelia was always tired and cranky after spending a weekend with him.

"Ow, Mummy. You're hurting."

Ignoring her protests, Cate grabbed Amelia's sandals, pushing them onto struggling feet and tightening the straps. "Right. Come on – breakfast. Quickly!"

Amelia reluctantly followed her downstairs, plonked herself on a chair in front of the soggy cereal, and whined, "I don't want Krispies. I want Cheerios."

"Just eat them."

Irritated, Cate saw it was nearly 8.30. She still had to drop Amelia at her childminder Julie's house, and then drive down the coast to Bishop's Hill Prison. She was going to be late. Throwing an apple and a sandwich in her bag, she turned to see that Amelia's hunched shoulders were shaking. Torn between anger and pity, Cate begged, "Please don't cry, Amelia."

"But I wanted Cheerios," she sobbed. "Daddy lets me."

Giving in, Cate grabbed a clean bowl, filled it with Cheerios, sloshing the milk on the kitchen counter in her haste, and placed the bowl in front of Amelia. "Now eat them. Quickly!"

Amelia's insistence on Cheerios had cost Cate valuable minutes. After dropping her off at Julie's she drove to the prison and rushed into the entrance.

She waited patiently, catching her breath. The prison officers behind the reinforced glass continued talking to each other, ignoring her, so she banged on the window and pushed her ID card under the grille.

"Cate Austin. Probation Officer. Reporting for my first day."

Once she was inside the prison Officer Dave Callahan showed her around. He looked to be in his early fifties, with suspiciously dark hair and a body that was muscle gone to fat. He had probably been attractive in his youth, and held on to the illusion that he still was. Flirting with Cate, he escorted her around the units, making a show of chivalry by opening every one of the barred gates, but not showing her the respect of addressing her by name. When she asked him to cut out calling her 'love' and 'sweetheart', he just laughed in reply. She was going to have problems with him.

"So what makes a pretty girl like you want to work in a prison?"

"Well, I would have been a pilot, but I don't like heights," she retorted dryly, as Callahan's booming laugh reverberated round the walls.

"This used to be a training farm for men who were going off to the colonies."

"Really?"

"Yeah, young farmers got taught to work the land, then pissed off for a new life in Australia. Wouldn't mind emigrating myself. Now it's two prisons, one for men and one for women. The men's side is 'open', so you'll see cons wandering around, just like those farm boys, getting ready to leave. Some have been inside for years, at the end of long sentences, but if they're here it means we can trust them to work locally. They're Category D – low risk."

"I'm going to be based on the women's side."

"That's a different kettle of fish altogether, that's why they're behind the wall. Female cons aren't categorised, but if they were those bitches would be category A. Evil, some of 'em. It's too late to teach 'em to be proper women. They'd rather be out burgling and scoring drugs than looking after their kids."

They walked down a slope leading to a separate building with a flat roof. The sign on the wall said "Hospital Wing".

Callahan unlocked the external doors and led Cate into a corridor of cells, where the walls had been painted white rather than grey. The hospital wing didn't deserve its name. It was still just a prison landing, but with posters telling visitors to wash their hands and a torn diagram of a skeleton tacked to the wall. The cells were still locked, with an observation window of about thirty centimetres by ten, meaning there could never be any privacy, even for the sick. A woman was in the office, bent over a newspaper. She was wearing a starched nursing jacket instead of the usual white shirt and black tie. Cate guessed that whatever medical training she had received would be scant and it was unlikely she deserved that watch fob pinned to her chest like a medal.

At the sound of their footsteps, she looked up and came forward. She was slightly built and wore black trousers with steel-capped boots. She reminded Cate of one of those games of Amelia's, where you were dealt the tops and bottoms of people, and had to match them up. With the top half of a nurse and the bottom of a prison officer, this woman was a match Amelia would never have made. She offered the woman a hand, and introduced herself.

"I'm Cate Austin. The new probation officer."

"Kelley Todd. Principal medical officer."

"It's my first day working here."

Todd dismissed her in one glance, as if to say she knew as much.

Callahan had pushed behind them into the office, and was leafing through the *Daily Star*. "How's that poor bitch who got roughed up?" he said.

"Susan Thomas? Well, she needed stitches, but she'll mend. She's keeping her trap shut, though – she won't say who attacked her."

"Mind if I have a go at jogging her memory?"

"Be my guest."

Callahan threw the paper into the bin and led Cate towards the furthest cell in the block.

The cell was quite large and the bed was hospital issue, with a mechanism for lowering the height by foot. In the bed, a grey blanket pulled high to her chin, was a young woman of about eighteen. She had black stitches criss-crossing a wound on her brow and forehead, and her jaw was swollen. What struck Cate most were her eyes, wide with fear.

"Watcha, Thomas. Say hello to the new probation girl."

Thomas cautiously watched Cate, and she responded by smiling warmly, willing the poor girl to relax. She wished she could have a moment alone with her, just to calm her.

"You gonna say who did this to you?"

Thomas's voice was barely a whisper. "No, sir."

Callahan leaned heavily on the bed, his hand pinning the

blanket at one side and his voice low. "You sure you won't be persuaded?"

Thomas shook her head as much as she was able, fighting tears.

"Okay…If that's your final word. You'll be pleased to know you'll be shipped out tomorrow."

The patient managed a slight smile, and Callahan chuckled, tapping Cate on the arm. "Let's get out of here." As he locked the cell door he said, "She's scared stiff, poor cow."

"You said she'd be shipped out. Where to?"

"Anywhere that's not here. It's standard to send cons to another prison after they've been roughed up. Gets 'em out of the way."

Callahan led her out of the hospital wing and into the fresh air, where seagulls screeched, begging for scraps. They walked across an unkempt grass area, where empty cigarette packs and other litter had been discarded.

"Animals. They just chuck the rubbish out of their cell windows." Cate looked up at the cells, where two arms from adjacent windows were reaching across, to each other, finally managing to grasp fingers. Callahan shouted, "Oy!" and they dropped their hold.

"This is the Reception Unit." Callahan led her to an area near the entrance to the prison. "Let's go see Wimpy Wayne."

In the room there was a long table with several empty plastic trays lined up, a few medical screens and, in the corner, a gormless-looking man in black-rimmed spectacles huddled over a pile of paperwork. When Callahan shouted, "Oy!" again, he jumped and a fly that had been resting on his head buzzed into the air. He pushed the glasses further up his nose, still holding the pen, a smudge of red ink marking his forehead.

"Come over here," Callahan ordered, and Wayne slid from his chair and obediently shuffled over, shoulders hunched. He still held the red biro, the end of which was chewed to pieces.

Cate offered a hand, which Wayne looked at with surprise before grasping. "Cate Austin. The new probation officer."

He bobbed his head enthusiastically. "Wayne Bugg. I do the processing for the induction procedures."

She looked around and nodded at the plastic trays on the long table. "What are those for?"

"When a girl – sorry – woman arrives we have to take away her possessions: jewellery, purse, belt, anything like that. They do get some of it back later but to start with they can't have any item that would make them vulnerable."

"Vulnerable to what?"

"Well, bullying, for one." Wayne sneaked a sidelong glance at Callahan who had been distracted by the fly, and was swatting it with his beefy hand. "Any jewellery could make them a target. But suicide is the biggest worry so belts and shoelaces are always removed. You'd be surprised how crafty someone can be when they want to hurt themselves."

"Wayne, you bloody bleeding heart," said Callahan, "you should have been a probation officer."

Wayne ducked his head, mumbled something about not getting good enough grades, and then looked back at Cate. "Most of the girls who arrive here are frightened. Even the ones who seem tough will cry when they're alone. It can upset them. The searching, the medical. Not that I do any of that – it has to be a female officer."

Cate smiled at Wayne.

Callahan scowled. "Fucking Care Bear."

They left the induction unit and turned into a narrow dim corridor, which led up to the security office. Cate suddenly felt tight pressure around her wrist and, looking down, she saw that Callahan had attached a handcuff and was sniggering like a school boy. As she struggled to free her hand, the cuff tightened. She felt her legs quake and stumbled, only to be wrenched upright by Callahan. "Good job I had this on ya, missy!"

Callahan's face was in hers, a wide smile, all teeth, red lips wet and eyes narrowed. He was getting off on her fear. "Nifty, aren't they?" he crowed, a thrill sparkling in his reptilian eyes.

"Get this fucking cuff off me!" she spat. In a second he had released her, still finding it amusing. She rubbed her twisted shoulder, fighting back hot tears that threatened to betray her. Callahan laughed and gobbed his used gum onto the floor.

As her heart slowed, she wondered why she wasn't marching to the Governor's office to make a formal complaint. She was silent, shocked at how powerless she felt in this place.

Callahan said Senior Officer Deborah Holley practically ran the prison, since she was in charge of security. Officer Holley was an intense-looking woman, with her shirt buttoned high on her scrawny neck and creases in her trousers like knives. She peered out of a nipped face, looking like a clerk. She didn't get up from her chair, but swivelled around to face Cate, shaking her hand once, a tight pull downwards. When Cate's hand was released it throbbed. On the desk, laid out in precise order, were a pen, a pad and a plastic lunchbox, on top of which was balanced a banana and a can of Red Bull. Callahan perched on the desk and immediately started to fiddle with the neat display. To Cate's surprise Officer Holley's look was indulgent, even when he picked up her telephone receiver and began tapping it with his finger. "Hey, Debs, did you know your phone's not working?" Callahan asked.

"Fucking thing. I need a new one but supplies say the budget won't stretch to it." Holley snatched a tissue and wiped the mouthpiece before replacing it.

"Yeah, they'd find the money quick enough if it was for a con, though. There's always money to spend on them." Callahan and Holley exchanged a sardonic look.

"We just went to the hospital wing."

"Did you see Thomas?"

"Yup. She still isn't talking."

Holley smirked. "Well, no-one likes a grass."

Callahan remained swinging his leg as Holley talked Cate through the security procedures. It was delivered in a dull monotone, a lecture on how inmates could not be trusted, how Cate must never agree to take a parcel or letter for an inmate…and on, and on, until Cate had got the message that they were at war and the inmates were the enemy.

"You met Chatham yet?" Holley asked.

"Not yet."

"He's the kind of probation officer we like. Doesn't get in anyone's way, keeps his head down. Even the Governor rates him."

"Yeah," agreed Callahan, "Chatham'll never work on the out again. Knows when he's onto a good thing."

"He understands that the bitches are banged up for a reason. They deserve to be here, especially the nonces. I hate kiddie killers. If it was up to me," said Holley, "I'd bring back the noose."

Cate's office was through several locked doors – open, remove key, go through, replace key and lock the door. If such a small, dark room deserved to be called an office: really just a cupboard housing a desk and filing cabinet. Even the computer was just a word processor with no Internet access. Officer Holley told her that 'civilians' are always a liability, so it's best if they have no external e-mails or mobile phones. The only communication Cate could have was within the custodial estate. From 9 to 5.30 this would be her world, and she was as cut off as the inmates. *Well, good, at least there will be no distractions. I can just do my job and go home.*

Into the desk drawer went lunch: cheese sandwich, an apple and a can of Coke. She had a half-eaten bar of chocolate in her pocket that she might polish off as well. Even though the canteen – or 'mess' as Callahan called it – served hot food, she was still new and the idea of sitting alone while the prison staff gossiped around her was not a tempting prospect. Maybe she would brave it when she had got to know people, she told herself. After all, it was only her first day so she must be positive.

On her desk she propped a photo of Amelia, enjoying an ice cream in the park, and a picture she'd drawn at Julie's last week. In it a girl was on a swing, being pushed by two people, one with a triangular skirt and the other with a tie. Presumably her mother and father. *To Mummy*, she'd written, *love Amelia*. Cate taped it to the wall.

There was a single knock at the door and then it opened. It was the Governor, whom she'd seen on TV every time a prisoner from the open side absconded.

Governor Wright was a large man, used to standing over people, and he stood over Cate as she sat at the desk, battling against feeling like a schoolgirl.

"Just wanted to see how you're settling in."

"Okay, thanks. Dave Callahan showed me round the prison this morning."

"Callahan's a good officer, keeps the landings in order. My days of pounding the landings are long gone," he said. "Back then, inmates were treated like the low-lives they are. It's all gone too far the other way now, if you ask me. Prison's more like Butlins."

As he spoke he pulled a Twix wrapper from his pocket, removed the remaining chocolate bar and ate it in two quick bites. Despite being very fat, the Governor kept preening his copper-wire hair, and his suit looked expensive, dark and well cut, with white pinstripes. At his wrists were glitzy cufflinks, and an inscription was sewn on the cuff: NKW.

"A word of advice. You civilian workers need to remember your place. It's all very well being the dayshift, but the prison officers are here round the clock, and it's them that's in charge.

I like to run a tight ship, and I won't stand for any nonsense from you Care Bears."

"By 'Care Bears' do you mean workers who are interested in issues beside discipline?"

"You'll get used to the prison lingo," he said dismissively.

"I'm looking forward to working here." She thought it was the right thing to say even if it wasn't true. "Preparing the women for release will be rewarding."

"Yeah, well, don't let yourself be sucked into feeling sorry for 'em. I've no time for their hysterics. All that weeping and wailing, most of 'em are mental. At least with men you know where they're coming from."

She suspected he wasn't fond of probation officers so she tested the water by asking about the other PO who worked on the men's side of the prison. Surprisingly he answered with some warmth.

"Paul Chatham's sound as a bell. He's been on holiday for two weeks, but he's back today. I told him to brief you on your first case. Now there's someone who knows how to keep his head down and his mouth shut."

"Is that what you expect from your probation staff, then?"

"It's what I recommend. If you copy his example you'll do okay, though I won't pretend I like women working in prisons. After all, what good are they when there's trouble kicking off? And some of these cons may look normal, but they're fucking vicious. No offence, love, but I'd rather have a man around when the shit hits the fan."

Paul Chatham had been working in the prison so long that Callahan said he was almost part of the furniture and, despite belonging to a low-status profession according to most prison officers, judging by what Cate had been told he'd evidently managed the shift from "outsider" to "one of us". While she was "sussing out the territory", as Wright put it, he suggested she and Paul Chatham could meet regularly as part of her induction. Their first meeting was imminent, and she only just had time to grab a coffee.

The coffee machine was a locked door away, and the drink too weak, but she bought one for herself and one for Paul, reminding herself to buy a kettle for her room to avoid this regular trip for caffeine. She was still blowing the heat off the coffee when he arrived, handing her a packet of custard creams.

"Welcome gift! You don't need to be mad to work here, but it helps."

Paul Chatham was a handsome man, with thick white-grey hair and a face lined from years of good-natured smiling. His eyes were an unusually warm blue, and he looked easy in his tanned skin. He accepted the cooling coffee and, in the absence of a second chair, perched on the desk. In the cramped airless room she could smell the musky scent of him. It was the closest she had been to an attractive man for a long time but she sensed that Paul's groomed looks were not intended to attract women.

"So, you've obviously fallen from grace with the powers that be," he joked. "What was your crime?" It was a recognised fact that the probation service seconded undesirable staff to prison posts, the lowest rung on the ladder.

"What makes you think I didn't ask to be transferred?" she answered warily. "It's an opportunity to really make a difference."

Paul laughed. "I didn't think things were that bad in the field! I guess you'll tell me when you're ready."

Paul was right. Cate hadn't asked to work at the prison. Not that she had been forced exactly, but her manager had made it clear that things needed to change. Since Tim had left her she'd tried her best to juggle the various elements of her life, always keeping Amelia her priority. But her late arrivals and early departures from the office, time off for sickness – Amelia's and her own – had worn the patience of her colleagues thin.

And she had been off for six months with depression. During her sick leave she was often seen by colleagues in the park with Amelia in her buggy, so they called her a slacker and when she returned she found her confidence had gone.

It was felt a move would 'do her good'. She read the signs – she could be left to her own devices if she worked in a prison, demands were fewer and, if she missed the odd day, the consequences were less potentially dangerous. Here the clients were captive, so there was no immediate threat to the public. Prison was a retirement ground for probation officers and she, not yet thirty, had been sent out to pasture. But she would prove them wrong.

Paul downed his coffee in a long swig. "Christ, what a dismal office. You should have opted to work on the men's side. At least I have a window."

"I'll get used to it." Cate replied dismissively. "We went to the hospital wing this morning, and there was a woman – Susan Thomas. She'd been badly beaten."

Paul shifted his position. "That's prison, I'm afraid. Have you met Officer Holley yet?"

When Cate nodded he grinned. "Her security lecture's a hoot, no? All that guff about nail files and mobile phones. As if we don't keep them in our lockers, and the prisoners stuff them under their beds. Still, we have to go through the motions."

Cate grimaced. "The highlight was when Deborah Holley showed me the cabinet of weapons prisoners had made."

"Ah yes. Razor blades wedged into toothbrushes..."

"The wire garrotte from stripped computer cable…"

"When it's the boiling water that does the most damage. And there's an urn of that on every landing!" Paul laughed.

"I think she wanted to scare me."

"Well, of course, pretty missy. She's more butch than me, not that that's difficult. Officer Holley wouldn't want you to think she's not got a tough job. So, did she succeed?"

"Not at all." Cate said, all too quickly. It was true that she hadn't shown any fear on the outside, but the lecture had made her uneasy.

Paul added sagely, "Welcome to the madhouse. There's some funny folk who work in prisons. Just remember which side of the bars you're on and you'll be fine. And don't go thinking you can change the world – if you fight the system, you'll lose. But you can still do your bit."

"The Governor said you can brief me on my first case?"

"Don't be too eager. It's a parole report on a nonce."

"Nonce?"

"Someone who's hurt or abused a child. Your report's on a child killer, Rose Wilks."

Cate's stomach tensed. "What's she like?"

"I've only met her once, when she first got here. She's been around the system a bit and it shows. Hardened, I'd say. She didn't say much, face like a slapped arse. This is her fourth prison in as many years. She's on the Rule."

Cate frowned. "I don't know what that means."

"It means she'll be on a special wing. Rule 42 is for vulnerable prisoners, and they're all kept together on D Wing. Some are there for protection from themselves, but child killers are usually being protected from other prisoners."

"Have you got her case file?"

"Just her discipline record. Welcome to prison life: files arrive late, if ever. She got eight years for manslaughter, already served four."

"So she could be out in just a few weeks, if she gets parole?"

"Parole board sits in five weeks, and she could be out in six. But she'll only get out if she's become a saint. She did murder a baby."

"You just said she was convicted of manslaughter, not murder."

"Yeah, well, you know what a jury can be like when a clever barrister puts on a show. She probably got a break because she was depressed when it happened. She'd already lost her own son and was obsessed with the victim, a boy who was born at the same time as him. She'd broken into the house to see him in the middle of the night. Then there was a fire and the boy died."

"God, that's horrible."

"Well, don't let it get under your skin."

"When can I meet her?"

Paul looked at his watch. "No time like the present. I'll walk with you as far as the education block. From there you're on your own."

Cate navigated her way into the education block, deafened by the constant noise. Iron doors echoed around the cold walls, women's voices called from barred windows, officers shouted, and above it all the seagulls screeched.

In the corridor she saw Dave Callahan, who was making a show of larking around with a nervy-looking colleague, a young officer in a shirt so new it still had the creases from where it had been packaged. When he saw Cate the young man stood straighter, and she saw his eyes flick over her body in that surreptitious way of sexually inexperienced young men.

Dave called across the corridor. "Hey, it's our new probation girl."

Cate ignored him and offered her hand to the shy young man. "Cate Austin. Probation Officer."

"Mark Burgess." His hand was limp and sweaty.

Callahan sneered. "Mark only left school a few weeks ago, isn't that right, lad?"

He blushed. "University."

"University educated and he wants to work in this shithole." Callahan laughed.

"Are you on a graduate programme?" Cate asked.

"Yes, two years as an officer, and then I'll be fast-tracked. I could be a Governor grade by the time I'm twenty-five."

Callahan laughed so hard he almost choked. "You'd better grow a beard then, lad, or the cons'll think it's 'bring your son to work' day."

Cate willed Callahan to shut up. She said crisply, "I'd like to interview an inmate for a parole report. Rose Wilks."

Callahan leered at her. "A number's all we need, darling. Preferably yours." He chortled at his own wit, turning to Mark. "Off you go, lad. Fetch the con for the lady. D Wing. Quick sharp." Mark scurried off and Cate walked smartly to the opposite room, to await Rose Wilks's arrival.

6

Black Book Entry

My black book, my precious notebook. Once it was just
empty pages, but now I'm filling it. This book is like a diary,
and also like a letter because one day I'll hand this book to
you, Jason. I like to imagine you reading it. But not yet. Not
until I'm free.

The jury eventually found me not guilty of murder. They
believed me when I said I loved Luke, that I would never hurt
him. But they found me guilty of manslaughter. I was there,
that night, when it happened. I am a smoker and a cigarette
started the fire.

It's three years, ten months and two days since that night,
but in six weeks I could be free. I need to get parole, need good
reports from Officer Callahan and most of all from probation.
I'm getting gate-fever and I couldn't survive being locked up
for another two years.

It's quiet. Most of the women are at classes, some are sleeping,
and I'm mopping the landing. Officer Callahan walks across
the clean floor with his dirty boots.

"I have something for you, Rosie," he says, leaning against
the wall with his hand on his crotch. I have to laugh, as it

wouldn't do to appear frosty. Callahan's my personal officer, so it's he who fills out my file and knows my case best. He waves the papers he has in his other hand: my parole report. I reach for it but he stretches his arm up.

"Patience, patience! No need to grab."

"Please can I see it?" I sound like a begging child.

"Of course, Rose. But first I'd like a kiss."

He often taunts the girls in this way. Usually I ignore him, but more than pride is at stake. Disgusted with myself, I graze my lips over his cheek, but he turns his face at the last minute and his mouth touches mine. His wet, greedy lips make me feel sick, but I smile anyway. I know who has the power here.

"I just met the probation officer who'll be writing your report, Rosie."

"Really?" This is important, but I don't want him to see how much. "What's he like?"

"It's a she. Bit wet behind the ears. I just gave her the grand tour and she looked a bit shocked that it's not like Butlins."

"What's her name?"

"Cate Austin. Ms Austin to you. You'll be meeting her after lunch. Bit of a bugger for you, I'd say. A woman'll always be harder on a child killer."

I look around to check no-one is listening.

"Don't worry, Rosie. Your secret's safe with me."

Finally, he gives me the report. I fold it, tuck it into the back of my trousers, and finish mopping up, feeling the paper against my spine as I work.

It's a good report. I am a 'model prisoner'; Callahan wishes there were more like me. I haven't been any trouble at Bishop's Hill, and I'm always polite and respectful. In conclusion, he supports my early release. I hide the report under my mattress. I can't risk another inmate getting hold of it; jealousy breeds anger and violence. But on its own this report won't get me released. The probation officer's report is the one that holds the most weight.

My palms go slick when I think about the meeting. An officer will come for me soon, unlock my cell and take me to meet her. She'll ask about you, Jason. And about Luke. It's what they've all asked, the psychologists and shrinks, over the four years that I've been locked up, hoping to find something that will explain what happened that night. They want me to say that I did it, that I left a cigarette burning, that I started the fire that killed Luke.

I won't lie. Not even to get out of here.

The scrape of the key in the lock is the only warning that it's time for my interview. Officers never knock, never wait for a reply. Even if a prisoner is on the toilet there's no respect for privacy, no basic good manners here. I have to stop writing in my black book, this long letter that I write to you all the time, even when I have no pen or paper. I'm always writing to you, always talking to you in my head. Dear Jason.

The new officer, Mark Burgess, opens the cell door.

"Come on, Wilks. Parole interview. Time to meet your probation officer."

I follow Burgess away from the cells and into the education blocks where classes and courses are held. He leaves me outside a classroom.

I peer through the window in the door and see her, waiting.

She sits by the far end of the room, looking out towards the perimeter wall, her face in profile. Her navy suit is buttoned up even though it's warm today, and she is tapping the fingers of one hand against her leg, as if to some silent music. My file is in her lap and my fate's in her hands.

7

Cate waited in the classroom while Officer Burgess went to fetch Rose Wilks. She walked to the barred window and watched the seagulls hopping on the ground then fly freely over the wall to the sea beyond. Women who were a danger to the public were locked inside the walls, kept away from the world. And she was locked up with them.

Just fifteen miles away Amelia was being looked after by Julie. Somewhere else Tim was getting on with his new life with another woman. Someone he said was easy to be with, who made him laugh and didn't take life so seriously. *I don't want to be here, I want to be home. I'm not ready to be back at work.* She buttoned up her jacket, smoothed it down. *I can do this. It's okay. It's just a job.*

Rose Wilks would be arriving any minute. Feeling tense, she rolled her shoulders and told herself she had interviewed parolees before, and that she would be fine. It was just like riding a bicycle.

She made herself sit, thinking it would make her feel more in control, and then she picked up the thin file, the only details she had on Rose Wilks apart from what Paul had told her. It was scant information, listing the institutions where Rose had been held: the high security prisons, Holloway for six months and Durham for two years; then upgraded to the open prison at Highpoint; then back to higher security here to Bishop's Hill on the Suffolk coast. Moving down through the prison system was normal, but Rose's transfer from 'low' back to 'high' security suggested a serious misdemeanour at Highpoint. The discipline record simply stated 'one adjudication' against her, but no further details.

Sensing a shift in the atmosphere, Cate looked up. A dark-haired woman was staring at her through the glass. After a brief second, the door was opened, and the glass barrier gone.

Rose Wilks was tall and well built. She wore her own clothes, a concession all female inmates were allowed, but they looked loose as though she'd lost weight since buying them: plain dark garments, revealing nothing. On the sleeve of her right arm was stitched a strip of red fabric. Cate didn't want to show her ignorance by asking what it signified.

The prisoner's face was set in a mask of control, dark eyes fixed their advantage, access denied. Her almost-black hair was loose around her face and shoulders, long and wavy, making her look hippyish with her sallow face and kale eyes. She looked about forty, but Cate knew from the file that she was only thirty-three. Around her neck Cate saw the glint of gold, a chain that disappeared inside the collar of her shirt.

The two women shook hands, and Cate, conscious of her tendency to sweat, hoped Rose wouldn't notice her moist palm. She directed the prisoner to a seat.

"Hello. I'm Cate Austin."

"Rose Wilks."

"I'll be writing the parole report on you. The board are sitting in five weeks."

"I know that. I've been counting down the days."

"I imagine so. How are you getting along at Bishop's Hill?"

The prisoner sat straight, poised. "Don't you know?"

Cate was not affronted by this challenge, "I haven't had your full case file yet, so all I have is a list of dates. I hope that when we next meet I'll have got the records from your last prison, but today I'll have to rely on you for information."

The silence provided enough space for the woman to flick

her eyes over Cate, evidently weighing her up. "I've been here sixteen months and I'm getting on as well as anyone could, locked away for something I didn't do. Now let me ask you a question. How old are you?" Her voice was tilted upwards with the trace of a Suffolk accent, leaving the question raised in the air between them.

This was a familiar one. Cate had joined the Probation Service just after graduation, but she looked younger than her twenty-nine years. Torn between the desire to let this woman know she was no rookie and that her age was none of her business, she compromised. "My age is irrelevant. But I've been a qualified probation officer for seven years, and written many parole reports. Isn't that what you really wanted to know?"

Rose smiled, her shoulders dropped a little. "So I'm in good hands?"

Cate knew this was an attempt to draw her in, but she was practised at rebuttal. "I'm sure you know my job is to write a considered report, recommending whether or not you should be released on parole licence. You've been found guilty of manslaughter and that's my starting point. What I'm interested in is if you'll reoffend. If you're sorry for your crime."

"And how will you know that?"

Now it was Cate's turn to consider. This question struck at the heart of her job, the weighing up of words and emotions. The delicate skill of peeling back the layers of another person's psyche, stripping back what someone had done to find out who they were and what motivated them. This was what she was good at. It was why she loved her work, or had done until Amelia was born. When Tim left she'd sunk into despair, robbed of her self-belief. She told herself now it was just the illness making her doubt her abilities. She was better now, ready to be back. She could do this.

"Trust me," Cate answered with a confidence she didn't feel. "I'll know."

"Good. Because I shouldn't even be here. I need to be free, prison is killing me. It's not easy being locked away."

Cate looked to the window as a gull flew past, screaming.

"Especially for someone who's been convicted of a crime like yours," Cate said, keeping her voice neutral.

"You mean with others thinking that I'm to blame for a child's death?"

"Yes. You must get a hard time."

"I don't tell anyone what I'm in for, that would be asking for trouble. I've spent four years pretending, avoiding the attacks that would happen if anyone knew. I had to invent a crime. Aggravated burglary is a more acceptable crime."

"Do they believe you?" Cate asked.

"People always believe lies. That's why the jury convicted me, when the truth of what happened was staring them in the face."

"I should warn you, Rose, that accepting your guilt is crucial to you getting parole."

"You want me to lie too. But I would never hurt Luke. I loved him." Rose was leaning forward, almost pleading.

Cate held her gaze for a beat. "I've been reading your disciplinary record."

"Ask any screw and they'll tell you I'm no bother. My cell is always neat and I'm a trusted inmate."

"You've had one adjudication. At Highpoint. What was that for?"

"Doesn't it say?" Cautiously, testing.

"No. Whatever it was, it got you sent back to a high security prison, so it must have been serious."

Cate waited for an explanation, but none was offered. She watched Rose remove a packet of Rizla papers from her top pocket.

"Can I smoke?"

"You know you can't. Not in here."

Rose looked up through heavy-lidded eyes that showed a flicker of contempt.

"Tell me about the adjudication, Rose."

An indifferent shrug, not matched in the eyes that stared out with sharp awareness. "As you just said, a case like mine doesn't go down well inside. One of the inmates will get an idea of what I've done. My face is recognised from a newspaper article, or a screw lets something slip. There's always someone wanting to make a name for themselves. I ignore it all: the looks, the knocks. Even the boiling water, and that hurts like hell. But this was different. What she said was wrong."

"What did she say?"

"She got at me when I was in the shower. When I was vulnerable. There were other cons around, watching. She called me a nonce. I couldn't let it go. It would have been like I was agreeing with her."

Cate remembered Paul telling her that "nonce" was the ultimate insult, reserved for those who had committed the worst crime of all, that of abusing children. Or killing them.

"Most people don't know anything about me and, as I said, I tell them I'm in for burglary. People don't mind that and, anyway, it's true. I was a burglar."

"What did you steal?"

Rose smiled slightly, touching her necklace. "Just a key."

"So what did you do to the woman who called you a nonce?"

"Only what I had to do. You can't show weakness in prison. I waited until she wasn't expecting it and threw hot water in her face. It killed me to do it, but I didn't have any choice. I couldn't let word get round that I'd let her get away with calling me that." Rose blanched, and clasped her hands together.

Cate watched Rose closely. "Are you okay?"

"No." Her eyes welled. "Everything depends on this. And

no-one understands that I wasn't in Luke's room for any bad reason. I loved him. I know I had no right to be there, but since I lost Joel…" The tears fell slowly. "Just to hold another baby. That was all. I would never hurt him."

Cate watched as Rose cried, her fingers itching to reach and comfort her until she reminded herself that because of her a child had died. She let Rose cry herself out.

Sniffing and drying her tears Rose asked, "Have you got any children?"

"It's not really relevant."

"I think it is. But you're not supposed to tell me, are you?"

There were three beats of silence between them. *This woman is responsible for a child's death. Why shouldn't she know that I understand what that means to Luke's mother?* "I have a daughter."

Rose wiped her eyes. "I had a son. Joel."

"Can you tell me about him?"

Rose shook her head.

"What about Luke?"

Again, she shook her head.

"Rose, to write your report I need to know how you ended up here. I need you to talk to me. I know that what I'm asking you to do is painful. But we need to make a start if you want to be released."

8

Black Book Entry

Cate Austin didn't ask about you, Jason. She didn't press me
to talk about Luke's death, which surprises me since there
are only five weeks until the parole board meet. But then
sometimes these professionals do wait, even when they are
desperate to know. They want to "establish rapport" as they
call it. As if that's even possible.

After I was convicted, when the case had been adjourned
for reports to be written and for the judge to decide what
sentence to give me, a psychiatrist wasted hours asking me
about things. My favourite bird, my worst subjects at school, if
I liked any special flowers. I told him I liked to see blackbirds,
that they reminded me of my mother, that I'd always hated RE
and liked roses, because of my name. Finally, satisfied that he
knew enough, he asked about the fire. It was like an exam, and
every question had a correct answer.

I think it'll be different with Cate. She told me that she
hasn't got my full case file, when she could have pretended
to know everything about me. She seems cool but under
the surface things are always different. I've met lots of
professionals, and I know them, what makes them tick. Men
are the easiest to handle. They prefer to think of women as

44

"misguided", rather than plain bad. They're always looking for reasons and excuses.

There was something about Cate, recognition between us like seeing a reflection in the funfair mirror, distorted, but still familiar. Just a hint, in the damp of her palm when we first met, in the pained way she looked when I cried. She's hiding something. Some vulnerable part, locked away. She said she has a daughter, but doesn't wear a wedding ring. Maybe she's divorced, been abandoned by a man. Betrayed. These things matter, Jason, with a case like ours.

I'm writing this in my cell now, sitting cross-legged on the bed. The bed is so small that with my back to the wall my knees reach the edge of the mattress. The cell door is locked, but I can hear the officers talking in the corridor. We inmates listen, quiet as mice, straining our ears for information. We know who's sleeping with who, who has family trouble, who's ill. All their secrets and lies. We know more about the screws than they know about us. Being in control isn't just about who wears a uniform.

When the corridor is silent I know the shifts have changed. It's the night shift now, and there's only one officer on duty. They're supposed to do an hourly check of the cells but they never do. There are often women on suicide watch, and they need close observation since there are many ways to kill yourself, and it looks bad on the prison record if a shoelace wasn't confiscated, if the syringe wasn't found. Prisons are frightening places, and some inmates prefer death.

If you want to survive in here you follow the rules – someone gobbing in your food is the least trouble you can expect. I tell the new girls this: For God's sake, don't borrow, no matter how badly you need that phone card to call and wish your mum happy birthday, and never deal drugs no matter how much you need that fix. You'll have to pay it back, but double, and then you'll borrow again and the debt will rise until you're on the wrong end of a sock with batteries in it. Or worse. Some girls have razors and, when they're not cutting their own arms, they'll go for you, especially if you're pretty, and boiling water hurts like hell, scarring you for life.

Best to learn quickly. It's dog-eat-dog in here. One girl with HIV threatens with a needle, so don't mess with her. In fact, don't mess with anyone unless you want your cheek cut open. Find someone to look out for you. Someone like me, who knows the ropes. The screws aren't going to do it, especially not at night and that's when a lot of bullying happens. If you're new you'll be asked to sing or face punishment the next day. The screw on night duty will sleep or watch TV, so don't expect them to take care of you. Night shifts are an easy ride. Unless they're on suicide watch, they're being paid to dream, only disturbed when the day staff arrive at 8 a.m.

I go to my window and push open the thin rectangle of unbreakable glass. It's small but the air comes in fresh and warm, and I breathe it in. From here I can see the block opposite, women standing, as I am, at barred windows. Some have sheets, which they have wound into ropes, using them to swing notes and stuff between each other's windows. One woman swings a small bundle across, probably cigs or chocolate, friendship or fear making her give away her supply.

I can't see my own neighbours, but I know who's in each cell. I can hear them whispering the gossip. Sometimes I just listen, but not today.

"Janie?" I hiss.

She immediately squeaks back, "Here, Rose," like a pupil at registration.

"Did you do it?"

"Yes. I didn't find much."

Janie often gets on my nerves, brown-nosing the officers, but I was still glad when she was also transferred to Bishop's Hill. Janie's someone I like having around; we get on and I can ask her for favours. We're friends, as much as anyone can be in prison. She's one of those unlucky women who wouldn't be in prison if she hadn't fallen in with the wrong sort. But then what other sort would choose Janie as a friend? She's small and forgettable, perfect for any number of crimes. She would be a loyal lookout, an ideal burglar.

Janie had fallen in with a gang led by a woman who was assistant manager at a jeweller's. She passed on the addresses of customers who had bought valuable jewellery and a burglary would follow. Unfortunately for them, on the last job, Janie was so nervous she shat herself. Left a pile of evidence on the grassy verge.

The problem with Janie is that she's weak. She can't resist pressure; she's a tell-tale. That's why she's with us on the Rule. Suicides and snitches, the bullied and the notorious. We all need to be protected, either from other people or from ourselves. D Wing is our special place, the inmates in the kitchens will spit in our food; we're despised.

After the police checked the faeces for DNA Janie was arrested. To get a lighter sentence she spilled the names of every gang member as well as the assistant manager at the jewellery shop. Grassing on that scale means she'll always have to watch her back.

Janie has some power with us, because she's an orderly. The officers, recognising her obedience, appointed her to this prized position. She cleans the admin block, the rooms of the psychologist and Governor, dusts the filing cabinets where precious files are kept. She's a good cleaner; she would scrub a toilet with a toothbrush if they asked, she's that type. But being submissive is also a flaw. What makes her a good orderly also makes her a good informant. Today she cleaned the new probation officer's room.

"Tell me what you found."

"Well, it's a small office, just a desk and a chair really."

"Did you check the desk drawers?"

"Yup. There was an open pack of custard creams, so I took some." She sniggers at her own daring.

"What else?"

"There was a notepad. With your name on it."

"What else was written on it?"

"I'm not sure. Nothing much."

I curse Janie for not being able to read very well. I'll have to get her to steal Cate's notes to know what she's written about me.

"And there was a photo of a little girl on the desk. Real pretty. Hair in bunches. Licking an ice cream."

"That'll be her daughter. How old did she look?"

"Four or five, I reckon. There was a picture on the wall, y'know a kid's drawing, with her name on it."

"You know the girl's name?"

"Yeah, it was on the picture. In big letters. A – M – E – L – I – A."

"Amelia."

Janie has risked a lot for me. If she were caught snooping she'd lose her cleaning job and probably be sent to segregation. She put herself in danger, for my sake.

"Good girl, Janie. You've done really well. Now you need to find out if Cate Austin has a man." I breathe in the free air and smile into the night.

Nights are so hard, Jason. I can't sleep. Do you still sleep with your body splayed in total submission? I would watch you at night, as you dreamed, amazed that you were mine.

I'll tell you a story now, write it down for you in my black book, which I'll give to you one day. It's more about a girl named Rose who lived by the sea.

My life before you met me made me what I am.

9

Black Book Entry

I was brought up in Suffolk, in a seaside town where my family owned a shop. Lowestoft had seen better days and the once-grand town houses along the front were now split into flats and lived in by single mums and teenagers on benefit. There were four of us: me, my mum and dad, and Peter. He was two years older than me, a beast of a boy with piggy eyes in a pale podgy face and a brain the size of a pea. He had my mother's pale colouring but none of her delicacy. He used to bully me endlessly, as older brothers do, but Mum said I had to make allowances because Peter was 'special', meaning he was stupid.

Our shop was by the beach, the type of seaside convenience store that sells everything, and Mum was supposed to look after Peter and me but she went through periods when she just couldn't handle us and would stay in bed. When she was well she'd be full of fun, taking us swimming in the sea, letting me play with her long sunshine hair. But those days would be suddenly eclipsed by her "loony spells", as Dad called it, when her hair would be greasy and her eyes dull.

I was just a child and didn't know much, but I'd noticed that one of the customers, Mrs Carron, popped in the shop a lot. She was a flouncy woman with musky perfume and pink lips. Lots of the housewives in the terraces would come in for loaves of bread or packets of biscuits most days. My dad was friendly with them all, and if he was even friendlier with Mrs Pink-lips, that seemed okay. Why should I think anything of him joking with her or staring at her bottom when she walked away? He was a man, after all, and she was one of those women who dolled herself up and laughed like a spoon in a glass, so it all seemed normal, nothing strange or bad. But Mum didn't think so.

I heard her shouting about it, and knew the words were bad even if I didn't know what "whore" and "slut" really meant, and my father shouting back, saying "Shut up!" and then calling her a mad woman and finally saying, "Well, who could blame me?" That was when she would cry. After these arguments she'd go to bed and Dad would go out. He never said where to, but he'd come back smelling of musk with pink lipstick on his cheek.

After arguing with my father, Mum looked different, angry and sad. She'd hold herself as if she had a heavy weight to carry and her mouth would be pulled down at the sides; she wouldn't laugh, like she did when she was well. I rode the roller-coaster of her moods. She could be warm and loving, when we would do exciting things. But on her "loony" days she'd look at me like I was a stranger.

When Mum was ill, Peter and I would have to stay in the shop and not get under anyone's feet. There were comics on sale and we would try to sneak a look but Dad would tell us not to touch, and we got bored. Peter would poke me, booming insults in his bass voice, nick my book away or tease me for being fat. Sometimes he would go with his mates to the beach, and I would be glad.

I didn't want to be in the shop. I wanted to be with Mum. I sneaked into her room and climbed onto the bed, snuggling under her duvet and playing at dens.

The blackbirds were back, building their nests. In the rain. I could see them from my mother's bed, flying in the grey-torn sky and darting to a bush. The slash of dark wings against lime and yellow, disappearing into the shrub, one going in, the other coming out, over and over. Wet feathers. Dripping leaves. The beaked grip on thin brown wood, the unlikely angle of the head as the twig slid into place. The black beady eye. A single jet feather lifted by the wind. I watched and shivered.

The window shook, but I was safe from the weather in my duvet den.

I cuddled close and Mum kissed my head. My nest, her bed. They wanted a home, those birds, a place for eggs, for chicks to hatch. "Oh my, just look," she said, so soft, "how they keep on and on. They believe in their little nest…and it's pouring now. How did they learn to be so determined?" She nestled in the downy pillow, and the exhaustion of speaking made her close her eyes.

A shameful thought: not like her. She never had any determination, always so tired.

Push it away.

I kissed her hand, light as a feather, and so cold. "Oh, Rosie," she said, her eyes still closed, "just to see them makes me so tired. Over and over, until the nest's built, and then the waiting…"

I knew about waiting. The sitting and being still and waiting until she was well again, until she was up and I was safe and could breathe again, and she was my mother.

The rain didn't stop.

Elaeagnus. "El – ae – ag – nus," she said the next day, sounding it out for me. That tree. That shrub, so thick and wide, outside the window. Yellow and small, white flowers that smelled of lime even stronger after the rain. I knew – I'd been there, before school. If only she would open a window. Since the sky was dried out, all wrung. But she wouldn't. Couldn't. It was her nest. Days she stayed in there. Days and days.

We watched, after school. Me in blue gingham and her in a white nightdress. She watched the blackbirds and I watched her for signs that she was ready to get up. To be well. More comings and goings from the blackbird nest, but only one this time. "The male. You can tell from the orange beak," she whispered, as if he might hear and be disturbed, "and it's bigger too."

What was bigger, when there was only one? Nothing to measure it against. How do you know what's big, what's right, what's wrong, if you've nothing to compare it with? But its beak, sure enough, was orange. Full, too, not with twigs anymore, but with worms and grubs, and I thought the chicks must be hatched. The bird was so quick, keeping on and on. "My chick," she said, stroking my arm, "my Rosie."

I thought of Peter, downstairs. Her clumsy, stupid other chick, who only came to see her when Dad made him. "Go say goodnight to your mum." Not like me, who couldn't stay away and was always getting told off by Dad for disturbing her.

I thought of Dad, working downstairs in the shop, and how he foraged like the blackbird each mealtime while Mum was in her nest.

"I wish," she said, and I held my breath, not having known her to wish for anything, so knowing it was important. "I wish I could look in that nest." She surprised me. "Climb up, into the Elaeagnus – no, fly up there like a bird and peer in to see how many chicks, how many preciously thin, hollow-boned babies are waiting, mouths wide for food."

She wasn't talking to me. It was to herself, to the air. To the birds outside that she envied. "I wish I could make them strong and healthy and able one day to leave. To fly away."

She started to cry, like always, and I didn't know how to

comfort her. How to stop her open mouth, which was crying out for something that I couldn't give her, because I didn't know what it was she needed, to make her strong. I had no comparison, to know what was wrong.

When I arrived home after school I would be tired and hungry but I would have to sit in the shop until closing time, my head resting on crossed arms as my eyes blinked away sleep. The regulars got to know me, and would joke about me being the youngest shop assistant in Lowestoft. My favourite place in the whole shop was on a wooden stool beneath the row of glass jars full of sweets: pink peppermint rock, square yellow pineapple chunks that made your mouth sore, shiny brown cola bottles you could spend ages sucking the sugar off, sherbet lemons the colour of Mum's hair and – my favourite – those sticky toffee bon bons covered in icing sugar which dusted your fingers.

The shelf was too high for me to reach, even from the stool, so they tempted me every day. Peter could reach, and he would get a sticky toffee, taunting me. "Not getting any for you. You're fat enough already!"

"Please, Peter."

"Get stuffed."

He'd chew his toffee loudly, with an open mouth, wide open, showing me the sticky mess inside until I wanted to slap him but if I did he'd go crying to Dad and I'd get told off, since Peter was a bit "special", meaning he was retarded. He was in a learning-support class in school and the books he brought home I'd read at infant school.

The only thing Peter and I had in common was that we both loved penny sweets. We called them that because each Saturday Dad would give us ten pence to spend, and we would buy a bag, one penny for each sweet we chose. I spent hours planning how I was going to spend it.

Peter would eat his sweets immediately, but I would squirrel mine away in an empty ice cream tub. Through the week I'd allow myself one or two, a bon bon or liquorice bootlace, but most would be hoarded, and soon my secret stash grew quite large. Each week, his bag empty, Peter would steal handfuls from my box. I learned to offer him some for favours: to have him reach me things, to borrow his personal stereo.

I took such pleasure in my hoard that I would often tip it from the box, just to look. My mother had coloured sweets too, in little glass bottles with tops that didn't ever come off when I tried to open them. She kept them in her bedside cupboard and would eat them when she was ill. I sometimes offered her one of mine, but she would always refuse.

That summer, when school finished and I was nearing my eleventh birthday, the days in the shop seemed to drag on and on forever. I willed Mum to get better so we could go out somewhere, but she had been ill for ages and hardly left her bedroom. At least we had the blackbirds to watch, and she let me go to her each evening once the shop was closed. Together we saw the yellow ball of the sun change to red and die. The moon replaced it, beautiful and large and shining on us, turning her nightdress to white sand, her skin to millions of pearly shells. The air was thick and warm and smelled of salt. It was safe up there. Downstairs Peter would be into something he shouldn't be or scoffing sweets. Dad would be working, stocking shelves and ordering, and then cooking our tea with the TV blaring out, but in Mum's room it was peaceful.

Dad didn't go up to Mum anymore, but slept in a chair in the lounge, and I thought it must be normal, mustn't it? Since Mum was ill and Dad worked so hard. But I worried about the pretty laughing ladies and wondered if he would fly away if he could, leaving Peter and me alone in the nest.

I thought he was a good man, but I couldn't be sure. I had no comparison.

10

Black Book Entry

My dad's shop was so small that even three customers made it seem packed, and it was always busy after school, when the bell above the door rang over and over like the collar bell on a cat that won't go away, but stays at the door waiting for milk. There were quiet times during the day, but after school the shop was busy with children in blue and white gingham dresses, or grey trousers and navy blazers, swapping silver coins for sherbet fountains or strawberry laces. The women squeezed the bread, sniffed the cheese, tested a grape. Dad smiled at them, ran a hand through his blue-black hair, shiny with wax.

Dad liked Mrs Carron. He stroked his hair even more when she was around, and she was always running out of things and having to pop in. If Mum asked who'd been in the shop that day I knew better than to say Mrs Carron's name. Not since the time Dad had to tell Mrs Carron to fasten her blouse because a button was undone, and she looked but the button was gone. Her blouse was gaping open at the neck and I even saw her red bra! I thought it was funny, and Dad laughed, and so did Mrs Carron, but when I told Mum about it she frowned, and her hands started to pluck at the sheet. I said, "But a red bra, Mum!" thinking it was a funny thing, because I'd only seen them in white or flesh-colour. Mum didn't smile. She asked where Dad had been just before Mrs Carron noticed her button was gone. That was easy, since I knew he'd been in the storeroom out back to see if he had any Earl Grey tea that Mrs Carron said was the best. I'd stayed in the shop, watching the till. Mum asked where Mrs Carron was, and I said she'd gone out back to make sure Dad knew which tea to look for. She came back to the shop all smiles so they must have found what she wanted.

Mum cried then, and I never mentioned Mrs Carron again, but I took it upon myself to watch her and Dad. To make it safe for Mum to come out of her nest, and be well again.

I used to go to the blackbirds' nest every morning before breakfast, and every afternoon, so I could let Mum know how the birds were doing. It was the only thing she seemed to care about. When I told her the eggs had hatched she was so pleased. I told her about the three chicks with thin scrawny necks and hardly any feathers. I felt like I'd given her a great gift, and we watched from our duvet-den, the parent blackbirds to-ing and fro-ing with their worms and grubs, happy, knowing the little ones were safe.

But you can't know anything for certain.

The day after I'd counted the three chicks, about a week after I saw Mrs Carron's red bra, I put on my blue gingham dress and went to see Mum before school. She was awake, but lying very still, and she gave me a little smile, then asked me to pass her pills.

"I think I might get up today, Rose," she said.

I jumped in the air, whooping with joy. The spell was broken, and today she would be back to normal. I knew from all the times it had happened before that when the bad "loony" days had passed she would be lovely. She would take me to the beach and buy me ice cream, and make up for all the days she'd stayed in bed.

I ran outside and tagged Peter on the arm and kept running, so full of energy that I could've run to the end of the earth that day, but all I wanted to do was get school over so I could be with Mum again. I knew she'd be waiting for me downstairs. Dressed and ready.

It was only when I was at my desk at school, kicking the back of creepy Alfie's chair, that I realised I'd forgotten to look in on the three chicks. But that was okay – I bet it was the first thing Mum would do after she got dressed. And Dad would sleep in her bed again tonight, and everything would be normal. I didn't even mind when Alfie passed a crumpled note to me, saying he fancied me.

After school I ran home, ran so fast I tripped but didn't care about a grazed knee. I ran right past Peter and his mates, and kept going until I ran straight into the shop, hardly hearing the bell, and straight into an empty room. Where was she?

I started calling, "Mum? Mum!"

I heard a sound coming from the store cupboard. A woman, and it sounded like she was in pain. "Mum? Is that you?".

I ran to help, opening the door as the sound became a cry of pleasure. I saw Dad's back, two hands on his shoulders. He was pushing someone against the wall.

"Mum?"

"Here, Rose." A voice from behind me.

I turned around. Mum was standing there, her hair still wet from a recent bath, clothed, smelling like a new day. But her eyes looked beyond me into the store cupboard, to Dad's back and the other woman's hands. "Rose, what is it?" I wished, how I wished, that I'd been able to keep her safe. She pushed me aside and then I heard a high-pitched scream. "You bastard!"

Inside the store cupboard Dad twisted his head, there was a scramble of bodies coming apart and clothing being pulled down. He came forward, his shirt untucked and his hair all messed up, and behind him I saw Mrs Carron, wearing nothing on top but a red bra and a satisfied smirk. Mum doubled up like she'd been punched, and started to howl.

I ran out of the shop, and round the back, throwing myself on the grass at the base of the Elaeagnus. Then in front of me, I saw them.

Tiny baby dragons. No hair, just thin necks, big black beads for eyes, and one wing outstretched. Two of them.

As I watched, a magpie came out of the Elaeagnus, a scrap of life held tight in its cruel beak, which it jerked, tossing the tiny bird to join its dead brothers on the grass.

The magpie flashed its beautiful, glossy wings, looked at me quickly, and was gone.

I cried for a long time, and the sun was setting when I finally got up from the ground and went to the tree. I stood on tiptoe and reached for the empty nest, cupping it in my palm and gently pulling it from the branches. It may be empty, but it was still a home. I would take it to Mum, as a gift.

No sign of Mum or Dad or Mrs Carron. No sign of Peter, who was supposed to stay in the shop after school. I would look in the flat, find Mum and give her the nest. I pulled back the curtain and climbed up the stairs, listening for any noise but hearing none. My stomach rumbled with hunger and I decided to dip into my ice cream box of sweets, hidden under my bed. But when I looked the box was gone. Peter must have it! He'd be hiding somewhere, stuffing himself on all my lovely sweets that had taken so many weeks to collect, and so much of my willpower to resist.

The kitchen was empty. So was the front room, just Peter's shoes lying on the floor where he had kicked them. I checked the bathroom, even looking behind the shower curtain, but he wasn't there. There was just one place left. My parents' room.

The door was closed and I pushed the handle down slowly, seeing from the shape on the bed that Mum was there, huddled up under the bedding. Poor Mum. The room was hot and stuffy as she wouldn't have the windows open. She didn't like to hear the outside world. She was lying very still, so deeply asleep that I couldn't resist going over to her, thinking I'd climb under the duvet and make it a den.

I placed the empty nest on her pillow, so she would see it when she opened her eyes.

She was so pale, her long blonde hair lying in a rope on the pillow. I tiptoed right up to the bed. She hadn't stirred and I suddenly wanted to kiss her. Surely that would be allowed, if I were careful not to wake her. I climbed onto the bed, and lay down close to her, afraid of being caught but entranced by my beautiful mother. If she woke she might shout for Dad to fetch me away, and I would get a good hiding. But it was worth the risk, just to be near her.

I touched her cheek with my hand, cool and dry. Her parted lips were cracked. I leaned over and brought my lips to her cheek, then to her lips, feeling the roughened skin on my mouth. But there was no warmth there either. I wanted to hug her, to press my warm body over her cold one. She held something in her hand, her fingers grasping the neck of a bottle almost empty except for a few of her pink sweets. I pulled at it, but it was as if her fingers had been welded to the glass.

Then, a muffled sound came from the wardrobe.

I froze, thinking of the monster I feared lived in wardrobes, as I watched the door inch open. Expecting a furry paw, or claws, I held my breath, cowering into my mother's stiff body. Instead, the open door revealed Peter. His mouth, smeared with sugar, was a round wound of an "O".

"I saw her do it," he said, "but I couldn't stop her, cos then she'd know I was hiding in here and she'd tell me off for eating all your sweets."

Between his feet was the empty ice cream box. His eyes were red and puffy and dried tears streaked his face.

"I saw her take all her pills, and now she won't wake up."

11

Black Book Entry

What I remember most about my mother's funeral was the hushed voices of dark-clothed strangers, huddled in corners of our flat, whispering as I walked by. No-one would talk to me so I sat in the corner of the front room and waited. Dad came over, swaying as if he'd had too much beer like he always did at Christmas, and patted me on the head, pulling my hair with his heavy hand. "You're a good girl, Rosie."

Mrs Carron came over, and handed him a whisky. I heard him say, "Thank you, Isabel," and that was how I found out her name, but she was always Mrs Carron to me. When she came to kiss me all I saw was teeth, and I moved away so she caught my jaw with a tight peck. She was younger than you'd think a widow should be, and though she was dressed in a black skirt her blouse was red and silky. She had shiny lips and big gold earrings and I didn't like the way she looked at my dad, like our cat used to look when it brought a bird in from the garden. She led him away, into the front room, and the door was closed behind them. When they'd gone I wiped my face where Mrs Carron had kissed and the back of my hand was smeared with pink lipstick.

I didn't know where Peter was and I didn't care. No-one in

the room came to talk to me, but I saw them look over often. I felt like I'd grown horns or something. And then a group by the door separated to let a round woman in a large fur coat enter. She had a tiny hat like a porkpie balanced on her head, and a piece of black lace over one eye, but I could still see it was Auntie Rita straightaway. I jumped right up and ran to her.

"Oh my, Rose, what a big girl you are! You're going to be quite the bobby dazzler in a few years."

She took a tissue from her shiny black bag and spat on it, wiping the remaining lipstick from my face and tutting. She smelled strongly of roses, and I wanted to bury myself into her soft coat.

"It's not real fur, but who'd know?"

"It's very soft."

"I need to take it off. It's too hot in here." She peeled back the fake animal skin, revealing a tight black dress and fat knees in thick tan-coloured stockings. "I must sit down, Rose. My legs are like lead weights."

Rita sat on a wooden chair, her massive thighs bulging over the sides, and stood me in front of her. She was ten years older than my dad, and lived further down the coast in Felixstowe so we didn't see her much, but she always had violet sweets in her handbag, along with her ciggies, and I loved it when she came to visit. I wanted to put my head on her bosom and be held there.

She touched my chin, turning my face upwards. "Have you been in the dining room yet?"

I shook my head. The dining room wasn't a big room and we only used it at Christmas or for special meals, though Mum sometimes sat in there with a book. The door had been kept closed all morning, though I'd seen people going in and coming out and thought the food must be in there.

"Then I shall take you. Your mum's in there and you need to say goodbye to her."

I gasped – Mum was in the dining room! I pictured her sat in her favourite chair, talking to all the people who'd been going in to see her. Why hadn't someone told me? I would run to her, let her scoop me in her arms and kiss my hair. She would say, "Where have you been, Rosie? I've been waiting for you," and I would show her the blackbirds' nest, kept safely for her.

I jumped from Rita's grip, ran out of the front room and down the hall, pushing past the sombre-suited strangers. I yanked the door handle of the dining room, desperate to see my mum.

The room was dark. The table was empty of food. Then I saw it. A dark wooden box, balanced on two chairs. I inched closer and saw white satin lining the box then the tip of my mother's nose. I didn't move, but stood on tiptoe and peered down at her face. She was so pale, so featureless. It was as if her face had been wiped clean of all its colour, leaving a wax mask. Her eyes were closed and her blonde hair was loose around her face.

"Give her a kiss."

I jumped when Auntie Rita spoke. She put her heavy hand on my shoulder, pressing me into her generous warm body. "Go on, Rose."

I inched forward to the coffin, afraid that Mum would suddenly move. I looked at her for a few moments and then leaned into the box, eyes screwed shut tight as I puckered my lips onto her cheek. I could feel the edge of her cheekbone, the cold skin hard and unyielding.

"Talk to her."

I began to cry. Hot tears fell down my cheek and into my mouth, which I wiped away with the back of my hand.

"She can hear you, Rose. And see you. Her body is empty, but her spirit is still here, in this room."

Through my sobs I said, "Mum?"

"That's it, Rose."

"Mum. I want you to come home."

Rita was right behind me, burying me into her. "Your mum is in the spirit world now, Rose. She won't ever come home but she'll always be with you, when you want her. And she will always be listening."

It was the first time anyone had told me that death could be like that. I'd thought of heaven as clouds or a large garden with lots of birds and angels. But Rita taught me about spirits. She taught me not to be afraid of death. I learned that heaven is a better, safer place.

Some birds steal the nests of others. It's in their nature. Killing the chicks in the nest is just what they have to do.

Some women think nothing of stealing a man.

Dad was in such a state in the months after the funeral that I should probably be grateful to Mrs Carron. She kept the shop going and cooked our meals while he just sat behind the counter staring into the dusty air. When the salesmen called he would look into their boxes with a frown, as if he recognised the strawberry laces and the snowy macaroons, but just couldn't remember what they were for. The shelves weren't stocked and the jars were empty. Mrs Carron quietly set about reordering supplies, and taking the cash to the bank on Tuesdays. In the evening she would write with small neat handwriting in the accounts book, while my father slumped in the armchair holding a forgotten cup of tea. She would smile at him, take the cold cup away, and make another. In time he began to drink the tea, eat the food she cooked, and he seemed to forget that she wasn't really supposed to be there.

I didn't forget. I watched her, knowing that she wasn't my mum. She had no right pretending.

I couldn't tell you the exact day Mrs Carron moved in. It should have been memorable, dramatic even, the moment when my mother was replaced, but she moved quietly like she was playing grandmother's footsteps. One day I turned around and she was there, ready to tap me on the shoulder, before I had a chance to scream.

Things were different for my brother. After Mum died Peter took things hard. He was so angry he would kick a kitten if it came too close, but when Mrs Carron came to live with us he was quieter. He wasn't a clever boy and Mrs Carron treated him like a baby, hugging him to her breast and ruffling his hair. She bought him an electric guitar for his birthday and he said it was his best ever present. He liked Mrs Carron; once he called her Mum and she kissed his cheek. I would never call her Mum. She had stolen my father.

When I think of it I'm back there again. I'm no longer in prison; I'm just a girl.

I need to know Mrs Carron's secret. I need to know why Dad loves her so much that he's forgotten Mum.

He doesn't know that Mrs Carron is not naturally beautiful. But I do. I've seen how she does it. I've watched her sleep, in Dad's bed, on the side where Mum used to lie. I've sneaked in and touched her bare back. Once she woke to find me standing over her, and she yanked the sheet up over her breasts, hiding her brown nipples, and called me a freak. I couldn't let that happen again.

Dad's wardrobe door doesn't shut snug, and I like hiding among his dusty jackets. I like the smell, like a library. Stuffy but safe with old air and too much heat.

Through the crack I see Mrs Carron slide into her dressing gown and peer at herself in the mirror. She sits, twisting her hair into a loose knot, clipping it high. Then she dabs from a glass bottle onto her fingers, smoothing musk over her neck and cheeks. I can tell by the eyeshadow she puts on what colour clothes she will wear, and today it's green. Her sparkly finger strokes her closed lids. But it's the lips I like watching best. She stretches her face, opens her mouth and eyes wide, like she's had a fright, paints pink over nude lips.

Then she takes off her gown and stands naked in front of the other wardrobe, so close I can see her chest rise with each breath. I can see the mole on her hip. I pray she can't hear the thumping of my heart.

Later, downstairs, Mrs Carron stops speaking when I enter the shop, and Dad eyes me cautiously. I place my money in the till and select a glass jar. I'm tall enough to reach now.

"Rose, you never bring any friends home," Dad says. "Is everything alright at school?"

"Yeah."

I busy myself in weighing out a quarter of lemons; the dusty sherbet rises in the bag. I can smell her musky perfume. I pop a sweet in my mouth and suck.

She says, "I know it must be hard for you, with your mum gone." Gone. I wince at the sharp tang of the sweet. "But we don't need to make the situation harder than it is."

My bedroom is next to Dad's and the walls are as thin as cardboard. If I peel the Bananarama poster from the wall, a bit of plasterboard comes away with the Blu-Tac. That was how I got the idea of making a hole in the wall. I couldn't hide in the wardrobe forever. It was too risky.

The knife was soon blunt and I had to fetch a screwdriver from the kitchen drawer to finish the job. I was careful to make the hole the right size – large enough to see through, small enough to be invisible. Luckily the wallpaper in Dad's bedroom is a floral pattern and the hole is in the centre of a blowsy flower. The hole is high, so I have to stand on tiptoe.

I hate the screech of Peter's electric guitar, but at least he's in his bedroom and not pestering me. I know he comes here when I'm not around. Sometimes he comes in to catch me off guard, loving it when I jump out of my skin. "What you up to, fatso?" he demands, and I holler at him to go away. I tell Dad, but he won't put a lock on my door, so I have to remember to wedge a chair under the handle.

I don't peep through my hole when Dad is in the bedroom, because that wouldn't be right. In the mornings, when I hear the clink of the milk deliveries van and the chirp of a radio from downstairs, then I know it's safe. Dad is in the shop and Mrs Carron is alone.

It was so cunning how she did it, moving in so slowly that I don't think Dad even noticed. First it was just a toothbrush and a comb, and then a few dresses squeezed in next to Mum's. But then, through my spy hole, I watched her taking Mum's dresses out and tossing them into bin bags. I saw her pause over Mum's best blouse, the white silky one that she wore at Christmas, and hold it against herself. I could see it would fit her, but still she threw it away, as if my mum could be put out for the dustmen to collect like everything else that had been discarded.

Later, when Mrs Carron was in the shop with Dad, I went to the bedroom.

Her clothes were not like Mum's, but shimmery and thin. "She'll catch her death in that!" Mum would have said, and there was nothing comfortable or warm. No trousers, either, just narrow skirts and tight dresses. One dress caught my eye; it was the colour of rubies, and silky. I held it close to me, just as she had held my mother's blouse. I could hear Peter's guitar and voices from the shop. It was the busy hour when school ended and kids arrived to buy sweets. It took just seconds to pull off my sweater and jeans.

Standing in just my knickers I looked tall and plump. I would soon need a bra, and my stomach was round. The dress looked awful on me, clinging in all the wrong places so I looked like an over-ripe strawberry. Red wasn't my colour; it drained me, left me looking bloodless. I squeezed the flesh bumps of my chest, wondered what kind of woman I would become. Mum hadn't worn green eyeshadow or pink lipstick. She didn't smell of musk. Suddenly, I was aware that Peter had stopped playing his guitar and his heavy steps were heading my way. I was struggling out of the dress when he opened the door.

"What are you doing?" he turned pink when he saw my bare flesh.

"I don't know." All I knew was that Dad loved Mrs Carron and I wanted to be loved. By putting on her clothes maybe I could understand. Make myself lovable.

"You're a bit old for dressing up, aren't you?" he snorted, "Freak!" He slammed the door behind him in disgust.

I stepped out of the crimson fabric, pulling on my own clothes as fast as I could. He was right; I was too old for this game. I was a freak, and no-one liked me. The only boy who ever fancied me was Alfie, the class idiot who had a permanent sneer on his pitted face. He openly stared in class, his fingers scratching his legs, and the other girls would whisper, "Your boyfriend's looking at you!" One day, in the playground, I punched one girl so hard her nose bled, but it was just after Mum died so the teachers didn't do anything. No-one bothered me after that, they just stayed away. Without Mum I was so lonely.

That night I had a nightmare. I was wrapped in red winding silk, and it was so hot my skin burned. Mum was there, trying desperately to cool my blistering arms, a damp sponge on my neck. I felt her arms around me, the safety of her love, and cried, waking to find that the arms comforting me were Mrs Carron's. I pulled back in a fury, the shame and guilt of betraying my mother. She tried to soothe me. "It's just a bad dream, Rose," she said.

I pushed her away like she was on fire, like her embrace could kill me.

It's not nice to admit it, Jason, but loyal people can also be violent; the same passion that makes a good partner also makes a jealous lover. And some of the things you need to know, some of my story, is ugly. It's not my fault that Mum died or that Mrs Carron tried to replace her. Of course I hated her; even being in the same room as her would unsettle me, prick under my skin like an itch. I spent more time in my bedroom. I studied the woman who had taken Mum's place, and tried to understand her power.

One Saturday morning, Mrs Carron was hiding. I'd looked all around the shop, even in the store cupboard, but she was nowhere to be found. We were playing hide-and-seek, though she didn't know it. I counted just the same: 1 – 2 – 3 are you in the kitchen? 4 – 5 – 6 maybe in the shower, behind the curtain – whoosh! Not there! Come out, come out, wherever you are 7 – 8 – 9. I can hear you…alone, in the bedroom.

I propped a chair against my bedroom door to stop anyone coming in, peeled back the poster and looked through my spy hole.

She lay naked and awake, her hand stroking her thigh. I felt my cheeks burn, knowing I shouldn't be watching, but unable to look away. She was sleepy, her eyes still closed, but her movements were like a waking cat that stretches and preens itself. She was touching between her legs. Mum always told me that only bad girls touched themselves there. Her fingers grazed over her left breast, and I wondered what it must be like to touch such softness. At that moment I would have given anything to be held, to be safe. But the only person there was me.

I touched my neck, my breasts. I knew Mum would say it was naughty, but she was gone and Mrs Carron had taken her place. Dad had forgotten Mum because Mrs Carron had made him forget. I hated her and loved her at the same time. She was my mother; she had replaced my mother. Her power drew me in; I sensed she knew something precious, something that I could learn. I lifted up my skirt. Even if it hurt, I wanted to know how it felt. I pushed my hand between my legs, into my knickers, feeling the soft tangle of new hair. An embarrassment in the PE changing rooms, a shame I hadn't accepted, in that instant became something else.

I couldn't see Mrs Carron's hand, but her body rocked over her fist, half her face crushed in the pillow. My fingers probed lower, but it was awkward with my eye to the peephole, so I grabbed the chair from the door to stand on. It was now much easier to copy what Mrs Carron was doing. I was surprised to feel that I was wet. Then, in an instant, I knew how to move. My body followed its own rhythm. Together we seemed to dance, swaying to the same music.

And then – Oh shit, no! – the unsecured door crashed open. Peter stood, mouth gaping, taking me in, standing on the chair, skirt hitched, hand low, with my eye to a hole in the wall.

"You sicko," he murmured, slowly. Then, louder, "Dad! Dad – come here, quick!"

But Mrs Carron, startled by the shouting, arrived first, belting her dressing gown as she appeared in the doorway. I saw her face, and she saw mine. She stared at me, standing on the chair by the wall, at the hole in the wall. She knew I had been watching her. She wasn't angry. She was terrified. Fear in her eyes like an electric shock. She was frozen, unable to look away as I straightened my clothing and stepped down from the chair. When I walked towards her she flinched back, like I'd burned her.

Dad arrived, breathless from bounding up the stairs, and before anyone else could speak Mrs Carron pulled at his arm, her voice low and urgent.

"Get her out of here. If she doesn't leave, I will."

12

Black Book Entry

I heard her coughing in the street and looked out in time
to see Auntie Rita's bulky frame struggle through the shop
entrance. The bell above the door trilled, and I could hear Dad,
downstairs in the shop, making a weak attempt to welcome
her.

In my bedroom I pulled my clothes and belongings from
drawers and shelves, shoving what I could into a black plastic
bag. I took the nest from where I kept it, hidden carefully in
my knicker drawer, and wrapped it in tissues so it wouldn't
get damaged. Peter stood in the doorway, watching with a
gormless look on his face. He hadn't spoken to me since he
discovered me watching Mrs Carron.

Downstairs, Dad put his hand on my arm briefly, mumbled
something about how I was a young woman now, and Rita
would see me right. He never knew what to say to me,
particularly since Mum's death, and what had happened that
morning had confirmed his view that I would be better off
living at Rita's.

Rita's house was two train journeys away from Lowestoft.
She lived in Felixstowe, alone, apart from her budgie Bill,

in a battered end terrace within earshot of the North Sea. At night you could hear the music and loud shouts and laughter from the amusement arcade. She didn't treat me like a child. She never asked me where I was going or what time I'd be back, and she sent me for chips or fags when other kids my age would be in bed. She didn't like to cook and most nights she'd say, "Shall we have a saveloy for tea? Run to the corner, there's a pet." The stalls by the pier sold all the types of food I loved: sausages, pasties and chips, fish, kebabs. The men who ran them all got to know me, would look at my thin blouse and throw in another helping for luck.

Rita spent most of the day in a saggy armchair, muttering that there was nothing good on the box, or leafing through a gossipy magazine. She ate and smoked in that chair. It fitted around her just right. I would curl up on the other chair, newsprint on my fingers as I licked the grease from the chips. Unlike Dad, Rita thought it was alright to eat in front of the TV and we would follow all the soaps in silence, the only sound being the crinkle of paper or Rita's occasional coughing fit.

On account of her back, which she'd done in cleaning other people's floors, Rita was on sickness benefit, and didn't go out much. But every Saturday a woman named Annie would call for her and they'd go to a 'session'. Rita would put on her only good dress, which I remembered from Mum's funeral, her face alight with a kind of glowing excitement. She'd sometimes come home a little sad and would go straight upstairs to bed, though the next morning she'd be her normal self. I liked Saturdays. It was the one evening I could be alone. I didn't think much about Rita and Annie's sessions, but I knew they were held at the local church hall, which made me think of Sunday school and jumble sales, so I didn't think anything that happened there could interest me.

"It's a séance," Rita told me, "we get messages from people who have passed over."

One Saturday I heard Rita coughing down the street and

was surprised, as she wasn't normally back for another hour. When she struggled through the door I could hear her wheezing as though she'd had a turn, but her eyes were wet and her face was pink.

"I've a message for you, girl."

She could hardly get the words out, and I helped her to the chair. She put a hand to her chest, and tried to speak normally.

"She's watching us, Rose. Right now. She's pleased."

A cold shiver ran down my back. There was only one "she" in our lives.

"She says you've grown into a real bobby dazzler. She says I'm looking after you just as she wanted. She told me to tell you she loves you."

I bit my lip so hard I tasted blood.

"Don't cry, poppet. She's happier where she is. Life is hard for some people, and living was such a burden to her. She's not in pain anymore."

Rita passed me a hanky that had been balled up in her sleeve. She was silent for a while, but I sensed she had more to say.

"She wants you to come with us, Rose. Next week. Your mum wants to talk to you."

All that week I thought of the coming Saturday, dreading and longing for it. The only thing I knew about the occult was from Gypsy Margo's brightly painted stand at the end of the pier where she told fortunes. But when we arrived at the church hall there was nothing bright or sparkly about it, and no crystal ball either. Just a room full of old ladies, chatting to each other over cups of tea. The medium, Maureen, didn't look special at all, and I started to think that she couldn't have any powers. She just looked like somebody's nan. But then she stood in the centre of the stage and put her fingertips to her temples, swaying slightly in her dowdy cotton dress. The whole room fell silent.

"Is there anyone here with a cat in the spirit world called

Suki?" Maureen said, like a teacher asking a class of pupils if anyone knew the correct answer.

Rita's hand shot up. "Here!"

Maureen came down from the stage and stood in front of Rita. "Suki's a beautiful cat, isn't she? Black?"

"That's right." Rita beamed with pleasure.

"She was much loved, wasn't she?"

"Oh yes," Rita dabbed her eye.

"But she says she's been replaced?"

Rita shifted in her seat. "I've got a budgie now."

"There's someone with Suki. She wants to speak to the girl next to you."

I felt Maureen's eyes weighing me up and shivered.

"Hello, love. I've got someone here who knows you. She says she misses you very much." I blinked away warm tears. "She says she knows it's been hard for you, but she's watching over you. Making sure you're okay." Suddenly her hands grasped her throat. "I've got a pain! Why have I got a pain in my neck?"

Rita looked sideways at me, but didn't speak. My voice was so calm it surprised me. "Suicide," I said. "She took a ton of tablets after she found my dad fucking another woman."

Maureen blinked. A ripple of suppressed chatter ran through the rows and I flew out of the hall as if the devil himself was at my heels.

13

Black Book Entry

You're visiting today, Jason.

You don't come often, just once a month, so it's rare enough for me to feel excited. That's the wrong word. Apprehensive is better.

I know you find it hard to see me in here, but you never miss a visit. I'd like to ask you why that is and if you feel guilty, after all, but I'm afraid to.

When I was arrested and remanded into custody, I thought I'd have to cope alone. But you've proved me wrong; you came back to me. You've been more faithful than I would have thought possible.

You don't try to make sense of what happened, you don't analyse it. It would be too hard to do that, wouldn't it? In court, when the prosecution tried to make a case for murder, you sat with your head bowed. Not once did you accuse me, not even with your eyes. When the foreman said I was not guilty of murder, you didn't look surprised. You just nodded your head as if to say, "That's right. She's not a murderer."

You never asked me about the night Luke died.

It's so hard for me to think about. Never being able to hold him again, to smell the sweet scent of baby talc in the folds of his skin. And yet I'm expected to talk about him to a stranger. I must, if I'm to be set free. Cate Austin will want me to say that I'm sorry, to "take responsibility" as these professionals put it, admit that I was deranged.

Is it true? Was I sick? Am I cured? And if I'm cured, how has that happened? From being caged like Rita's poor budgie for almost four years with no treatment, no therapy except fifteen minutes with the psychologist when I arrived at each new prison.

In my cell I have my memories. I have my nest, so small and perfect, which I hold in my hands, thinking of my mother. At night, lying on the three-quarter bed, army issue, I sift through what I remember like treasure and find the pearl. My boy. At night, in the dark, he's mine again. I can hear him breathing next to me. I can feel him suckling milk from my breast. I nurture him, keep him alive, until daylight breaks through the bars. No-one grieves more than me.

In the room used for family visits I sit in my own clothes but with a red tabard over my dress to show I'm a prisoner. As if there could be any doubt. I fit in here, but you are the odd one out with your curly golden-red hair. Like a visitor from across the seas, a strange warrior, you shine in this grey building. The newer prisoners, seeing you for the first time, look over. They're asking themselves how I've managed to get a man like you when I'm so plain. You're tanned from working as a brickie, building a new shopping mall in Ipswich. May sunshine has turned your arms brown. Your hair is shorter now than it has been, but it still springs from behind your ears, catching the sunlight coming in between the bars.

You take my hand. Yours is warm. "How are you, Rose?"

How do you cope, I wonder. I thought you would leave me, but now I think you'll stay with me no matter what. There's something strong binding us together.

"I'm fine. What about you?"

"Good."

We sit in silence for a while before you think of something to say. I like to hear about the squabbles on site, the problems the foreman is having with the workers from Poland. Then it's my turn to speak. "I've met the probation officer who'll write my parole report."

"Oh?"

"I've only met her once, so far. I'm her first case since she got posted here. She'll want to meet you."

"What's it got to do with me?"

I stroke your hand, soothe you. "That home visit is important, Jason. It has to go well or I won't get parole."

"What's she like?" You sound nervous.

"Younger than me, pretty. But she's guarded – a tough nut to crack."

You look around, see Natalie Reynolds at the next table. She says hi and you smile back. At the other table Susan Thomas is having a visit from her mum, and she's brought Susan's daughter. I watch for a second as the little girl climbs into her mother's lap and touches her bruised face. "Did you fall off your bike, Mummy?"

Susan was promised a move to another prison, in return for her silence, but she never got it. She was attacked in the shower, when all the inmates were locked up.

I squeeze your hand. "She'll ask you about Luke. And Emma."

You clear your throat.

"Will you be okay, Jason?"

"Why wouldn't I be?" you say, as if Emma is of no consequence. You never could talk about how you feel. But the thought of you saying her name, talking about your marriage, causes a physical pain in my chest. I need to know that you are mine, still mine.

I stroke your hand and then I kiss you, savouring the pleasure as our lips touch. Most of the officers allow this, apart from

76

Officer Holley, who insists inmates stay in their seats. We're in a corner and it's the new officer, Mark Burgess, overseeing the visits, so I slide from my place and sit on your lap, circling my arms around your neck. Over your shoulder I see Officer Burgess is too busy reading to stop me. With my mouth over yours, I carefully undo your belt, one eye on Burgess.

"Rose, stop. People'll see."

Natalie is having a visit from her boyfriend. She whispers in his ear and they both turn to see, sniggering. I feel your penis stirring through my dress and I push back, gently at first, then harder. You try to look around to see Burgess but I'm in control and I circle my body in tiny, tiny movements. Your eyes go blurry as you gasp in more air.

The other visitors and inmates nearest our table see what we are doing. Susan turns her daughter's back to us and her mother gives me an evil look.

I want you, as I've always wanted you. I miss you, have missed you every night. I want you so much that my hands are shaking. "I love you, Jason."

You breathe heavily into my ear, and a groan escapes from your open mouth. Is it me you're thinking of, or Emma?

I hold you tightly as your breathing steadies.

We stay locked like this until the bell rings, and you have to leave me. Again.

14

Cate Austin was working at her desk at Bishop's Hill. It was barely 10 a.m. but she already felt exhausted. She was full of a summer cold, and soggy used tissues clogged up the waste bin. Since Amelia had started going to the childminder's, one or both of them always seemed to be sneezing or coughing. Today Amelia had been quite unwell when Cate left her at Julie's and she felt guilty for not keeping her home, curled up on the sofa, watching her favourite children's TV programmes.

She had held Amelia tight before passing her over, relieved but pained at how easily her daughter clung to Julie's embrace, as if she belonged there.

Reaching for another tissue, Cate thought about how she always seemed to fall short of what was expected – especially as a mother. The failure of her relationship with Tim meant that Amelia had only a part-time father. *Still*, she thought, massaging the swollen glands in her neck, *I'm only doing what millions of other women have to do. Juggling.*

She knew she wasn't really well enough to be at work but there was no way she could have called in sick. She'd had too much time off in the months before her prison secondment, and anyway this morning she was meeting with Rose again.

Gathering her papers and the remaining tissues from her desk, she went to check her pigeonhole. Inside the mailroom a few officers were chatting, including Deborah Holley and Dave Callahan, who looked over and winked. She smiled politely, and then turned her back to him, reaching for the box with her name on it. Empty. Officer Holley separated herself from the group and approached her. In her hand she held a bundle of papers fastened by a red band.

"I think you want this," she said, holding it out.

Cate grasped it quickly, reading the name: Rose Wilks.

"Remember what I said, Austin: don't feel sorry for her. She's a nonce and deserves everything she gets."

The file was thin and Cate thought there should surely be more than this on a woman who had spent four years in prison. She looked up, intending to ask Officer Holley about this, but she had gone.

"Morning, sunshine. How's the world with you?"

She was pleased to see Paul Chatham smiling at her. "Oh, you know. Another day, another dollar."

"A bit more than that, I hope. Unless they've brought in performance-related pay when I wasn't looking. Anything planned for the weekend?"

"Bed, I think. I feel lousy." As she spoke she tore the manila envelope and removed the sheaf of paper.

"Is that the file on your nonce?"

Cate nodded.

"Thank your lucky stars it's not too long. Must be straightforward. Tell me over coffee later."

Sitting back in her broom cupboard of an office, Cate quickly separated out the file into four neat piles: prison record; pre-sentence reports; witness statements; then came the psychiatric report, thick vanilla paper with a letterhead proudly announcing the psychiatrist's credentials, written after Rose was found guilty of manslaughter to help the judge decide on a sentence. The report described Rose as "plain-featured" and "of heavy build"; "Miss Wilks is a tall woman with hazel eyes and dark hair". The psychiatrist said that Rose had engaged with all the questions asked of her. He concluded, "It is my opinion that the fire which resulted in Luke Hatcher's tragic death was an accident, triggered largely by the defendant's depressive state and dependence on sedative medication, making her clumsy and slow to respond after her cigarette set fire to the carpet. This woman does not belong in the criminal justice system and I recommend a suspended sentence."

The door behind her opened and a cup of coffee appeared, as if hovering in mid-air.

"Hello, Paul."

His face appeared. "How did you know it was me? Here you go, love."

The coffee was strong and sweet and very welcome. Paul perched on her desk, looking at the four neat piles of paper. "Touch of obsessive-compulsive, I reckon."

"Guilty. I like to have everything in order."

"Oh, me too. You should see my underwear drawer, it's colour-coded."

"Really?"

"No, not really. I never wear underwear."

Cate slapped his leg. "Wind-up."

"So what are these piles? Men who've asked you out, men you fancy, men you wouldn't touch with a six-foot barge pole?"

"Paul, stop it. It's Rose Wilks's case file."

"Anything juicy?"

"That pile is the psychiatric assessment. It really pisses me off. I mean, what difference does it make if Rose is attractive or not? It went on about her hair, her face, how tall she is. Put a few letters after your name, and you can write anything you want."

"Sounds like you're letting the case get under your skin, babe." He picked up the second group of papers. Clipped to the top page was a newspaper cutting with ragged edges where it had been roughly torn out. Someone had written in biro, "*East Anglian Daily Times*".

A baby died yesterday in a house fire in Ipswich, while his mother was lifted to safety through a bedroom window. Fire crews from the area were called to Clifton Drive at 4.20 a.m. on Friday. The fire was confined to the first floor of the detached property. Crews were at the scene until 6 a.m. Fire fighters wore breathing apparatus to tackle the blaze, but the four-month-old baby boy was already dead by the time they managed to reach his bedroom.

Paul put the file down. "No wonder you're worked up. That's horrid. But you need to keep a distance. It's only work."

"I know. Don't lecture me."

Paul had a point, though. Reading about a child's death inevitably made her think of Amelia. She was meeting Rose Wilks at the next bell, and she needed to get caffeine in her system and her daughter's face from her mind before the interview.

Rose was waiting in the classroom, which had evidently not been cleaned since their previous meeting. Cate noted the growing number of fag ends on the floor but the same lesson plan on the board. After sitting opposite Rose, she took out her notepad.

"I got your case file today. I've just read the psychiatric report."

Rose rubbed her lower lip with a finger, and looked to the window. "The psychiatrist wanted me to say I started the fire deliberately. He said he would understand. Everyone knows about post-natal depression, don't they? But I couldn't lie. I would never harm Luke."

"But Luke did die, Rose. And you were convicted of manslaughter."

"You have a child. Do you really think a normal woman could deliberately harm a baby?"

"I do," said Cate. "If she was unwell, or addicted. Or depressed."

"It goes against a woman's nature. Women who kill kids, they're evil. You know that, you're a mother. We're programmed to protect children. To take care of them."

"I don't see things quite that simply."

Rose looked closely at Cate. "I've never understood women who don't want to look after their children. Like career women. How can they do that, leave a child with someone else? Maybe they have to because they haven't got a man. What do you think?"

Cate realised that this comment was for her benefit, and was interested that Rose was taunting her. She was about to speak when the door opened, shattering the moment. Officer Mark Burgess rushed in, worry etched on his face.

"There's been a call from your daughter's childminder. She's had an accident."

"Is she hurt?" Fear curled a cold hand around her heart, squeezing tight.

"She's been taken to hospital."

Cate fumbled with her papers, dropping her pen as she rushed to the door.

"Cate?" Rose had silently moved behind her and was standing at her shoulder, bending forward, speaking softly into her ear. Turning, Cate looked up into Rose's face. Rose took Cate's hand and opened it, pressing a pen into her palm.

"You forgot this." She touched her hand a beat too long. "I hope Amelia's okay. I'll be praying for her."

Cate hurried away, desperate to get to her daughter's side. She didn't even wonder how Rose knew Amelia's name.

When Cate arrived at Accident and Emergency, Amelia was nowhere to be seen. She went over to where a receptionist was taking a call, impatiently tapping her fingers on the desk, eyes darting and ears pricked for Amelia's voice. She was in a state of controlled panic and had driven as fast as her conscience would allow, forcing herself to brake at the red lights rather than rush through. There had been no vacant spaces in the car park and she had pulled onto the grass verge.

Finally, the receptionist ended her call. Mistaking Cate's pale face for a patient she said crisply, "If you take a seat, I'll get a nurse to see you."

"My daughter's been brought in after having an accident. Amelia Austin."

The woman zigzagged a red nail down a list. "She's with the doctor now. Room 3 – just down there." She pointed to a corridor on Cate's left.

Cate was halfway to the cubicle already. *Please*, she silently begged, *don't let Amelia be badly hurt.*

"Mummy!"

Her daughter lay on a hospital trolley, being examined by a doctor. Sitting by her side was Julie, the childminder.

"Is Daddy here too?"

"No, love." Cate reached for Amelia, cradling her close and kissing her hair, smelling fresh sweat on her scalp. "Oh sweetheart, what have you done?"

Amelia cried into her mother's jacket, as Cate watched the doctor twisting her daughter's foot, its sole against his palm. "Ow!" cried Amelia.

"Is it broken?" Cate asked.

The doctor prodded the puffy ankle. "Maybe a small fracture. We'll need to take an X-ray and we'll put an ice pack on it to take down the swelling. It will need to be strapped up and she'll be hobbling around for a few weeks, I'm afraid."

"What happened?" Cate asked Julie.

Amelia's muffled voice said, "I fell, Mummy. A boy at the park knocked me off the climbing frame."

"I don't think he meant to," said Julie. "It was an accident."

"You should have been watching her, Julie."

"I was!"

Cate couldn't even look at her. "I need to feel Amelia's in safe hands when I'm at work."

"It was an accident, Cate. Don't you think I feel bad enough already? I wish we'd never gone to the park, but Amelia was feeling better and I thought the fresh air would do her good." Julie reached forward and stroked Amelia's arm. "We thought we'd have a little playtime, didn't we, angel?"

Amelia smiled at Julie, forgetting her pain.

Cate shifted in her seat. "You can go now, Julie. I'll take care of her."

As Julie rose to go, Amelia reached out for her, clinging to her with the tenacity of a limpet. Cate tried to smile, telling herself it was a good thing that Amelia had a strong bond with her childminder. "Okay, Julie. We'll see you tomorrow."

"You sure you want me to leave?" Julie looked hesitant.

"Just go," said Cate, fighting a rising tide of jealousy. As she held her daughter tight she whispered a hundred sorries into her hair.

15

Black Book Entry

I learned a lot from Rita, but mostly I learned about death. She wasn't afraid of it like most people are. Even when the doctor said she had lung cancer she wasn't scared. Her only worry was what would happen to me when she was gone. It was the summer after my GCSE exams and I'd done well enough to stay on at school for the sixth form. I was good at the sciences, especially chemistry. Mr Wilson said I was a natural, and I liked the experiments, lighting the Bunsen burner with the air hole closed, then opening it, the gas burning in my sinuses as I watched the flame change from yellow to blue. I was going to do A-level chemistry, and I wanted to be a pharmacist. To help people get better.

Rita was dying. Her coughing was something we both dreaded, the awful hacking that went on and on. She said it was only cigs that made her lungs feel clearer. The doctors tried to make her stop smoking, but what was the point? She said it was a pleasure, and she had few enough of those left. But she would rub my hand when she said it, and I knew from her look that I was a pleasure to her as well.

Rita wanted me to go to university, and she'd worked out that there was only one way for that to happen: I had to go back to Lowestoft to do my A-levels and live with my father. I heard the pleading, whispered conversations on the phone and knew she was talking to him.

"But she's your daughter! She's so clever, you should hear what the teachers say," she said. "An education will be the making of her." Another time I heard her say, "She'll be all alone when I'm gone, doesn't that bother you?" and during the final conversation she said, "Shame on you! Her mother must be turning in her grave."

I was glad when she slammed the phone down. I didn't want anything from him anyway.

When Rita's breathing became too difficult she was admitted to the general hospital in Ipswich and put on oxygen. I stayed in the house alone each night, going every morning on the bus to Ipswich, a new magazine rolled up in my pocket. Rita lived in a council house and, although the housing benefit was paid for the month while she was in hospital, I knew they'd soon want me out. Rita would never come home, and I'd have no right to live there once she was gone, and Dad didn't want me back.

It was a long summer the year I was sixteen, and I spent every day by Rita's hospital bed watching her slipping away from me. The nurses worked around me, putting watery hot chocolate by my side, and taking it away cold. I wasn't thinking about food, but each evening Annie would bring over a plate of whatever she'd cooked at the house: chops and carrots, liver and mash. I could hardly get it down but she would watch over me, clicking her tongue if I paused for too long. She didn't ask how Rita was. She knew it was just a matter of time. But she would rub my hands and ask about me.

Although Annie had known Rita since they were both girls she wouldn't come with me to the hospital. She just said she preferred to think of Rita at home; that was how she wanted to remember her. It was only later that I discovered the real reason.

When I arrived in the hospital room I heard the grating noise in Rita's throat and knew it was bad. I pressed the red buzzer and a nurse came quickly. She took Rita's pulse and then turned to me.

"That noise," I said, "is she choking?"

"Not choking, love. It's a rattle – it means she's going to go soon."

I took Rita's hand, and saw that her fingers were swollen. "Look," I said to the nurse, "what's happening to her?"

"Her body's had enough, love. Just sit and talk to her. Make her passing easier. There's nothing more you can do."

I sat on the chair, stroking Rita's puffy wrist, listening to the life caught in her throat. Finally, within the hour, the noise stopped and I knew she had gone.

When I got home that evening Annie didn't force me to eat any food, but hugged me tight and kissed my forehead. "It'll be better, Rose, in time. You'll see." But I didn't believe her. Rita wasn't just my auntie, she'd been my best friend. She'd helped me navigate through the last few years, and I'd started to think about my future. With her gone, I was shipwrecked.

For the first two weeks I only left bed to use the toilet or get more smokes. Smoking reminded me of Rita, and it was the only thing that slowed my breathing. I didn't open the post; it could only be bad news. The council would want me out and I had nowhere to go.

On the third Saturday Annie came calling, shouting through the letterbox until I had no choice but to let her in. She took one look at me and frog-marched me to the bathroom, leaning her ample body over the enamel bath and twisting the hot tap on full. She tipped in a generous amount of Rita's pink salts, dissolving them with her hand.

"Now, Rose. Rita wouldn't like to see you moping like this. You need to sort yourself out. I want you to have a bath and get dressed. Quickly, mind. We can't be late."

"Late for what?"

"What do you think? It's Saturday." And that, of course, explained everything. I knew I had no choice so I got clean and clothed and followed her out of the house to the church hall.

The meeting hadn't started yet, and the huddle of women turned to greet Annie. When they saw I was standing behind her they hugged and soothed me, sympathising with my loss. But there was an excitement in the room, like before a party, and one of the women squeezed my elbow. "I hope she comes," she whispered, and Annie smiled back at her.

Soon, Maureen went to her place on the stage and everyone took their seats. I felt the hope and expectation in the bodies around me. And that night I understood the comfort of it.

Rita didn't come, and neither did Mum, but Annie had a message from her dead husband. I found out why she hated hospitals; he'd gone in for a hip replacement, but caught a virus there and never came home. She'd vowed never to set foot in a hospital again. But those sessions gave her comfort. She laughed when he told her she'd gambled too much on the dog race that Saturday. Another woman was asked not to forget her sister's birthday and that she wanted yellow flowers on her grave. Another had her new haircut complimented by a lover. Even the ones who didn't get a message weren't crestfallen; there was always next week. And what they'd witnessed reassured them that the dead are with us always.

Later, when the messages started coming from Rita and occasionally from Mum, I knew that I wasn't really alone. I also learned not to fear death. Rita could now smoke to her heart's content and she'd never cough again.

One Saturday Annie was chatty as usual, taking my arm as we walked. "Now Rose, I've done a bit of checking around and there's a job going at The Grand."

"The hotel on the seafront?"

"That's it. It includes a room and I think you should go and see about it. You need to look forward now, duck."

Annie helped me a lot after that, and she never forgot to call for me on Saturday evenings. I took the job at The Grand and forgot my dreams of going to university. The pay was poor, but included board and lodging. They started me as a waitress but after customers complained that I didn't smile, they switched me to being a chambermaid.

I'm so grateful for that time now, for all I learned. Everything was new. I even had a new home in the staff quarters, a room filled with Rita's furniture and my most prized possession: the birds nest, carefully stored in a drawer.

I sometimes think back to the faded grandeur of The Grand: the Edwardian brickwork, the large staircase that swooped down into reception, the steel kitchen with its pots and pans hanging overhead. The fizz of water boiling over, the sizzle of chips in oil, the reek of kippers each morning. And I think of you, Jason. How you smiled like you'd just woken, the graceful movements of your long, lean body. How your hair was always tied back, golden-red curls escaping.

You came into my life and changed everything.

16

Black Book Entry

Survivors recognise damaged people and the first time I saw
your face I knew you were hurting.

My heart was beginning to mend. Mum's death was still
very sore, as was the loss of Rita, but I comforted myself
with the thought that they were with me always. Sometimes
I forgot that they were spirits, and set out extra plates or two
coffee mugs. Death didn't stop me talking to them; in fact, I
was closer to Rita and Mum in the spirit world than I was to
my father and brother, who lived just an hour up the coast. I'd
never returned to Lowestoft, but I knew that Peter now ran
the shop. I wondered if he still stuffed his hand into the glass
jars of sweets, or if he'd outgrown his love of sugar. Dad and
Mrs Carron had a bungalow close by, and helped out when
needed. Peter was married. The wedding was a small affair,
he explained on a scrap of notepaper. I was invited to the party
afterwards but I didn't go.

I don't want to bore you. The part of the story before you
arrived into my life must be so tedious for you. But it's all
necessary, Jason. So many things have to be told, I shouldn't
waste time. Let's move on.

At The Grand I'd become a permanent fixture. If people thought I was sullen or rude, it didn't matter, as I was good at my job. I never took a single day off sick, and I didn't mind working on Christmas Day. I was a good chambermaid; I liked the work, making the rooms neat and tidy, seeing different clothes swinging in wardrobes and wondering about the guests with all their strange and unknowable lives. I never took anything, but sometimes squirted a bit of perfume from the dressing table on my wrist, or had a little look through a suitcase. Just curiosity really; who wouldn't have? Sometimes guests complained about jewellery cases being moved or underwear being mislaid, but no-one took the complaints seriously. All chambermaids snoop – it's only natural. And I liked looking at guests' jewellery, their bits and pieces. It was an innocent enough pleasure.

You get to know a lot about people when you clean up their mess. Mrs Stokes was someone I knew well, though we never had a conversation. When I cleaned her room she would be in the dining room, wolfing a full English breakfast, before trekking down to the beach hut she'd hired. I knew this, because it was what she wrote on the postcards, half-finished on the dressing table, each one scrawled with the same message. She visited every summer for three weeks, but only brought two dresses and one summer raincoat that she would drench in Yardley's English Lavender. The bath was always dry, the soap still wrapped, as if using perfume meant she didn't have to wash. Halfway through her holiday she would rinse her knickers in the sink, leaving them dripping on the radiator, drenching the carpet. They crunched like stale crisps when I folded them back into the drawer. She should have bought more; it wasn't like she was hard up. She had two hundred pounds stashed in her suitcase, and she was hardly going to spend all that on postcards and cream teas.

Mrs Stokes liked to read, those thick books with a woman on the front in jodhpurs or a skimpy nightdress. When she'd finished with one, she'd throw it away and start another. I would spy them in the bin, like a gift left just for me, but would resist the urge to hold the book until I'd finished my job. I built up quite a collection that way. I also had an assortment of shampoos and expensive shower gels that guests had left behind, some hardly used.

Another guest I got to know well was Miss Talisker. She would only stay for one night at a time, and it was always a last-minute booking. She'd arrive early. Sometimes I wouldn't have finished cleaning the room from the previous guest. She only ever brought one piece of luggage: a leather vanity case, post-box red and very classy. Even if I were still polishing she'd start to unpack it. I'd dust the dressing table, watching her in the mirror as she took out her gold lipstick, her silver cigarette lighter, the white and purple box of cigarettes: Silk Cut, her favourite brand. She'd place a skimpy nightdress, sometimes still with its price tag, on the pillow. Then she'd go downstairs to wait for the man, always the same one. He would come much later, and when she returned with him to the bedroom I'd be long gone. The next morning, while she was at breakfast, I'd clear away the empty champagne bottle from her room and put the flowers into a nice vase. She never bothered to take them home, which I thought was a waste.

Sometimes, if I was ahead of schedule, I'd slip between the sheets and close my eyes. Miss Talisker's perfume smelled of pine forest, or maybe that was her lover's aftershave. The sheets had the sweet aroma of burnt fruit, so I thought that must be what sex smelled like. I thought about it happening to me, in that bed, and wondered what it would be like.

One morning I was paired with Hannah, a new girl. She was pale with dark hair and a stud in her nose. I was nearly twenty and she was a few years younger, and they put us together so I could show her the ropes. We started off in this woman's room who we all knew as Kiki. She was a regular guest, as she sang at the Spa Pavilion during the summer season, and at Easter too. Of course, we thought Kiki was very glamorous, going on the stage every night, and she smoked these thin cigarettes that come in a cream tin. I took a tin from the waste bin once. I kept it for years. All her dresses were long and sparkly, and I showed them to Hannah. We took a few out, holding them against us. Hannah was shorter than me, and slim, so when she held a red cocktail dress against her I could tell it would fit like a glove.

"Try it on," I urged, knowing she was itching to.

"I daren't, Rose. What if Miss French finds out?"

Miss French was the housekeeper, a dragon of a woman who scared most of the staff half to death. She was always kind to me, though.

"She won't know. Go on. I bet it'd look great on you."

Hannah quickly threw off her uniform, a white blouse and navy skirt, revealing frayed knickers and a grubby bra.

"Help me, then," she said, and I eased the red satin over her body, tight as a second skin. My hands shook as I tied the thin strap around her neck, an imperfect bow at the nape. I pulled the zip, watching her pale flesh being closed in by the silver teeth.

We both watched her reflection in the mirror, astounded at her transformation. She looked wonderful.

"Wait!" I said, rushing to the bedside cabinet. At the back of the drawer, behind her dirty laundry and the mandatory bible, Kiki hid her jewellery in a pink leather box. I pulled it out and unclasped its gold fastening. I knew exactly what to choose and it took just moments to hand the sparkling earrings to Hannah, who pushed the silver wire through the pierced hole in her neat lobes. I watched her swishing her head to the pleasing jangle of the diamantes.

"I look beautiful," Hannah said. I wondered why she was surprised.

The room was hot with our excitement, our daring, and in the impulse of the moment I reached for Kiki's makeup bag on the dressing table and took out a lipstick.

"Rose, don't. What if someone sees?"

"You can wipe it off afterwards. It's just for fun."

But I was deadly serious, and I concentrated so hard I bit my own lips when putting the glossy red stain on hers. The lipstick, which had a perfume like hot plastic, stretched her mouth. I made her lips bright and glossy, and as red as the blood on my own. I reached behind her head, tugging the elastic band that was holding her hair trapped, and it fell loose around her shoulders. She didn't look in the mirror, but at me, and I felt a surge of pride that she wanted my approval.

"You look like a film star."

She smiled, only half believing. Young, but at the same time knowing what womanhood could bring her.

"Oh Rose, I wish I could have things like this. I wish I could always be pretty."

I cupped her chin with my palm, kissed her cheek. "You are pretty, Hannah. Always."

And then I tasted the red lipstick with my bloodied lips, my mouth stained by hers and hers by mine, the perfume in my throat like a swallowed bud. We fell back onto the bed and I pulled her on top of me, kissing her deeply, my hands locked around her back. She placed her hands on my shoulders, pushing me away, but I knew she was shy and it was what she wanted so I held her tighter, her body writhing on top of mine, her mouth moving on mine as I kissed her hard. Still she pushed and pulled and then she wrenched herself away, still in my grip, and the fabric ripped, an awful tearing sound as the fabric at the seam gave way, leaving a gaping gash down the side of the dress.

She stood, shaking. "You weird lessie!" She held the torn red satin in her hand and looked at me, pale-faced, and very close to tears. "Look what you've done!"

I jumped off the bed and ran to Mrs French's room. The heat of anger and shame scorched my cheeks. But Hannah was wrong, I wasn't a lesbian. Watching her in that dress, seeing how pretty she was, made me think of Mrs Carron. Made me think that life could be different for me, if I could make myself like that. If I could be pretty and lovable.

I barged into Mrs French's office, where she was seated writing at her desk, hardly catching breath, "Come quickly, Miss French! Hannah has done something awful."

She threw her pen down and followed me back to Kiki's room, where Hannah was sitting on the bed, still in the torn dress, weeping.

It took Mrs French a moment, but I have to hand it to her, she kept her dignity.

"Hannah, I want you to clean your face, take off that dress, and come down to my office. Immediately."

Of course, Kiki had to be told what Hannah had done and the hotel had to pay for a new dress. Miss French had to let Hannah go, as she obviously couldn't be trusted, trying on residents' clothes like that. I admitted that I'd watched Hannah get into Kiki's dress, and that I should have fetched Mrs French straightaway.

"I suppose you felt afraid to stop her?"

"Yes, Mrs French."

"You're a good worker, Rose. And you've been with us – how long?"

"Four years, Miss French."

"Well, Rose, I have to give you credit for coming to get me when you did. But I've decided to move you to another part of the hotel. Somewhere where these silly girls who've had their heads turned can't influence you. Chef is shorthanded at the moment, so I'll see about a move to the kitchens. Would you like that?"

17

Black Book Entry

I didn't think I'd get on in the kitchens at first, but soon found my way. Chef liked me. I never answered back, just got on with the task in hand, never gossiping or slacking like other staff who came and went. When someone new arrived they would be introduced to me. "Rose has been here forever. Any questions, just ask her." I'd take them under my wing. I'm like that. Staff moved on all the time; waitresses were especially fickle, and I hardly got to know their names before they left. I suppose one pretty, bubbly girl is much the same as the next.

I'd moved out of the staff accommodation and got my own place by then. Each night, smelling of oil and garlic, I returned to the small flat I rented, close to the sea. It was only a street from where I'd lived with Rita. It was my home. I suppose life was okay; I was rubbing along quite well, so it was quite a shock when my world was turned upside down.

I guess it was fate that brought you to me. You needed saving and by then I was ready to love.

Bartenders have to smile, and yours was quite convincing, but I could see behind it. You had the weathered face of a sailor, ruddy cheeks and a strong jaw. Your golden-red hair was beyond control. Most people wouldn't think that such a roguish-looking man nursed a secret pain, but I knew it. As I said, survivors can sniff out the damage. I sneaked from the kitchen and saw how your face dropped when you had your back to the customers. People assume life is easy if you're handsome, but I could tell it wasn't true for you.

I finished my shift and walked through to the front of the hotel, into the empty bar area. You were turned away, polishing a glass, intently rubbing it as if you were conjuring a genie. What would be your wish? I wondered.

"Can I help you, pet?"

"Half of cider, please."

You turned on the tap, shoulders tense, and the amber overflowed the glass. You wiped the lip of the glass with a napkin, and placed the drink in front of me.

"Can you put it on my tab? I'm staff." I showed you my name badge, and you wrote it down. You relaxed, knowing that I wasn't a paying guest so you didn't have to put on a show, your head dipping as you picked up another glass to polish, your hands working quickly. I wanted to put my fingers on yours, tell you to stop working. There was no wedding ring on your finger.

"So, what do you do in this God-awful place, pet?"

"I'm in the kitchen."

"I didn't mean the hotel. I meant the town."

"Oh, Felixstowe's not so bad."

"I think it's a shithole." A vein on your forehead throbbed blue.

"Where are you from?"

"Newcastle."

I sipped my drink. "What brought you here?" I asked, watching your strong face, the arrogant arch of your nose.

"My wife."

I hadn't expected that. The cold cider iced my stomach.

You looked at me, more intently than before. You were already used to disappointing women and a half-smile played on your lips as you watched my crestfallen face.

"She's a dancer. But now she's dancing with someone else."

"Oh. I'm sorry."

"Yeah, me too. The old bastard didn't waste any time. We only moved here three months ago and now she's living with him." You poured what remained of a wine bottle into one of the gleaming glasses and swigged it down in one gulp. "The bitch."

You were so raw, your pain so fresh, that I winced for you. I thought about putting my hand on your chest, telling you your heart would heal. Who knew better than me? But I stayed silent.

I drained my glass, picked up my coat, and left.

The next day slimy Simon was working behind the bar, and my shift dragged, but the following lunchtime the waitress – Melissa or Kate, I can't remember – bounced in, ponytail swinging. For once I was glad of her chatter.

"That blond guy's behind the bar again! He's so lush. I thought he fancied me until he stopped me getting a nip of vodka – said I'd have to pay. Bloody cheek. I bet he helps himself when no-one's looking."

I worked on after my shift had ended, waiting until the bar would be quiet. When I got there you were wiping down the counter. You looked up, and didn't put on your false smile. I was glad.

"Drink?" you asked, and I nodded, watching you pour two glasses from an open wine bottle. I didn't normally drink wine.

"Rose red." You slid the stem between my fingers as you spoke. I felt the tip of your thumb graze my hand. "I'm Jason, by the way."

"Cheers, Jason," I lifted my glass and sipped the drink. "What did you do yesterday? I noticed it was your day off."

You raised your eyebrows. "Been checking up on me, have you?"

"Maybe," I said. "I wondered what you'd found to do in this 'shithole'."

"Not much. Listened to music. Slept."

"There is stuff to do around here, you know."

"Oh yeah? I'm not sure I believe that."

"Let me show you then. When's your next free day?"

It was March and it had rained every day for a week, the sky swaddling the town in grey mist. I took you to the beach, where we watched the angry sea, tasted salt in our mouths. Head bent, hands deep in your pockets, you told me about Emma, your ex-wife. I had no idea then how much she mattered.

You said she was a beauty, a slight whistle on the wind, like you were thinking of a prize gelding you once saw race. I knew about men and beautiful women; I'd seen how one had stolen Dad away. Mrs Carron's beauty had been manufactured from bottles and peroxide, her body wrapped in silk and drenched in scent. My mum's beauty was too subtle to hold him, too pale and distant.

We bought coffees from a kiosk, needing to hold something warm, and we kept the hot steam close to our faces. Spring had forgotten to arrive. I went to the public loo, feeling the temperature drop by degrees in the stone building. I briskly rinsed my hands in icy water, splattering the mirror as I shook them dry. I caught my reflection briefly, and then looked closer. No, I wasn't beautiful. My hair wasn't a style, and just hung around my face. My eyes were green like slime and my skin was pale. At best, I was plain. So plain that if you hadn't been so hurt, you would never have looked at me twice. But my plainness, my tall awkward body, would help me. Emma had left you for another man, but I never would. I would always be grateful for any interest you might show. A woman like me could never hurt you.

The pub had called last orders, so we staggered into the night air. At the hotel I sneaked in the Staff Only door, following you down the corridor. You were staying in one of the bedrooms that came with the job. I'd lived in one myself once, and it was strange to be on the staff corridor again, the brown nylon carpet snagging underfoot.

You were drunk. At the pub you had downed five pints in rapid succession, so your key slid as you tried to find the lock, but I didn't offer to help.

Eventually you managed to open the door and find the light switch, throwing your keys and wallet on the bedside table. The small room was a mess, although the dingy flowered light shade barely shed enough light to see much. The floor was littered with pizza boxes and kebab wrappers. I kicked a can, spilling final dregs of lager onto the floor. You frowned, as if suddenly seeing the room through my eyes. There was nowhere to sit other than the bed. It was unmade: a bunched-up duvet, a crumpled under-sheet, and I resisted the urge to straighten it. As you reached to switch on the CD player a pile of clothes got knocked to the floor. I bent to pick them up.

"Don't."

I froze.

"I don't want you to do that."

I righted myself, waiting as you collected your jeans and shirts, piling them back up.

"I need a coffee. You?"

I nodded. My voice had deserted me since I entered your room, and I was glad when you left, listening to your padding feet down the corridor to the communal kitchen.

I breathed in and the smell was delicious. The heat from the boiler pipes warmed the room, intensifying the smell of you. I was used to the aroma of a kitchen and could smell orange and basil from your aftershave, but underneath the earthy scent of sweat. I gingerly found a way to the bed, where the smell was strongest, neatened the duvet and sat on the edge. I bent low over the pillow, and saw fine gold threads of lost hair. I wanted to wind one around my finger.

I looked around, greedy to find out who you were: a guitar with a broken string, a portable CD player with a scattering of discs beside it, an empty bottle of Jack Daniels with a stub of candle pushed in the neck. The only things in the room that made it yours, along with a few bits of clothing and a razor on the enamel sink. Everything else was rubbish, newspapers and cans. Your wallet was on the bedside table, with your keys. I picked up the wallet and opened it. Inside was a clear plastic window, meant for a driving licence or credit card. But you had a photo. A redhead woman, pretty and delicate, wearing a white dress, clutching a bouquet. Wide, hazel eyes, and a full smile, revealing a row of perfect white teeth. Emma.

Hearing the kitchen door bang, I returned the photo and positioned the wallet. I thought about how I must look, nervously perched on your bed. Would you wonder why you'd invited me? I must look desperate, asking for it. The travel clock on the floor said it was nearly midnight. You came in holding two mugs, handing me the one with the chip.

"The milk smelled funny, so it's black."

"Fine. Thanks." I blew on the steam, knowing I wouldn't drink it anyway. My stomach was in knots. You put on a CD, some bluesy music, and sat on the bed next to me, your shoulders hunched as you sipped coffee.

"I should be going, Jason."

"What about your drink?"

I took a gulp and the near-boiling water burned my tongue.

"I'll walk you home." You sounded reluctant.

"No need. I always walk home alone after my shift."

"Yeah, but it's midnight."

I stood, wanting to escape, to breathe easy, to be alone, but I also wanted to be with you. You took off your jumper; the T-shirt underneath was tight on your body. You weren't going to walk me home, then. You rubbed your eyes. "Christ, I'm done in."

I didn't want to overstay my welcome. I walked home alone.

18

You'd only arrived in Suffolk a few months earlier and had no friends in the area. I wondered why you didn't go back to Newcastle but was afraid to ask. Even though I knew you must still love Emma, I didn't want to hear about her. Didn't want to hear you say that you hoped she'd come back to you. Didn't want to think about that photo you carried in your wallet.

We went to see a Bond movie at The Palace, the two-screen cinema in Felixstowe, a crumbling place where a weathered woman still offered tea or coffee on a tray before the main feature. You took a sideways glance at me. "From the ark, isn't it?"

"I like it."

The Palace was never more than a quarter full. There were only a handful of people watching the film, a group of teenage boys at the back, and us. Once the light came down, I could hardly focus on James Bond, fixated instead by your bare arm leaning on the armrest between us, your long legs stretched out in front. Though facing forward, my eyes flicked sideways to your splayed limbs, your fidgety hands. I was like a schoolgirl, daring to imagine your hand on my thigh. I shuffled lower in my seat, pretending to concentrate, when all my thoughts buzzed to you. It was ninety minutes of torture.

"Nightcap, pet?"

"Great. The Grosvenor?"

"No. My room."

This time the room was tidy. The bed was made, clothes hidden, CDs in a pile. A bottle of red wine stood waiting, with two mismatched glasses. You knew I'd come back with you. *Oh God, please let me do this right.*

I was a freak. A 28-year-old virgin with a lanky body and breasts like half-risen pastry. I was odd, but then my life had been odd. My best friend was a seventy-year-old widow and the only boy who ever fancied me was creepy Alfie.

You uncorked the wine, an expensive bottle that had come from the hotel cellar, and poured, downing a glass before handing me mine. Your stained mouth was tight as you re-filled the glass. The warm alcohol hit my curdling stomach, tasting like medicine, and I felt sick. Pressing play on the CD player, the same music as before, you sat next to me, close enough for me to see the stubble on your chin, the patch of freckles on the bridge of your nose. I wanted you to touch me, but I was so afraid. My feet felt itchy, ready to take flight. I crossed then recrossed my legs before standing.

"I think I'd better go, Jason."

I got my jacket from the floor, checked my keys in my pocket. In seconds I was at the door, my hand opening the latch, nearing safety, turning to say goodbye, when you were there, in front of me, too close. I was backed to the door, when your hand slapped against it, slammed it closed.

"I don't want you to go."

You came closer, your breath in my mouth. I could feel your heat, my own temperature soaring. The kiss was full and fierce, your tongue quickened in my mouth as your hands stroked my neck, over my back, under my top. I felt like you were falling on me, crushing me, and I was glad, hardly coming up for air.

You pulled away, steadied yourself, and opened the door. It was time for me to leave. It was over. I looked at your downcast face, saw your eyes slide away.

"See you tomorrow?" I begged.

You shrugged, nudged me into the corridor and left me standing in front of a closed door.

The next day you didn't show up at work. At first I thought maybe you'd just switched shifts, or that you were too hung-over, but when you didn't show the following day I knew something was wrong. I'd lost you. The opportunity had slipped through my grip. You had gone. You had left me. It was my fate to be alone.

I made mistakes in the kitchen, cut my finger on a paring knife, sliced meat into vegetarian meals. Eventually Chef threw down his tea towel. "What is it, Rose? You've been a klutz all day. It's not like you."

I chewed my nail. "For God's sake!" he yelled, ripping my hand away from my mouth. "Whatever it is, don't come back until it's sorted."

I left the kitchen, heading into the main part of the hotel where some guests were checking in. The receptionist was busy handing a key to a man in a morning suit, and I ducked through the door that led to the staff accommodation. The nylon carpet crackled under my feet as I walked past an open bedroom door, where two waitresses leaned out of the window, smoking and laughing. Someone was in the communal kitchen, bent over a cereal bowl, but it wasn't you.

Your door was shut and I stood listening to the silence. I leaned my forehead against it, and, without hope, I lifted my knuckles to the door and tapped lightly. No response. Panic rose in my throat. I would never see you again.

I rapped louder, the blows of my fist matching the beat of my heart.

"Jason? Jason? Jason. Please. Jason." Several doors opened along the corridor, but I couldn't stop, my voice getting louder and louder.

When you flung open the door I nearly fell in. You stood, naked except for a hand towel held around your waist, bleary-eyed from sleep. "Christ, Rose. Where's the fire?"

I pushed past, diving into darkness. I was shaking, as you called down the corridor, "It's okay, everyone. It's fine." Then you closed the door and turned back to me.

"What's up?"

I stood still, trying to control my breathing. "Nothing. I'm sorry."

You sauntered sleepily back to bed, dropping the towel on the floor as you slid under the duvet, pulled it high to your cheek and yawned. "I'm knackered. I didn't get to bed till five."

You closed your eyes. The room was warm and dim, cocooning us. I knelt on the floor beside the bed, my face close to yours.

"I thought you'd gone away. When you didn't show up for work…"

You didn't open your eyes. "Yeah, well. I'll say I was ill."

"Why haven't you been at work?"

"I was with Emma."

My chest felt tight. "Are you back with her?"

"It was only while her bastard husband was at work. After we'd slept together she kicked me out. Bitch." You rubbed your face into the pillow. "Last night my heart hurt and this morning my head hurts."

"I would never throw you out, Jason," I said.

You looked up from the pillow. Your hand snaked out of the duvet, tugging my arm. "Come here."

Awkwardly, I joined you under the duvet. You pressed into my back, and I felt sweat on my palms. Through my jeans I could feel the contours of your knee, your thigh. Your mouth heated the skin under my collar. "You'd never leave me, pet?"

"Never."

Your hand moved to the buttons of my shirt, unpeeling

me. You unhooked my bra, pulled it away, so I was loose and exposed. Your mouth explored my breasts. You nuzzled my nipples, sending shivers through me. My stomach contracted as your hand found the zip of my jeans, tugging and pulling until I helped you fling them off. You rolled me onto my back and stroked my hips, your mouth travelling low to the waistband of my knickers, a wet line where your tongue traced the elastic.

My hand cradled your head as I felt your tongue lick my inner thigh, desperate for you to carry on but desperate for you to stop. You released me from the thin cotton, your mouth following your hands.

I went to an unknown place, somewhere above, and thought of nothing, but felt – oh, how I felt – every particle in my brain begging me to stop as my body gave itself to you totally. My heart and mind were hypnotised, seduced. I saw the soft shades of the rainbow.

Soon, you were rising above me, supported by your forearms as you lowered yourself down and into me. It hurt and I sucked air, tensed against the motion of you. A new stinging, an aching fullness.

I listened to your breathing, your guttural grunts as I realised you were about to orgasm. Then, after your shuddering release, you collapsed on top of me.

I held you tight, kissing the damp nape of your neck, saying your name over and over. "Jason, Jason. I love you, Jason. Say you love me, Jason."

You closed your eyes and whispered, "Oh, Emma."

You missed work again and got sacked. So you packed your few belongings into a carrier bag and came to live with me.

We never spoke about you saying Emma's name. Nor did I tell you about it being my first time. But you must have known. And I knew I loved you, but you loved Emma.

19

I'm in my cell, lying on the bed.

Janie is with me, her head resting on my shoulder, and we're sharing a joint. She's listening carefully, as I read the latest letter from her father. She doesn't read well, and his letters show that he's barely literate himself. The lined sheet is covered with disjointed sentences and misspelled words, some thickly scribbled out by black biro. Thankfully, they're always brief.

In two months Janie will be released, and the education staff have realised that she's not equipped to deal with life on the out. To try to prepare her, they've organised day release for her to attend a course in basic literacy and numeracy at the further education college in Ipswich. She hates it, but she goes obediently, on the train, across town on a bus, to sit and learn lessons she should have done a decade ago. "How are the classes going?"

She grimaces like a child forced to swallow medicine. "It's so hard, Rose," she says, "but my teacher's nice. I'm allowed to wait in the classroom during break, cos I don't like to mix with the other students. Miss Reed has a kettle and a jar of coffee in her desk, and we sit and have a drink together. Sometimes she brings chocolate biscuits."

Typical, Janie has become teacher's pet.

"How difficult would it be," I ask, "for you to take a little detour? Into Ipswich, I mean. A bus ride away from the college."

"Easy," she boasts. "Last week when I got to the train station, I nipped into McDonald's and spent my bus fare on a Chicken Deluxe. I hadn't had one for months and it was lush. I had to walk to the college, and I was nearly an hour late, but Miss Reed didn't say a word. She didn't even call the prison to rat on me."

Janie is such a child that she gets away with light monitoring. Everyone is fooled by her stupidity. That will be useful to me.

I turn my attention to her dad's letter, and begin to read.

As usual he makes excuses for not visiting her, claiming poverty and distance as the reasons. In the next sentence he's telling her about his holiday to Spain. Sometimes I skip bits that I think will hurt, protecting Janie. I make other stuff up: "I hope you're being a good girl," I improvise, "and remember that I love you." It's a small gift, but she's pleased. I don't think a lie is wrong if it brings happiness.

I fold the letter back into a square, slip it into the scruffy envelope, and hand it back. Janie clasps it to her girlish chest. I touch my joint to her lips and tell her to breathe deep, which she does. She coughs, pushes the spliff away. I stroke her head back into my lap, playing with her mousy hair.

"There, there, lovely," I murmur. This is when I like her best. She pulls her knees to her stomach and closes her eyes as I take a long drag, allowing the drug to leaden my limbs. "Your daddy loves you," I tell her. "He'll visit soon."

"No. He won't," she says, surprising me with her insight. "But I don't care." She looks up, eyes wet. "No-one's ever taken care of me like you, Rose. This is the happiest I've ever been."

"But we're in prison."

She brings her head to my shoulder. Her breath warms my neck. "I'd rather be here with you than free and on my own."

I let her nuzzle my neck like a puppy, her slim arms sliding around my waist. What a sad life it is if you'd choose this over freedom. I kiss her head, smelling the cheap prison-issue soap. Janie would do anything I asked. Such love is a gift indeed.

This is what I've become, a scheming creature. I have to plan for the parole board, behave well and answer questions in a calculated way. I don't recognise the girl I once was. How naïve I used to be.

I look at myself in the mirror and I look old. Although I'm still quite young, I feel ancient. Prison has aged me, it's made me cynical. Ugly places make people do ugly things. So do ugly experiences. Do you think beautiful places lead to goodness? Remember Felixstowe beach, white shingle and yawning blue skies that make you ache, they're so perfect. Remember the warm air breathing over our faces. We were happy, weren't we?

Prisons are the ugliest places on this planet. All grey concrete and steel. The clangs and clicks, shouts and screams, doors banging, the locks and keys. It's always cold. A bad place crammed with women who've done bad things. And the workers, who chose to be here, locked away with the rest of us, even if they do hold the keys.

I wonder what made Cate Austin want to be imprisoned. Not that she'll ever tell me since her job is to get me to talk. She's a listener. A judge.

She buttons herself down to keep herself strong. Even though she lives outside the walls she doesn't bring the season in with her like other staff do. And though she can choose what she wears, she wears similar clothes every day, a uniform of navy jacket and white shirts, dark trousers. She stands apart from the others, the teachers and psychologists. Her hair is cut at an angle into a bob, which she scrapes back behind her ears. It's the colour of autumn and could be pretty.

I need to know more about her to influence my report. She keeps her cards close to her chest but sometimes she lets one slip. Her blind panic, for instance, when her daughter was hurt, how she ran to the door, forgetting everything, a part of her that she would prefer to keep hidden. Vulnerability. We're both careful about what we hide, what we reveal. She has a job to do, a reputation to keep. She has to draw me out, know when to pounce. But the prize I play for is freedom. For me the stakes are higher. I'm playing for my life.

Her job is to take me back to the past. She takes me back to when I was centuries younger, when my face matched my age, and I had hope for the future.

20

Black Book Entry

I was finally normal. I shared my flat with a man, I had a lover. Your toothbrush crossed with mine in the beaker. My flat wasn't much better than your room at The Grand, but I kept it tidy and clean. It was the upstairs part of a seventies house, with the front room as the lounge, a bedroom at the back and a small box room where I kept Rita's things. Now your guitar was there, your empty suitcase. I crammed our tiny kitchen with treats from the hotel. Chef was always generous and I had vanilla pods and cinnamon sticks, saffron and even a bottle of Madeira. The flat was fine, apart from the downstairs neighbours, who would sometimes argue at two in the morning and then make up even more noisily.

You still hadn't found a job, but we got by. Chef knew you from when you had worked behind the bar, and would ask after you, giving me a couple of steaks or a leftover piece of salmon to take home. Sometimes I'd sneak a cigar as a special treat. Working in expensive hotels had given you expensive tastes.

You were bored with nothing to do all day. When I left for a shift, I felt guilty leaving you slumped on the sofa in front of Jeremy Kyle, strumming the guitar. I worried, too, about how you spent your days without me, knowing that you still kept Emma's photo in your wallet, and your mobile phone was never out of your reach. If it buzzed you would check the text, but never tell me who had sent it and I didn't ask.

Three weeks after you moved in I had a visitor. It was about seven in the evening on a Saturday, and you were watching *Top Gear* on TV while I washed up, when the doorbell rang. It rang so infrequently that I guessed it would be Annie.

I wiped my hands dry and skipped down the stairs. I opened the door smiling, wanting Annie to see men's shoes by the door, hear your voice calling. But her face was dark as thunder. For a woman in her sixties with a wide girth, she was formidable. She bared her false teeth at me.

"Rose. What the bleeding hell is going on?"

My smile was slapped away by Annie's tone. I'd never heard her so angry before.

"Young lady, you are coming with me tonight."

I tried to protest, but Annie reached her fat arm past me and plucked my coat from its peg. "Now. We can't be late."

"Wait a minute." I reluctantly pulled the coat on and bounded up the stairs away from her. You were lying on the sofa drinking a beer. "Jason?"

You didn't look up from the screen.

"Do you mind if I go out for a few hours?"

A weary smile appeared. "Course not, pet. You go."

"I won't be long."

"Take your time." You reached for your mobile phone and started to scroll through your messages. I bent to kiss your cheek, and then trailed back downstairs to Annie. I cursed her for stealing time I wanted to give to you.

The front door was open and she was standing in the cold air. She held her arm for me to link and we walked quickly to the séance at the church hall.

"She's glad to see you here," Maureen said.

I knew who "she" meant. I'd been coming here for so many years that Rita needed no introduction. And the regulars, women who remembered my aunt, turned and smiled at me. "She's been waiting. You haven't been for a while."

Annie glared at me and I blushed. "I've been busy."

Maureen nodded. "Rita says she knows. You've met someone."

"Yes."

"Rita says he's very handsome, but his hair is like a girl's."

I laughed – that was Rita all over. She liked men like prize-fighters, bulging muscles and shorn scalps.

"Your mum's here too, Rose."

The hairs on my arm bristled. Mum didn't come as often as Rita, and when she did she usually stayed silent. "What does she say?"

"It's about him. The man."

"Yes?"

"She doesn't like him, Rose. She says he doesn't cherish you like he should."

I hated to hear the truth, pushed it away. "We've only known each other a few weeks."

"Your mum says he loves someone else."

"He's just got divorced. He hasn't got over it yet."

Suddenly, Maureen came close, fear in her eyes. "Your mum says it's dangerous. You should stop: walk away while you still can. She wants to protect you from pain."

I felt Annie's papery hand caress mine. Maureen's eyes were still on me. Their intensity was suffocating.

"How can I make him stay?"

Maureen was silent. The whites of her eyes became crescent moons. When the irises returned they fixed on me, and I thought I saw my mother. "There will be a child."

My heart leapt. "Our child. Jason's and mine?"

"His child. It will bind you forever, but pain will follow."

What did she mean? The pain of childbirth?

"Your mum says you should leave him."

I pulled my hand from Annie's grip. "I can't do that."

Maureen was so close I could smell her breath, spicy with rum. "Leave him now, while you still can. Once the child is born it will entwine you together and you will never be free."

She was so close, her eyes boring into me, that I couldn't bear it.

"Okay," I said, just wanting her to leave me alone, "okay."

Maureen stared at me for a long time, and then she smiled. "Your mum has gone now, Rose. There's someone else with me. Is there anyone here with a cat in the spirit world called Ginger?"

She moved on to someone else and the spell was broken. The only person still looking at my burning face was Annie.

"Do you see why I made you come?" she whispered, her fat thigh pressed to mine. "Every week it's been the same. And I said to Maureen that you needed to know, duckie."

"I want to go home. I won't stay for tea and biscuits."

Annie hugged me tight, "Go on, duck. You do what your mum said. Remember: she knows best. You hurry along now."

I did hurry. I wanted to see you so badly I tripped on the pavement, rushing down the street. But I would never do what Mum asked. However much you loved Emma, I couldn't ask you to go. I had promised never to leave you. I loved you and I would make you love me. I would bind you to me forever, not through marriage – Emma had proved how weak that tie was – but with blood. Flesh and blood.

Mum had given me the answer to my problem. If we had a child, you would stay with me. I would be safe.

I turned the key in the lock, my hand trembling, and called out your name.

But the flat was in darkness. You had gone.

21

Black Book Entry

I'd been in bed for two hours when I heard the key in the door. I kept my eyes closed, lay still, listening to the sound of the bedroom door over the carpet, the rustle of clothes being dropped. You got under the covers, keeping to the edge of the mattress. I moved against you, an arm over your waist, burying my face into your hair. I rolled you onto your back, kissing, touching.

"Where have you been?"

"Hmm?"

You pretended to be asleep, but your breathing was too shallow. The delicate scent of green apples was on your skin. You didn't respond when I touched you and your penis was wet, already spent. I shook your shoulder.

"Let me sleep, pet."

"Tell me, Jason!"

I straddled you, my knees fast against your flanks. You stared up at me, unmoved. "For pity's sake, Rose, I'm tired."

"And why are you tired? Where have you been?"

You opened your sad eyes. "Don't, Rose…you know where…with Emma."

"That slut…that whore…" and I remembered Mum saying those same words to my father.

"She doesn't want me, Rose," you said, voice wavering. You closed your eyes and tears trickled down your cheeks.

"Oh God, please don't leave me, please…" I started crying and shaking and stuttering. "Jason, I'm sorry. I shouldn't have said anything."

"After she'd used me she asked me to leave."

And then you started to cry, rolled onto your side, clinging to me like a child. You were still depressed, still so new to pain, and Emma had hurt you again. You let me hold you, comfort you.

I did the only thing I could: I reclaimed you, sucking in the pain. I stroked and caressed your shaking body, burying my agony as I pulled you into me. An animal marking her territory, wiping out the other female's claim. I made you make love to me.

When I arrived at work the next day my anger was like a tumour full of poison ready to seep into my blood. If I tried to speak, bile rose in my mouth. I banged and crashed around the kitchen. Finally, when Chef was on his break, I took a steel ladle to the towers of fine bone china, delicate plates with blue detailing around their edges, piled high ready for service, and lashed out. The crash of the falling tower, the shattering of broken china, was a perfect release. Standing in a ground zero of devastation, tears dripping but anger spent.

Chef ran in, began to shout and then saw my stricken face. "Don't cry, love," he said, "accidents happen."

That night, when you cried in my arms still scented with Emma's perfume, some kind of sorcery must have taken place because that was when I conceived. I felt something happen inside and I knew it was the baby Mum had told me about.

You never did say that you loved me, but there is something

stronger than love. Need. You needed me. I had rescued you, salvaged you from the wreckage of your broken heart.

I want you to understand, Jason. To see how the seeds were being sown for what came later. Given a choice, I wouldn't tell this story in words. I'd show you pictures to remind you – us throwing stones on the beach, watching TV in the dark, that night when you sobbed in my arms. I'd silently show you these pictures, and you'd understand.

Words aren't easy; they can be twisted. The truth is that I loved you. I didn't expect you to love me back. All you needed to be was faithful.

22

Black Book Entry

I was ten weeks pregnant, but I hadn't told you. I hid it well, and I've always been on the heavy side so it hardly showed. I wanted to keep my secret for as long as possible, but I kept sneaking away to look at the pregnancy test, that precious plastic stick with the indigo line. It was a talisman, the proof that I was lucky after all. I had finally been blessed.

We were in bed one Sunday morning, and I was trying to cuddle up, but you kept pulling away. And then something in you snapped like you couldn't stand it anymore.

"I can't do this, Rose. There's something I need to tell you…"

"Shhh…"

I stroked your hair, kissed your cheek, all the time feeling the distance your heart was placing between us, fearing what was to come. You still checked your mobile constantly for text messages, the picture of Emma was still in your wallet.

"I'm leaving, Rose. It's no good, trying to pretend. There's nothing for me here."

My hands clasped around the gentle curve of my stomach, the baby inside. "Please stay, Jason. I'll do anything if you just stay."

"No, Rose, you deserve more than that…"

"Just you! I don't even deserve that…" I moved closer, pressing against you like a needy child.

"Christ, Rose, have some dignity. Don't be so pathetic."

"But I am pathetic." I tried to cuddle up, but you pulled back to your side of the bed. "I love you."

"But I don't want you, Rose. I love Emma."

How easily you said it. My next breath came quick, but I kept calm. "I know that. It's okay."

"Rose." You were exasperated with me, holding me away with both hands. "What will it take to make you see this won't work?" You rolled on your back and stared up at the ceiling. "I need to get away from Emma, from the hold she has on me."

"Don't talk about that."

"Get your head out of the sand, Rose. I never lied to you: you know I've been seeing her. We've had sex a few times, but she always sends me away afterwards. Anytime she has an argument with that bastard Hatcher she's texting me."

I could hardly breathe, staring up at the dark ceiling, your cruel words pinning me down.

"Whenever she's pissed off with him, angry at all the nights he's working at the school, she gets in touch. And she knows I still want her. I can't cope with it anymore."

I remembered the night of the séance. The scent on your skin.

"Where do you do it?" I don't know why knowing was important, but it was. I needed to picture the scene in my head.

"In their bed."

"Their bed?" I sat up on an elbow so I could see your face. "You go to their house?"

"Afterwards, Emma cries. She always says it's a mistake, that she loves her bastard husband. That she won't have sex with me again; it must be the last time. I try to persuade her. I can't carry on like this, just waiting for her to text me. I think it's best if I get away from this place. Don't you see, there's no future for us."

But you had nowhere to go and I wasn't going to give you up that easily.

"Jason. We're going to have a baby."

I watched your face, saw the disbelief in your eyes.

I placed your hand on my stomach. "You're going to be a father."

You thought it was a trick until I showed you the pregnancy stick as proof. But then you did something I hadn't expected; you cried. You reached for me, clinging to me like a child, and sobbed. You put your hands on my stomach and I felt their heat.

Then you put your lips to my neck, in the dip above the collarbone. Your breath was hot. "We're going to have a baby." You said it like a prayer, soft and musing. I was light-headed with relief, caught up in the embrace.

"But I don't love you, Rose."

You sounded so sorry, so pathetically sorry for me. Like it was something you couldn't control.

"Could you?" I asked, barely audible. "Could you love me?" A begging plea. I had no shame.

You didn't answer for a while. "I swear to you, Rose – I will love our child." And you touched me again, on my stomach, making a pledge. I knew that you wanted the baby. Really wanted it. Even more than you wanted Emma.

I could have said that I didn't want you to stay with me for the sake of the baby, but that would have been a lie. I wanted you at any price, even without love. And if a baby kept you with me and away from her, then that was enough. I would make you love me. Or at least I would make you stay.

I cradled you, rocking slowly, thinking of our baby. I wasn't going to let Emma take you from me.

As you slept, all my gnarled and broken thoughts turned to her. The bitterness of jealousy was turning to the sweeter taste of hate. The woman you'd had before me. My tears kept coming as I rocked to the sound of your breathing. Gold curls had fallen across my wrist and I thought of Samson's strength, of how, like Delilah, I wanted a knife, a blade to take your strength away, to stop you from leaving. But my weapon was more subtle, hidden deep in my womb.

23

Black Book Entry

Over the following months you were so careful with me. There were no more arguments, only silence. I thought we were going to be a normal family, just like I'd always wanted. For once, everything was going my way. The baby that I carried was safe, nothing could harm it.

Pregnancy made me happy. It also made me primitive, like a vixen preparing a burrow for her litter, all soft and warm with my secret, but snappy and on edge with the outside world. I stayed at home, lying on the sofa with my knees tucked under and a blanket over me. I didn't want to go out; as the nights drew in, the winter began to bother me and I would turn the heating as high as our old boiler could muster, put jumper over jumper to keep the cold out.

At twenty weeks we went for a scan. The jelly was cold on my tight stomach as the radiographer pressed with her probe and a grainy image appeared on the monitor.

"Now, I'm just going to do some basic checks and then I'll tell you what I see."

The probe beeped and she and I intently studied the screen. A fuzzy white image bounced up and down on a sea of black and white blobs. I saw an arm raise, a leg kick out.

You absorbed the image on the screen, your hand clamped to my leg.

I saw our baby's profile and then, like it knew we were watching, it turned its face towards us. I could have wept.

The radiographer moved her probe to the baby's back, measuring its spine. "Everything looks good. The spine is complete, and the head and heart look good too. From the length I'd say nearly twenty-one weeks."

I nodded. "My due date is March 22nd."

"And do you want to know the sex, if I'm able to tell?"

I knew he was a boy as surely as if I'd already met him. But you nodded, needing proof.

The radiographer concentrated again, her probe moving low on my abdomen, searching.

"Rose thinks it's a boy," you said.

She smiled. "Well, Rose, you're right."

My heart whooped in joy as my good luck took my breath. I wanted so much to have a boy like you.

How awful it would have been to bring another Rose into the world.

The hotel kitchen, for years my second home, was now a cage, and work had become a chore. My hands, scarred with ancient burns, trembled as I melted fat, fearing the spits. I skirted the pointed steel edges of the tables, wary of the knives I had previously handled without a care. I was vulnerable in pregnancy. Happiness was so new to me that I was terrified of it being stolen away.

It was hard for you, I know, stuck in the house all day, and I began to worry. You'd stopped showering and caring what you looked like. Your mobile phone was in a drawer, switched off, and I knew you were doing that for me. For our son.

I made sacrifices too, just to keep you busy: we'd go to the local pub on the corner where I endured the drunken shouting, or to the cinema where I'd flinch at the loud soundtrack assaulting our baby's paper-thin ears. I'd read somewhere that a baby in the womb can hear the outside world. I worried about giving him frightening dreams, and I couldn't soothe him. I sighed with relief when the credits rolled and the lights went up. I went to watch those films for you, to keep you from thinking about Emma.

Still, you were leaving me. Not physically, but slipping into a world which I feared. It was the world my mother had visited on her "loony" days. I heard the flatness in your voice, your dull eyes, and remembered Mum's depression, how it stole her away forever.

So I got you a job.

Chef knew of a fancy French restaurant that needed a wine waiter, but you hadn't got the relevant experience. I lied to Chef about your qualifications. He eventually wrote you a personal recommendation, and on the day of the interview at Auberge I gave you half the rent to buy some clothes for the interview. You came home a different man. Wearing a white linen jacket and beige trousers, you could have passed for a Frenchman and the restaurant owner offered you the post on the spot.

Since I told you I was pregnant you never spoke about leaving me again, but your love for Emma was still between us like a sheet of glass. I checked your wallet, and saw her photo was still inside, staring back at me with wide hazel eyes, her blonde hair as yellow as the sun. With your new job you came home late but I never looked at the clock when I heard your key in the door. You started carrying your mobile again, and it would beep if you got a text, but I still never asked who it was. If you'd been with her I didn't want to know. You came home to me, that was what mattered. I was carrying your child.

It was February when I started to think about the box room I used for Rita's things, and decided to make it a nursery. I was heavily pregnant by this time, and pulling boxes and suitcases around was tough, but I sorted through, chucking away what I didn't want. I wanted to start afresh, and I felt finally able to let go of the past. I gave away the lamp from Rita's sitting room, a sewing box that I'd never seen her use, her footstool. I called a local charity shop, and two volunteers came to collect the furniture, cheerfully loading their van with her walnut dresser and oak rocking chair. Without those old things the room was bare, a blank canvas. A new beginning.

The next day I entered a shop I'd stood outside many times, looking at the window display of Victorian rocking horses and jointed teddy bears in jackets. I gripped my purse where I kept the grainy ultrasound picture, and thought of the tiny arm that had waved to me on the screen. The memory gave me courage. The smartness of the shop was daunting. The glass doors slid aside and the air conditioning assaulted my sinuses but I didn't care. My eyes greedily consumed the mock rooms, each one individually designed for an absent child.

"May I help you?" From the cluster of idle shop assistants a smart brunette came over, an eager smile tilted on her pink lips.

"Oh, I'm just browsing." I took a step back.

"Any particular colour?" she persisted.

"Blue." I said. "Definitely."

"So it's a boy?" She came forward as if to touch my bump, and I shrank back. "Then I must show you our fabulous New England range. It's just arrived." I followed her, watching how her hips swayed as she trotted along in her high heels. Her ankles were slim, and I guessed she had no children of her own.

The room she showed me was perfect. Cream walls were bordered with swans and geese drawn in duck-egg blue, and matching curtains. The cot was a reddish brown, the colour of maple syrup. I touched the wood, feeling its comforting sturdiness.

"Isn't it just to die for? It's cherry wood, imported from America. And we have a matching changing table and chest of drawers."

I turned the tag over, handwritten in black ink. It was over two thousand pounds. "Wow," I said, stunned.

"It may seem a lot, but you're buying a piece of furniture that will last for generations. Just think, your grandchildren will use it. It's an heirloom."

I stepped back, in love with the cherry wood, the duck-egg blue and the tiny birds. But I didn't even have two thousand pence in the bank, let alone two thousand pounds. I felt shabby and poverty-stricken, sorry for the poor mite in my belly.

"We do have special hire purchase agreements," she said, lowering her voice. "You could pay monthly."

When you arrived home I kissed you, holding you as close as my bloated figure would allow. "I have a surprise for you, Jason," I said, reaching to kiss the tender place behind the ear.

"Have you now?" you murmured, hands sliding under my top to my enlarged breasts and nuzzling my neck.

"Not that." I took your hand and led you down the hall. "Something much better. Ready?"

I kept my grip on the handle until I could bear it no longer and threw open the door with a flourish. Inside the tiny room the cherry wood cot dominated the space, made up in readiness with blue bedding. The curtains hung from the small window, slightly too long, and squeezed next to the cot was a nursing chair, also in cherry. A row of immaculate white sleep suits hung on gingham hangers from a white rail, and on the cot sat a jointed teddy bear wearing a blue waistcoat.

In the middle of the room was the pram. It was from the same shop and the pattern was Burberry check. I touched it and imagined myself pushing it through town.

You stared in silence, taking it all in, until finally you spoke in a voice that seemed to come from miles away. "Rose, what the fuck have you done?"

I felt like you'd hit me.

"We can't afford all this stuff. How did you pay for it?"

My voice was shaking. "I got it on hire purchase, over four years."

"Four years? That's a fucking lifetime. How much did it come to?"

I didn't tell the whole truth. "Two thousand."

"You've got to be fucking kidding me! You're giving up work in a few weeks, and you know how dodgy the restaurant trade is after Christmas. Two thousand pounds? Christ, that's three months' rent!"

"Jason," I pleaded, "it's for the baby. I want him to have the best."

"Oh, grow up, Rose. He won't care about this crap." With one hand you dismissed the room, all the hours I had spent getting it ready. "He'll be happy in a travel cot as long as he's loved."

I suddenly saw my beautiful room through new eyes. It was grotesque.

"I'm sorry, Jason." I put my hand on your arm but you pushed me away. I fell back, catching myself on the pram as I stumbled to the floor.

"You just don't fucking think, do you? It's all about you, isn't it?"

Suddenly, a sharp pain stabbed my abdomen and I gasped, clutching my stomach.

"Don't push the sympathy button. I'm going out."

The pain came again, and I doubled over, one hand holding the pram chassis for support.

"Give it a rest, Rose."

But the pain, worse than any period cramps, circled my abdomen and I crumpled, unable to stand, terrified.

"Jason. Oh, God. What's happening?"
"You're trying to keep me here, that's what."
I bent my head low to the carpet, eyes screwed tight against the sudden grip of agony, and heard the front door slam shut.

24

Cate drove past the flats on Coronation Road and parked further down the cul-de-sac. She didn't want to be seen gathering her paperwork and applying lip balm and mascara, which she had forgotten in the rush for work that morning. Amelia's ankle was now strapped up and she was on four-hourly doses of painkillers, so the night before she had slept with Cate, whimpering even in her dreams. Watching her daughter she was smothered with guilt. Not just because she hadn't been there when Amelia had fallen, but also because Tim had left them.

Cate had dropped Amelia at Julie's along with a large bottle of medicine and promises that she wouldn't be late this evening. To Julie she had been polite but cool, still unable to lose the feeling that if Julie had taken better care of Amelia the accident wouldn't have happened.

She didn't want to be outside the flat on Coronation Road, she wanted to be at home with Amelia, both of them snuggled on the sofa and catching up on sleep. She studied her bruised eyes in the rear-view mirror. She looked as bad as she felt, and pulled her fingers through her hair in a futile attempt to tidy herself up.

She hated home visits. It was all about territory and the visitor was at a disadvantage. The only time in her working life that she'd been assaulted was when she visited a prisoner's father, to check the home was suitable for his son's release.

From the second she walked in, the father had been wound up and aggressive, and when she had tried to make a swift exit he shot from the chair and had her pinned to the wall. The stocky man had his fist in her face when her adrenalin kicked in. She pushed free and ran for the front door just as his knuckle connected with the brickwork. Afterwards she pulled her car in a lay-by, and briefly but fiercely cried her eyes out. Then she drove back to the office.

Nothing like that will happen today, she reassured herself. She'd probably just find a lonely husband desperate to have his wife back at home.

Coronation Road was a crescent of seventies housing in the town centre, part of which had been converted into flats for rent. Lots of students lived in the area, and the unkempt gardens were testimony to this. Flat 38b was accessed from a side entrance and as Cate approached she saw a man's face dart back from the upstairs window. He had been looking out for her, but still she rang the doorbell.

The door was opened by a tall man, over six foot, and slim, probably in his mid-thirties. Good-looking, he had high cheekbones, framed by a thick fringe of golden-red hair that partly obscured his eyes. Not the kind of man she'd pictured with dour Rose.

"Mr Wilks? I'm Cate Austin, from probation."

He took a second to look her up and down then opened the door just wide enough for her to enter. The hallway was cramped and junk mail littered the carpet.

"Don't mind the mess." He looked down, as if he'd only just seen it and it had nothing to do with him. Like he was showing her into someone else's home.

He led her up the stairs slowly, reluctantly maybe.

In the upstairs hallway a denim jacket was slung over a chair, a phone poised on a stack of telephone directories, plastic bags stuffed down the back of the radiator. "And it's

Clark, not Wilks," he threw over his shoulder. "Rose and I aren't married."

Cate realised that Rose hadn't told her this.

He led the way to the small front room, which would once have been a bedroom but now served as a lounge with a beige chenille three-seater sofa with fringed cushions and a stiff armchair. From the TV in the corner came the lively chatter of a daytime soap. The room was furnished with fifties furniture and there were piles of oddments and paperwork on every surface.

Jason stood awkwardly, as if he'd entered a conversation he wasn't part of. "You want a drink?"

"Please." Normally on home visits she refused hospitality, but this time she accepted. It would give her a bit of breathing space, time to take a measure of the place.

She sat on the sofa, which dipped under her weight so she could feel the springs beneath.

A few photos and cards were propped on the windowsill, others had fallen over and lay on the carpet. The TV chattered away as she took in the mess of CDs scattered on the carpet, stacks of local newspapers, an empty pizza box. The signs of a man living alone who hasn't quite got the hang of looking after himself. Where the coffee table wasn't covered it was marked with rings and in its centre was an opened can of lager, an ashtray full of dog-ends, and a mobile phone. Next to her on the sofa was a box of tissues and a pile of unopened brown envelopes, probably bills.

Jason Clark was gone for what seemed ages, but the kitchen was only a thin wall away. She could hear a cupboard door and a fridge being opened and closed. When he returned, he took up position on the furthest point of the sofa, placing a mug on the table. He hadn't made a drink for himself but took a cigarette from a packet of Silk Cut and lit it.

He propped his elbows on his knees, his chest rising and falling rapidly, dragging on his smoke.

"As I said in my letter, I'll be writing your wife's – sorry, partner's – parole report."

"Yeah. She said."

"I've met with Rose twice so far, and those conversations will provide the bulk of the information for the report. But I also want to include your opinions in it."

"What for?"

Cate answered carefully. "Sometimes partners have mixed feelings about release. Rose has been in prison a long time. Having her back would mean an adjustment for both of you."

He bit the edge of a fingernail, then, catching himself, stopped. "I've got used to it, I suppose."

"But Rose being in prison must have turned your life upside down?"

"I suppose I'd already found out that life is shit, and her being in prison was just another thing to get used to."

"Not easy, though," Cate suggested.

"I visit every month, and send her cards and that. Do my bit." He sounded like he was justifying himself.

Cate sipped her coffee. It was very strong and the smell of the cigarette made her head woozy.

"Rose tells me you're a builder?"

"At the moment. I mainly work in the restaurant business, but it's a bit quiet at the moment. No-one's got any money to eat out."

Cate sipped her coffee again. She was asking questions to which she already knew the answers, but they broke the ice. No-one wants to hear that a stranger knows things about them; it's unnerving. So Cate asked another question to which she knew the answer. "How long have you and Rose known each other?"

Jason frowned. "Five years nearly."

"And you met when she was working at The Grand?"

"What is this, Mr and Mrs?"

"I'm just checking I've got my facts right."

"That's a first – one of you lot caring about getting it right. Yeah, okay, I was working in the bar when we hooked up. When they laid me off I moved in here with Rose." He ground his cigarette butt into the ashtray.

Cate was cautious now, realising that Jason was angry. He resented being asked questions, but she still had to ask. "And then she got pregnant?"

"Yeah, after we'd been together a couple of months."

"That would be a strain," Cate suggested, "an upheaval like pregnancy so early on in the relationship."

"You reckon? We were chuffed, even if it had happened a bit quickly. She wanted a baby – we both did." His eyes moistened and he palmed a tear away.

"I'm sorry for your loss."

Jason looked up for the first time, and she saw sadness settle on his features. "Everything would have been different if our son hadn't died."

He stood up, a large man who needed to break free from the moment. He paced the lounge and went to the windowsill, picked up a silver framed photograph and handed it to Cate. "He was just two days old when that was taken."

The photo showed a tiny baby in a plastic incubator, a tube taped to his cheek. Rose was also in the picture, leaning over her son, trying to smile but failing. She looked younger, prettier, despite the dark circles under her eyes. Her long dark hair hung into the crib. Cate handed the picture back to Jason.

She watched him holding the photograph of his dead son, thinking how vulnerable he looked. She recognised the need to protect your child, how strong that urge was, and here was a man who had failed. In that moment she realised that they were alike – the expression of loss written on his face was the same as hers, as she'd dashed to the hospital after Amelia's accident. At least Amelia was well; this man's child had died.

"Do you mind if I ask you about Emma Hatcher?"

He flinched, then sat heavily on the sofa, still clutching the photo frame, and reached for the opened can of beer, which he swigged. "I don't have anything to do with her now."

"What about her friendship with Rose? Was it strange, having your ex-wife and new partner become friends?"

He looked at Cate with something like disgust. "It wasn't like that. You people, always making out something sinister going on. It was just a coincidence, Emma and Rose being together in hospital. I didn't even know they knew each other. Not until right at the end."

"So Rose kept it from you?"

He finished his beer, wiped a hand on his jeans, as if there were some stubborn stain there. "I suppose she was worried about upsetting me. When I met Rose I hadn't got over Emma. She left me for a bloke she met at the school where she worked and I was pretty cut up about it."

"Dominic Hatcher."

"That bastard. He knew she was married, but that didn't stop him making a play for her. Rose didn't know that the Emma she had met in the hospital was the same Emma who'd been my wife. She only found that out much later."

"Do you really believe she didn't know?"

"Rose is not a liar." His face reddened. "And neither am I."

"But at some point Rose did realise that her new friend was your ex-wife?"

He seemed thrown by the question. "Well, yes, she found out when she got to know Emma better. I don't know exactly when. But when they first met in the hospital she could never have known. I mean, why should she? She'd never met Emma so she didn't even know what she looked like. And she was remarried by then so she had a different surname."

"Would you say Rose was prone to jealousy?"

"What's that got to do with anything?"

"I need the bigger picture to form an accurate assessment of the case. I need to know if Rose could still pose a risk to Emma if she is released."

"Rose would never hurt Emma."

"I need to assess the risk," Cate repeated.

"She didn't mean to start that fire, you know."

"The jury accepted that. But she was still going into the Hatchers' home at night. She was going into Luke's bedroom and nursing him. And the fire was started by Rose's cigarette."

Jason bit his lip, staring at his own packet of cigarettes on the table. "It was a horrible accident." He chewed the fingernail, viciously pulling the flesh. "Look, the reason Rose got a bit obsessed with visiting that house was nothing to do with Emma. It was to do with Luke. Our sons were born at the same time, that was all."

He touched the photograph down on the coffee table with his finger then pushed it away. "Their boy was the same age as Joel and Rose kept in touch with Emma. I suppose she felt that Emma understood what she was going through."

"Didn't you understand what she was going through, Mr Clark?" Cate said softly.

He pulled his hand across his thigh, and Cate saw a sweat mark where his palm had been. "Course I did. It killed me too, you know. But women talk more, don't they?"

"You found it difficult talking with Rose?"

"You're twisting my words! All I'm saying is I wasn't the one who had him growing inside me all those months. I didn't get to know him – I only saw him for a few minutes in intensive care at the end of each day. Not that his death didn't tear me apart. But it was worse for Rose."

He looked like a man trying to keep himself together, his hands were wrung together and his eyes wet, his whole body hunched over like he was weighing up whether to erupt into tears or punch the wall.

"I'd really like to ask you about Emma."

"For fuck's sake!"

"Where did you meet?"

Jason stood up and left the room. She could hear him

moving around in what she assumed was the kitchen. A cupboard door was opened and closed.

Jason reappeared, holding another can of lager. He took a deep swig. "I met Emma when I was twenty-five. I was working at Newcastle Arts College. She was in her final year there, and I had some work in the Union bar. I first noticed her because she always drank Vimto and vodka and I thought it was the most disgusting drink I'd heard of."

Warm lager at ten in the morning sounds worse. "What else?"

"She'd come to the bar after rehearsals, still in her dancing clothes. Some of the students acted like they knew everything, and treated us staff like shit, but she didn't."

"She was different from the others?"

"Seemed so. One night we just got talking, and that was that."

"That was what?"

He sighed, agitated. "Look. We were very young. We became serious too quickly, and then got carried away and got married. In a registry office with a few friends and no family."

"Go on."

"You really want your pound of flesh, don't you? After she graduated she got a job teaching dance at a boarding school just outside Ipswich. I hadn't even heard of the bloody town but I didn't mind moving, I can find work anywhere. Course, if I'd known what was going to happen, I never would have agreed."

"She met Dominic Hatcher?"

"Cracking on to a married woman like that. The old pervert should have kept his hands to himself. He was deputy head at the school, and it all happened very quickly. I tried to make her see sense, but she said she'd been 'bowled over'. That was how she put it."

"That must have been awful for you."

"She didn't care about that! Said she couldn't help herself. So she moved in with him. That's what Emma's like, act now think later. It was a quick divorce – she accepted the blame, cited her own adultery, so it only took six months. She was married again before the ink had dried. Not that she didn't regret it."

"How do you mean?"

Jason swigged his lager then slammed the can on the table. "Nothing."

"And when did you meet Rose?"

"Emma had just left me. I guess some would say I was on the rebound. But then, we've stood the test of time. Not like Emma and me. I didn't even know she was still with that jerk Hatcher until I saw them at the trial." He paused. "Emma looked awful, she could barely walk. I think she was pretty heavily sedated. We didn't speak to each other."

Cate nodded. "That would have been difficult. I always think it's bad the way everyone is together in court waiting rooms. Victims and defendants together, it's cruel." As she said it, Cate realised she was thinking of Jason as a defendant. He was Rose's partner, and may have known what she was up to.

"So after you and Emma separated, you met Rose. Why didn't you marry her?" It was an impertinent question, but she thought it could be significant.

"Once bitten, as they say. I just didn't see the point. I'd found out the hard way that a wedding ring is no guarantee that a relationship will survive. Rose would mention marriage every now and again but I don't think it really bothered her. I've stayed with her, haven't I? We didn't need a ceremony."

Cate wondered if Rose was really as unconcerned about marriage as Jason said. The fact that Jason was once married to Emma must be significant to Rose's stalking; it couldn't just have been about Luke. But she didn't want to push Jason too far on this first interview, sensing that he could lose his composure if she questioned him too closely. She turned the focus away from him. "How do you think Rose has coped with prison?"

"Alright. Better than I would, I reckon."

"She's surprised you?"

"She always surprises me." He allowed himself a slight smile that looked like pride, and met Cate's eye for the first time, catching her off guard with a question. "Do you enjoy working in prison?"

"I only started a week ago," adding quickly, "but I'm sure it'll be fine."

"You're not how I imagined a probation officer." He was looking at her intently now, and she felt her colour deepen. He leaned closer and she could smell his boozy breath. "What does your husband think of you working in that place?"

Her right hand went instinctively to her left, to the finger where no ring had ever been. "We're not here to talk about me."

"You people!" Jason erupted, "You come in here and ask all these questions, opening up a can of worms when it'll only cause trouble…" He stopped, closed his mouth tight.

"Why do you say that?"

"I'm not saying anything else. You could never understand."

"Understand what, Jason?"

"You want to know everything but it won't change what happened, will it? You can't bring either of the boys back. You have no idea what it's like…"

"Losing a child must be the worst pain."

"She'll never have another. You know that, don't you?"

"No. I didn't know…"

"She can't. When her womb ruptured, or whatever it was happened, they couldn't fix her. Even before Joel died we knew there'd never be another baby for us. Can't you see why she got so attached to Luke?"

"It must be terrible to be told you can't have any more children."

"What do you care, you patronising bitch." He moved towards her, his hands bunched into fists.

Must get out of here, I need to get out. She grabbed her bag and stood up. As she moved for the door her bag caught her half-full mug of coffee. It fell and dregs of coffee spilled onto the carpet.

She watched, feeling the blood in her cheeks, as Jason got on his knees and began blotting up the spilt coffee with some tissues. "Now look what you've done! What a fucking mess."

He stopped blotting the carpet and collapsed into a heap, fighting back muffled sobs. Cate could just make out the words as he covered his face with his hands. "What have you done? Oh Christ, what have you done?"

25

Arriving back at Bishop's Hill after her meeting, Cate couldn't settle. Her computer screen remained blank, despite her intention to at least begin Rose Wilks's report. Her mind kept flitting back to Jason. His anger, her decision to leave quickly and spilling the coffee all over the carpet. The abrupt end with Jason crouched on the floor, fighting back sobs.

He hadn't been able to cope with the interview, and was defensive from the outset. He was near tears when he spoke of his dead son, and also when she'd probed about his marriage to Emma. He was a hurt and angry man. But still he stayed with Rose, and didn't condemn her for stalking Emma. Cate wasn't clear how he'd been able to forgive her. In fact he acted as if Rose had done nothing wrong, even though he knew she had entered the Hatchers' home and nursed their son.

Cate hadn't known that Rose was unable to have children. Her own stomach contracted at the thought of forever having only emptiness inside. Jason would have found that hard too, but there was something else about his behaviour that made her wary. He was hiding something and she recalled his parting words.

The parole board met in just three weeks, and she had a report to write. She needed some answers.

Cate picked up the telephone and dialled Jason's mobile number. No-one picked up and after several rings it went to the messaging service.

"Mr Clark? It's Cate Austin. I'm sorry our interview ended as it did. I wonder if we could arrange another meeting? I could come at 10 a.m. Monday, if that suits? If I don't hear otherwise, I'll see you then."

She replaced the receiver, which had the print of her sweaty palm on it. Restless, she needed to move, and decided to head into the main part of the prison. She phoned D Wing.

A gruff voice answered after one ring. "Yes."

"Cate Austin, probation. I'd like to pop up and read Rose's unit file."

There was a pause. "You mean Wilks's file. No first names in here."

Cate sighed, annoyed at being patronised. "I'll be up in a few minutes."

The line went dead abruptly.

Going into the heart of the prison required much key-turning and slamming of doors, as the dark corridors led deeper into the main accommodation block. Dave Callahan had told her this was called the "landings", the rows of cells stacked on top of each other around an open square used for "association", which was the area where prisoners could come together to bully or bribe, gossip or goad. In the association area were a pool table and a large TV set, switched on to *This Morning*, and blaring out so loudly it hurt her ears.

Surprised to see so many women glued to the screen, Cate looked at her watch; it had just gone midday. Education classes had finished for the morning and lunch would soon be served. A game of pool was in progress, a game she hadn't played since college and had never liked. Two women were watching, one slouched in a chair and the other perched on her knee. The seated inmate took a luxuriant drag on a cigarette and placed her mouth over her companion's, blowing second-hand smoke into it in a long sensuous stream. Cate knew what a blowback was, but hadn't seen two women do it before.

As she crossed the square a wiry peroxide blonde, poised over the green baize with a pool cue ready to hit the ball, leered up at her. "Fancy it, miss?" The others giggled, egging her on. She held out the cue. "You look ready for a poke. Just try to get the ball in the hole."

"Any more talk like that and I'll be making a note in your personal file," Cate replied, nervous but determined not to show it.

As Cate continued walking, trying to keep her head high, a balled-up piece of paper fell to the floor just in front of her. Looking up, she saw a woman on the first landing, arms dangling over the railings, staring down, watching for her reaction. Beside her, she recognised Janie, the cleaning orderly, also watching closely. The woman with the pool cue called tauntingly from the pool table, "Your first love note, miss. What's it say? Someone want to suck your pink titties?"

Cate ignored the comment and saw Janie turn quickly away and disappear into a cell. She walked on to the unit office where Dave Callahan was seated at the desk reading *The Sun*. He had the same air of lazy arrogance she remembered from her first day.

He barely looked up. "Reynolds was just trying to wind you up, darlin'. She's harmless."

She decided to go on the offensive. "I called earlier. Whoever answered the phone was a jerk."

"That'll be Kevin. Don't worry about him." He pushed the cigarette packet towards her. "Want one?"

Tempted, she shook her head. "I'd just like Rose Wilks's case file."

"No problem." He reached into the steel filing cabinet. "I'm her personal officer so any questions, I'm your man."

"Can you remind me what a personal officer does?"

"Oh, you know, checking she's okay. Reviewing her status – she's enhanced, you know. A con can only get that if she's reliable and no bother, so she's won herself some privileges

142

despite being a nonce. She's Red Band – that means she's got a trusted job, that we can rely on her."

"What job?"

"Rosie works in the mess – best job going. They sneak the leftovers back onto the Unit, which is a good way to make friends. And she's got plenty of those, if you know what I mean." He added a lecherous wink.

Cate opened the slim file. The index sheet listed "personal officer interviews", described in one or two words: induction; upgraded – wants to work in kitchen; low mood – chatted it over; worried about Jason.

She pointed to this entry. "What was that about?"

He took the file, sucking a pen as he thought. "The usual. She thought he was playing away."

"Was he?"

Dave shrugged. "How the fuck should I know? Probably. Can't blame the guy. Four years without it…we're all red-blooded males, you know." The calendar behind the desk, showing a topless model with her hand in her knickers. Suddenly Cate felt self-conscious.

"So, you married, love?" He swivelled his chair to face her, legs wide apart, and leaned back. All she could see was his protruding stomach.

"No."

"Boyfriend?"

Cate hesitated, tempted to lie, but didn't. "No. Not that it's any of your business."

He reached into the desk drawer and took out a mobile phone. "I'll soon sort that out for you. What's your number?"

To her horror she saw he was already typing something, probably her name, into the phone's address book when a voice interrupted him. "I thought we weren't allowed mobile phones in the prison, Dave?"

Officer Mark Burgess, pink in the face but trying to sound assertive, stood in the doorway. Caught red-handed, Dave

Callahan threw the phone back in the drawer. "We're not, son, so just you keep it under your hat, alright? I'm off for a slash." He got up and left.

Mark came into the room. "Alright?"

"Not really. It's just this place. Everyone behaves so… inappropriately. Sorry. I must sound uptight."

"You sound fine to me," he said, blushing.

Cate eyed his pimply face, and thought of the taunts she'd just endured. "Do you ever get any hassle from the prisoners?"

"Sure. But it's only banter. I don't take it seriously."

Maybe that's where I'm going wrong.

"Oh, no, here comes trouble," said Mark. He was looking across at the association area. Cate went to join him in the doorway.

Rose Wilks had arrived and was in an argument with Reynolds. Rose looked angry and had her victim backed against the pool table. Reynolds seemed cowed, her head bowed submissively. Standing a little away from the action was Janie, and she was holding her arms out to make a barrier, to make sure no-one tried to intervene.

Mark, surveying the scene with no obvious intention of intervening, said, "Wilks is the top dog round here. Reynolds should know better than to mess with her."

Rose was facing up to Reynolds, who held the cue in front of her as if for protection.

"I think Rose is having a go at Reynolds because of me. I'm going to do something."

"Don't be stupid, we're on our own here. It'll sort itself out." His voice was high with anxiety.

Ignoring him, Cate walked up the stairs to the cell. But the confrontation was over and Reynolds was walking her way, dragging her feet. The other women watched her progress with interest. She came to a halt in front of Cate.

"Sorry if I was rude to you, miss. You won't get no more

144

trouble from me." She looked down at her feet, her voice barely audible.

"What's your name?"

"Reynolds."

"First name."

"Natalie."

"Okay, Natalie. Thank you."

Natalie Reynolds scurried away up the stairs, where Rose and Janie stood waiting. Cate watched as Natalie disappeared into a cell. Rose was standing in the doorway, looking down at Cate. She gave her a brief nod before turning and following Natalie into the cell, banging the door behind her.

Lunchtime. Callahan had told her on her first day that the smooth running of the catering department was vital to the prison's stability. The most privileged inmates, those who could be trusted with knives and boiling water, worked in the kitchen.

Cate and Paul Chatham stood behind the counter and surveyed the overcooked options. She ordered a stodgy combination of cauliflower cheese and chips.

"On a diet, sweetheart?" he asked, when they'd found a table.

"Comfort food," she admitted. "Aside from being knackered, I've had a tough morning. My visit to Rose's partner ended in him crying on the floor and me legging it before he hit me."

"Oh dear, not good."

"No, not great. I've just arranged to see him again on Monday."

"Want me to come with you, babe?"

"I think that would just aggravate him. I just hope he's calmed down by then."

"Well, at least you've got the weekend to recover. Have a fun time with your daughter doing whatever it is that yummy mummies do."

"No chance of that. I've got a crap weekend ahead, as I'm on my lonesome. Amelia will be with her father. Tim likes to show his new girlfriend how good he is at happy families, even though he broke ours up to be with her."

"Ouch."

"You could say that." She speared a chip into the cheese sauce in reply, eating without pleasure. "At least I don't have the hassle of a man in my life."

He made an exaggerated move backwards. "Point taken. Well, sweetheart, I've got good news for you. Tomorrow afternoon, I'm having a little drinks party. Now why not come along and see if I can't find you a nice man who is worth the hassle."

Excusing herself, Cate went to the toilet. Washing her hands, she caught sight of her reflection in the mirror. She needed a haircut. She needed new clothes. She looked tired. Since Tim left her, Cate hadn't even been asked on a date. At first this was a relief; she was bruised by betrayal, and Amelia gave her all the love she needed.

But now she felt her heart healing, a scab raised across the sore. She sensed that soon she would emerge, as if from a cocoon, and want to be wanted. Of course, there were plenty of men working at the prison, but even the few weeks she had been there had shown her that they weren't her type – too macho, too much ego. But then, what was her type? After ten years with Tim she wasn't sure anymore.

Paul, despite his handsome looks, did nothing for her. And anyway she was sure he was gay. This was something you'd obviously want to hide in a prison. His references to his 'partner' always made her assume it wasn't a woman.

Cate felt withered inside. She hadn't had sex in nearly four years and she missed it.

26

Black Book Entry

The first thing I was aware of was sound, soothing and familiar.
The low melodious hum of women's voices, murmuring. The
next, a dragging sensation across my abdomen. As though my
brain had taken a few moments to wake, pain dawned slowly
but soon scorched around my pelvis. The hurt wasn't constant
but constricted and tightened with each excruciating breath.
Where the hell was I?

Without opening my eyes I tried to pull myself together,
think about what had happened. Laid out and vulnerable, I
was flat on my back with something heavy pinning me down.
The surface supporting me was firm, and I was just about
to try moving when a sharp pain stabbed my womb, and I
groaned. I opened one eye, and then the other. There was no
immediate difference, no revelation. I stared into a hole. My
vision adjusted to the dark, and then made out a curtain on a
steel frame, half closed. Through the gap shone the soft glow
of an angle poise lamp, around which hummed the voices of
two whispering women. Everything looked so familiar, but I
couldn't find the right words to describe the place.

When I woke again, my eyes opened almost instantly.

The room was less dark. I tried to move, but the pain across my stomach stole my breath and I whimpered like a puppy. Turning my head slightly, I saw that there was just one woman now, writing something, her head bent as if in prayer. I now knew where I was: in hospital.

I felt something in my right hand. I couldn't look down but coaxed my fingers across its smooth plastic surface with an indentation in the middle, which I pressed. The nurse's head jolted up; it was an alarm then. She was on her feet, the sound of rubber on plastic, flip, flip, flip, and then her face came over me. She touched my left arm, checking the dressing there, and I saw I was attached to a drip. She looked too young to be a nurse, with her rosy skin and purple glittery eyeliner. Staring briefly down, unspeaking, she took my wrist, looked at the silver fob pinned to her dress, seemed satisfied, and released my captive hand. Then she spoke, a low whisper confirming that it was night-time.

"Thirsty?"

I hadn't thought about it, but once I heard the word I realised my mouth felt like sandpaper. I nodded, teeth held against the possible pain of moving. She reached for the clear plastic jug on the bedside cabinet, poured water into a plastic beaker that she placed by my side. Then with practised skill she pulled me forward, adjusted the pillows behind my head, and released me back so I was half-sitting. She held the cup for me to sip tentatively at first and then, when I realised there was no pain, more deeply.

She took the beaker away before I'd finished, causing some water to dribble down my chin. "Don't overdo it. Your body's still in shock. You've had a major operation."

And then it hit me like a lightning bolt. My baby. I grabbed her hand, spilling some water. "Please, where is my baby?"

She reached for a tissue. When she bent over me I thought it was to hug me but no, she just wiped my cheek, placed the used hanky in her pocket and a fresh one in my right hand.

She hesitated, so I knew something was wrong. She didn't know how to break bad news to me.

"The doctor will be coming to see you in the morning. She'll be able to give you much more information." Then she said in a rush, "Your baby's in intensive care."

"My baby. How is he?"

She bit her lip. "The doctor will explain everything. Your son is in the best hands."

My son. I do have a son. "Where is he?"

"We have a very good unit here. He couldn't be in a better place."

I closed my eyes. I couldn't remember anything that had happened except the sudden pain and the knowledge I had to get to hospital.

"When you came in, your labour was established, and your baby was in distress. Your womb had torn so you had to have a caesarean under general anaesthetic. The doctor will explain more when she sees you, but your body's been through an intense ordeal, which is why it's taken you some time to come around. You'll start to remember more, but give yourself time. A general anaesthetic can be quite debilitating."

"Why is he in intensive care? What's wrong with him?"

The nurse put her hands on mine. I felt her roughened fingers stroking my wrist. "Your uterus was badly ripped. It's unusual, especially with first births, but it happens. That's why you went into labour early. We can cope with quite early labours these days, but your baby was in distress and needs a bit of help. He's being well looked after, so you should try to rest now."

I listened to the flip, flip, flip of her departure and tried to think of nothing.

Later still, I was woken. It was the same nurse, moving briskly, and I noticed her dark hair was tinted with pink tips. The room was bright with morning sunshine.

"Are you hungry?" She had a Suffolk voice, a local accent, and it comforted me. I shook my head; it wasn't food I needed. "You really should eat, you know." She emptied the half-drunk water back into the jug and picked it up. "I'll just be a sec. I'll get you some more water."

When she was gone I saw that I was in a room on my own, but that through the open door, opposite the desk, was a long ward. I could hear talking and the squeaking wheels of a trolley.

The nurse returned. "Are you sure you won't eat? Shall we try?" She had a plate of buttered toast in her hand, but I shook my head; if I ate I'd be sick. She seemed to consider what to say, chewed her lip, then put down the toast. "You must be very worried, but he really is in good hands."

Tears drowned my vision. The pain across my stomach tightened. I couldn't bear to hear those words again. Sobbing, half aware of her placing a firm arm around my shoulders, I heard her whisper over and over again, "It's okay, it's okay."

Distraught as I was, I still recognised the lie.

Drifting in and out of sleep, I wasn't aware of time passing. The pain from the caesarean had eased and I had been given pills in a small plastic cup. Antidepressants maybe. Or morphine. Either way, they dulled the pain and my face was dry, tearless. The smell of school dinners and a plate of greyish meat and potatoes arrived. My stomach contracted but I managed to push some of the gravy around and eventually tasted some. It was unpleasant but my mouth salivated anyway, tastebuds urging me on after too long without nutrition. It amazed me that my body wanted to survive, even when it was damaged.

I knew I'd done well when the nurse, the one from the night before with the purple eyeliner and pink-tipped hair, took the plate and rewarded me with an indulgent smile. "There now. You must be feeling better."

On her badge was the name: Nurse Hall.

Once my tray was removed I had a visitor. Not a nurse; this woman wore a white coat, unbuttoned to reveal a smart suit beneath, and I couldn't think why anyone would dress like that in a hospital. Her lipstick matched the maroon of her shirt, although her nails were cut short and bare of varnish.

I watched her take out some papers from her briefcase and remove the top off a pen.

"I'm Dr Marion Cross. Did the nurse tell you I was coming?"

I shook my head.

"I'm here to talk to you about your son."

Oh God, I thought, simultaneously desperate to hear and dreading what she was about to say.

"He's in a critical condition, but stable."

So my baby was clinging to life. Dr Cross brought her chair closer to the bed.

"You went into early labour because your womb had ruptured. The thickest part of the uterus wall had torn, and you were haemorrhaging. We performed an emergency caesarean, but your baby was deprived of oxygen when your womb ruptured."

"Will he die?"

"What happened to you was a rare occurrence, but rupture can be disastrous for both mother and child. About one in twenty babies don't survive."

I closed my eyes. My stomach ached.

"But he's stable, and we have every hope he'll be fine. Miss Wilks, I'm afraid your uterus was not repairable."

"What do you mean?"

"You were bleeding extensively. An emergency hysterectomy had to be performed. I'm so sorry."

No womb. No more babies. The full force of this information hit me so hard I struggled to breathe.

"The drip in your arm is providing you with antibiotics, to make sure you don't catch any infections. But the wound looks to be healing."

"Can I see him?" I gasped.

Dr Cross nodded. "Of course. You can be taken to the ward in a wheelchair, and you need to be very gentle with yourself. Both you and your baby have been through a terrible ordeal. I should warn you, he looks fragile. Try to express some milk. Breast milk is far better for him than formula, and it will help you to feel involved in his recovery."

Recovery. The word was a talisman.

"He's small, and he needs help. His birth was problematic, and we won't be able to assess any impairment just yet, but he's a fighter. His dad has already seen him; would you like us to call your partner to say you're awake?"

But it wasn't you I wanted.

Nurse Hall took me down to intensive care in a wheelchair. I didn't speak on our way there. There was nothing she could say that would help, but she chatted anyway, telling me of the dog she just bought, and how it pissed on her bed when she was at work. When we arrived at the unit she wheeled me to a sink, and we both washed our hands. Then she pushed me to the incubator.

Inside was my baby boy. He didn't look like the baby I'd imagined. He wasn't pink and fat. He looked so tiny, so thin. The bones on his face too clearly defined. His eyes were closed. He was pale, almost blue. From his nostril a small tube was taped to the side of his face. My heart pounded, my breathing strained.

"He's so small," I whispered.

"Yes, he is. But babies are amazing, you know. They're tougher than they look." She put her hand on my shoulder, leaned forward and lifted the card attached to the incubator. "He's just over four pounds, he needs to gain weight. How do you feel about expressing your milk?" She pointed to a big machine in the corner with a hose attached to a large suction cup, looking like something that belonged in a cow shed rather than a hospital. "Would you like to do it now? The sooner the better, before your supply dwindles. Then you can feed him."

The machine was named Daisy, a reference to the fact that it reduced the woman to cow status. I was still in the wheelchair, so Nurse Hall brought it to me. She lifted my gown, exposing my breasts, and placed a plastic cone over each breast in turn to suck out my milk. I hadn't read about breastfeeding yet – I thought I had plenty of time – but Nurse Hall talked to me throughout. "Keep looking at your son, it will help to stimulate the supply. That's it, good girl."

I focused on my baby while being milked. Not a baby at my breast, but a plastic suction cup.

"The substance you're producing now is called colostrum. See how yellow it is? It's very rich, and gives your baby just what he needs. He only needs a small amount – his stomach is only as big as a grape." I watched her pour the milk in a syringe. "He's being fed naso-gastrically at the moment, to give him a rest, but it would be good to progress him to a bottle when he's stronger. He's too weak to feed from the breast just yet, but we'll try him soon."

She lifted my son from the heated incubator, quickly swaddled him in a blanket and handed him to me. He was so light, like a tiny bird. There were fine hairs covering his frail body and his nappy swamped him.

Together we fed him, Nurse Hall placing the syringe into the tube and gently teasing it out, droplets down the tube like tears. He hardly seemed to be taking anything but she was satisfied. "Have you thought of a name for him?"

"I like Joel."

Nurse Hall smiled. "He looks like a Joel."

Suddenly, giving him a name, an identity, was the most important thing in the world. I needed to make him real. I looked into his face and called him by his name for the first time. Joel. My son.

27

Cate decided to take Paul Chatham up on his invite to the drinks party.

It was just past three when she left her house. She would be early, but couldn't think how else to kill the time. Paul lived close to the town centre and she soon arrived outside his modest semi in Acacia Way. The house was modern, yet the shrubs and trees were established and rampant, and the front door was a bright yellow, making it stand out from its more conservative neighbours.

Ringing the bell she racked her brain for Paul's partner's name – something unisex like Nicky or Jo. A neat, middle-aged man opened the door, dressed casually in deck shorts and a linen shirt and holding a pair of secateurs.

"I'm really early, I know. I'm Cate."

He offered a smooth hand. "Welcome. I'm Sam. Paul has told me all about you." He glowed with health and exuberance, and his springy dark hair and warm brown eyes gave the impression of an affectionate puppy. She liked him instantly.

He led her through to the back of the house, down the hall with its immaculate cream carpet and through the Shaker-style kitchen in pea green, tiles underfoot. On the granite counter stood several bottles of wine, sherry and cling-filmed bowls of nibbles.

The back double doors were flung back, and sunlight flooded through. In the garden Paul was lounging on a steamer chair, reading a newspaper. Although initially surprised to see her he immediately looked delighted. "Cate, by Jove! I didn't think we'd have the pleasure. What's your poison?"

Sam came forward, listing the drinks on offer. "Or there's a lovely Sancerre in the fridge."

"Great," she said, looking around the immaculate garden. "Wow."

"Do you garden?" Sam called from the kitchen. Cate shook her head as he came towards her and put the cool glass in her hand. "Well, you won't have the time, what with working and being a single mum." There was no judgement in his expression, just observation.

She drank the wine more quickly than she should have, hardly tasting the grape, but enjoying its relaxation of her limbs. Sam busied himself with pruning, staying close by to listen to the conversation. She already felt a bit drunk, and wanted to release all the thoughts buzzing in her brain like hornets.

"Now, Cate," said Paul, touching her knee with the tips of his fingers, "I've been thinking about your lonesome status and I may have the solution. Have you thought about finding a nice prison officer to satisfy you?"

"Oh, please. They're all so macho, I think the testosterone would choke me."

"Tut tut, no stereotyping here, please. I happen to know a very nice officer who thinks you're the dog's bollocks."

She groaned. "Let me guess. Dave Callahan."

"Heavens, no. That rogue? I was thinking of a sensitive soul by the name of Officer Burgess."

"Mark? But he's just a child!" The idea of him fancying her was amusing.

"He's about five years younger than you, that's all. And once his skin clears up he'll be quite handsome. There's lots to be said for a toy boy, isn't that right, Sam?"

Sam minced back towards them, his gait obviously an

exaggerated parody to make her giggle. He perched on the end of Paul's chair and took the glass from his hand, sipping thoughtfully. "The thing with love is," he said, looking at Paul, "you can't control it. It chooses you."

Paul reached out and took his glass back. "And who said anything about love? What this girl needs is a good shag."

Cate spluttered into her glass.

"Christ, Cate, you're only – what? Twenty-seven?"

"I'm thirty in August."

"You should be having fun, not moping about because your daughter's with her father. You should find a decent bloke and get laid. It'll do you good." As Paul finished speaking the doorbell rang.

"And here," said Sam, "could be our first candidate."

By 5 p.m. the garden was buzzing with an eclectic collection of Paul's colleagues and friends. Although there were a few people from the prison, Cate noted that they were all, like Paul, defined by difference. There was Ray, the shy librarian who plodded the prison landings with his book trolley in the vain hope a prisoner would want to read about Anna Karenina rather than the Krays. There was the eccentric sociology teacher, with his piggy eyes and Father Christmas beard whom the inmates universally respected. Then she spied Wayne Bugg, the 'Care Bear' officer from the induction unit who was ridiculed by staff and prisoners alike. Yes, Paul has chosen well. These people would not be offended or prejudiced by his sexual orientation. She noticed that the Governor had not been invited. Nor Dave Callahan, which was a relief.

When Mark Burgess arrived she was struck by what a schoolboy he looked. Without his uniform of stark black trousers and white lapelled shirt he should have looked more grown-up, but his casual clothes only replicated another kind of uniform: his black jeans and navy T-shirt had a boyish quality, and someone so skinny should really avoid such a tight fit. He seemed to be in a mild panic, his eyes darting about for a familiar face, and when he caught her eye his relief was obvious.

She watched him bound over, a glass of beer sloshing in his hand. Up close he was shorter than he seemed in the prison, no longer bolstered by standard issue boots.

He took in her appearance with an admiring glance. "You look great."

She was embarrassed. "I don't feel it. I'm a bit drunk."

"Only a bit? Well, we'll have to fix that then, won't we? Wait here." She watched him rush back into the house and disappear into the kitchen.

As she stood waiting, Sam caught her eye and winked. "Oh, please," she mouthed, "rescue me," just as Mark resurfaced with a large glass of white wine and a second glass of beer and dashed back to her side. Sam was about to walk over when another guest approached him, engaging him in conversation. Sam looked over at Cate and pulled an apologetic face.

"I'm glad you're here," Mark said, standing a little closer than was comfortable.

She smiled weakly and saw with amusement that he wouldn't need much encouragement to think he stood a chance with her. He was like a puppy dog. *To get through this party I just might have to drink more alcohol.* At least she could have a lie in tomorrow.

She shouldn't have had so much to drink.

Cate was lying flat on the bed and the room was spinning. She prayed she wouldn't be sick but the posters on the wall didn't help – pictures of semi-clad women on motorbikes and one she recognised as a C-list celebrity.

"Drink this," Mark said, handing her a glass of water. The mattress sagged as he sat beside her on the cheap slipperiness of the single duvet.

"Thanks, Mark. I really couldn't have driven home."

She had ended up in his bedroom, too intoxicated to drive, too drunk to care. But she told herself she could handle him; he was just a boy. As the water hit her stomach it churned.

"I think I'm going to be sick."

Mark grabbed the waste paper bin, half full with sweet wrappers and sock labels. Bending over, she vomited, and he put a hand on her back. She was too sick to push him away, as she brought up the bitter taste of regurgitated wine and cheese and pineapple. A sour taste coated her mouth, the dizziness not gone, and there was sweat on her forehead. She fell back on the bed.

Still with the bucket in his hand Mark fell back with her, and kissed her clammy face. She moved her head away, and he placed the bucket on the floor.

To her horror he started to unbutton his jeans. She groaned, thinking that she had brought this on herself.

"Mark," she said feebly, "I'm not feeling well."

He was down to his boxer shorts and she was amazed that despite just seeing her puke he had an erection.

Cate thought about Amelia, and the heat of shame made her feverish. What was she doing? For God's sake, she wasn't a teenager. She was a mother, and here she was, half-drunk, in some guy's bedroom.

"Can I just hold you, Cate? Please?"

He was so pathetic that when he lay beside her on the narrow bed she didn't pull away. At least she was fully clothed. His hands clumsily wormed their way under her skirt, up her bare leg.

"Mark, I don't think this is such a good idea."

She pushed his hands away, tugging her skirt back down, but as she sat up her head violently spun, and she collapsed back onto the bed. She'd had more to drink than she'd thought.

His puppy-dog eyes burned into her, his clammy arm over her breasts, as the nylon sheet wrapped around her legs. "Come on, Cate." He lunged at her, his mouth open, and she

158

saw some food caught in his front teeth, smelt a brewery on his breath. His weight pinned her down, and she tried to push him away but his hand burrowed under her top, clamped on her left breast. He started to squeeze, and she felt herself being crushed.

"Mark! You need to stop this now."

His slobbering mouth swamped her, muffling her words. As his saliva ran down her throat she gagged, pushing him off her, off the bed, and into a thudding heap on the floor just before she leaned over and vomited the last of her stomach contents all over him. The taste was foul, and her head pounded. "Oh God, Mark, I'm so sorry."

Mark lay on the floor, his face and shirt matted with puke. He wiped a sleeve over his face, then, seeing the sleeve, pulled his shirt off his back revealing a concave chest speckled with black straggly hairs.

"I'm so sorry." She looked at the carpet. "I'll help you clean the mess."

She was empty and sore. Her head was splitting and she was parched, longing for a drink and a sleep in a dark room – alone. She had to get out of there, but she couldn't drive in that state. She could use her mobile to call for a taxi but the idea of waiting while one arrived was unbearable.

She forced herself off the bed, retrieved one shoe from underneath and another from the doorway. She couldn't look at Mark, still sitting on the floor with his head in his hands.

"Look, Mark, I'm afraid you've got the wrong idea."

He was embarrassed and angry. "I have to get a decent sleep anyway," he slurred. "I'm on duty in the morning."

She didn't look at him again, but fumbled down the hall to the front door, into the night air outside.

28

Black Book Entry

You came to the hospital room, looking pale and anxious. "How are you, pet?" You struggled to look me in the eye.

"Sore."

You pushed your hands into your jeans pockets, staring at the carpet. "They don't seem to know why it happened or anything."

"Just bad luck."

"Do you think, when I pushed you…" You didn't finish the sentence.

"Can you help me get up?"

You supported me as I sat up, then took my weight as I struggled into the wheelchair. You were so gentle with me. "Alright, Rose?"

"I'll be better when we see Joel."

You pushed me down the corridor, past the maternity ward, scooting round a woman who was vacating an individual room. "Sorry, pet," you said to her, "these things are like shopping trolleys." When we arrived at the door of the neo-natal unit you stopped and looked at me, your eyes clouded with crushing sadness. "I'll never forgive myself for all this," you said.

Inside the unit it was quiet. The babies were too poorly to cry. A nurse, making notes at her desk, lifted her head as we entered, and smiled.

"How is he?" I asked her.

"Joel's had a stable night. We're happy with his progress."

You squeezed my shoulder. Then you pushed the wheelchair next to the crib. Joel was sleeping, the tube in place and a machine keeping beat with his heart. You looked down at our son. "He's so beautiful."

Your eyes welled up, as you stroked a finger down his cheek, across his brow, touching the tip of his nose. "Hello handsome."

Eyes still closed, Joel's mouth made a circle as he yawned. You gasped as if it was a miracle.

I watched you fall in love with your son, and the mix of pride and pain was unbearable. If only you could look at me like that.

"Joel?" you said. "I'm your daddy. You sleep and get better, little man."

If you were surprised that I'd named him without talking to you first, you never said.

We sat by his crib, me in the wheelchair and you on a chair, your hand still touching Joel. The nurse came over, checked his feeding tube and watched the machine for a few moments.

"Is he going to be alright?"

"He's doing very well, his sats are a bit low but we're helping him with that. He'll be running around kicking a ball before you know it."

"I hope so." I saw that expression in your eyes, that same raw pain as when Emma first left you. I knew that I must be strong for us both. The nurse went to check on her other patients.

"He'll be fine, Jason. He's in good hands."

You couldn't take your eyes off our boy, and kept stroking his tiny arm.

"Will you be okay at home?" I asked. Since you'd moved into my flat I'd done all the cooking and housework, as well as paying all the bills.

"The fridge is almost empty, but we can live on takeaway for a few days."

"Not 'we' Jason. I'm not leaving here yet."

"God, of course not, pet. Ignore me. I don't know what I'm saying."

I leaned forward and touched your cheek with my lips, stroked a golden curl that had escaped from behind your ear. In just one year I'd become your mainstay. Since moving in with me we'd never been apart. I'd created a role for myself as lover, friend and confidant all rolled into one. It didn't matter about love: you needed me.

But I couldn't think about returning home. My whole world, my whole purpose for living, now lay in an incubator which kept temperature constant, every breath monitored, situated worryingly close to the duty-nurse's desk, while inside, alone, Joel struggled to hang on to his fragile existence.

"Christ, Rose. If I hadn't lost my temper with you." You bowed your head. "This is all my fault."

You wanted forgiveness. For the first time that look of grief in your eyes was anticipating my reaction, not remembering one of Emma's. I could see that things had changed between you and her, you and me. How sad, that it took a sick child to finally sever her grip.

"I'll never forgive myself if he dies," you said.

I placed my hands on your head, your curls twisting around my fingers, and pulled you close as you crumpled, a grown man becoming a boy, tears falling as I held you tight. And then you said it. "I wish I could love you, Rose."

I froze. It was still hard to hear you say this. When you pulled away, you looked back into the crib where Joel was still asleep. "I will love him, though. More than I've ever loved anyone."

You had to leave to get something to eat, since the hospital only provided food for patients. As with all institutions, the hospital honoured the tradition of presenting its inmates with food at times better suited to young children, so dinner was at 4.30. The meal came on a grey plastic tray, accompanied by a shallow clear cup holding three tablets. They were the only colour in the scene, Smartie-like in their brightness. Unthinking, I bolted them down with the tepid water and handed the cup back to the nurse. Satisfied, she left, leaving me to survey the food.

The meal was an uninviting splodge of brown, beige and white. Mince and potatoes, a slice of anaemic bread and a small plastic tub of margarine. In another container a dark red jelly wobbled under Dream Topping. Food for the sick. Well, I was sick; I realised that. But my sickness was inside. I was sick with fear for my little boy.

I felt Rita and Mum watching over me, and sent a prayer to them. *Please let him be okay.*

I couldn't think of anything but Joel. We'd spent most of the day in the intensive care unit, staring into his cot, feeding him with his special bottle or expressing my milk into Daisy. But now you were gone and I was in my room, resenting every moment that I was away from him.

There were happy voices coming from the ward. They were strange to me, those voices cooing over healthy babies, as they would be to a foreigner. Those mothers were swamped with cards and flowers, when I hadn't got one. The birth of a sick child isn't something to be celebrated. That's why I was separated. Segregated. Those women wouldn't want to be near me; my bad luck could be contagious. But I was glad to be in my own room. From the elevated bed all I could see through the window was sky. I was several floors up, and remembered the view of this rectangular block from the ground, when I carried Joel inside me. When he was still safe.

Intensive care was on the same floor as the maternity wards. The thought of his tiny, fighting heart grabbed my own, which kicked into rapid palpitations as I thought of the thin valves pushing life around his body.

Making me jump, the nurse came to reclaim the tray. I registered the uniform without directly looking at her and was surprised when I recognised the voice. It was Nurse Hall, who had been so kind on that first terrible night. "You've eaten well – quite a feat in here. And you have more colour today. Feeling a bit better?"

I nodded, risked a smile. After all, Joel was alive.

"Good. Maybe you'd like to try getting dressed? And I think we can get rid of the wheelchair now."

I shuffled down the corridor, making my way to the neonatal unit. As I walked by the maternity ward I saw visitors sitting on beds and auxiliaries were in the ward handing out teas. People wandered past me clutching flowers and boxes of chocolates in pastel paper. Reaching the junction of wards I followed the corridor marked "Paediatric", under the picture of a stork whose beak pointed the direction.

The wards in the maternity block, all named after Suffolk rivers, came off a main spur; those wards were for the healthy babies. I walked past two nurses who were deep in whispered conversation. Next was the individual room where you had struggled with the wheelchair, nearly bashing into the woman who was leaving. It had been empty when I passed it earlier. The door was open and in the room a woman was talking tenderly to her baby.

I stopped, transfixed, thinking I'd seen her somewhere before.

She was dressed like me, in hospital gown and slippers. We were like inpatients in an asylum. She looked up and smiled. There was a baby in her arms, its blue hat snug over escaping wisps of hair. It's easy to smile when your child is perfect. His beauty drew me forward.

"Is it a boy?" I said.

She nodded, pulling the blanket aside slightly. He was bigger then Joel, and bonny. He began to mewl and she cooed at him, reaching for a bottle on the bedside cabinet, lost to her son.

"Congratulations," I said as I left the room, passing a man who was heading towards it. He was an older man with snowy hair, smartly dressed, holding a huge bunch of yellow roses in his arms. He brushed straight past me, knocking me off-balance, as he marched into the room where he swept up the woman and her son in a possessive embrace.

29

Black Book Entry

In the neonatal unit six perspex incubators lined the sides of the room, four of them empty.

I walked to Joel's crib by the nurse's station, where he was pale and unmoving. I turned briefly, saw that the nurse was engrossed in paperwork, her head bent low over the desk. I wanted her to talk to me, to ask her if there had been any progress, but I didn't like to disturb her.

When Dr Cross arrived to do her daily round, she came to me first.

"Hello, Miss Wilks. How are you?"

"Fine," I said. But I wasn't the patient. "How is he?"

She picked up a clipboard from the edge of the incubator and glanced at the charts. "Joel is doing as well as could be expected. The blueness on his skin suggests he may have some weakness in the heart, but we won't conduct any diagnostic tests until he's stronger. His breathing is slightly laboured but that should improve, as he gains weight and his strength increases. The machine there is just helping him along, breathing for him when he weakens."

I looked at the monitor with its green light and computer printout and tried to think of something to ask, but there was only one question I could form in my mind and I was scared to say it. Taking my silence as satisfaction Dr Cross moved on to the next crib. I felt a hand on my shoulder; it was the nurse, now finished with her paperwork. "Do you have any questions, Rose?" She must have read my mind, or it must be what all mothers wanted to ask, because she went on, "He's in the best place, you know. A few years ago and we didn't have the technology, so his chances would have been slim. But these days we can do so much more. It's just a question of taking each day at a time."

I watched Joel's eyelids flicker and peel back. He was awake. His navy eyes flickered over my face, wise as an old man's. Surely his memory was unformed, yet still he lifted tiny fists as if in recognition. I placed my hand on the side of the crib, and gave him a finger to grip.

"Joel," I whispered, testing the sound on my tongue.

Back in my room, Nurse Hall had only just left when another woman appeared. She stood in the door, dressed in white like an angel. The sun was in her eyes and she blinked, smiling. I recognised her immediately. She was the mother with the beautiful son. I couldn't place her, but I felt that I knew her from somewhere.

She stepped into my room uninvited. I tensed, like a threatened animal. When she sat next to my bed I saw how small she was; despite recent pregnancy she was slightly built and her features were as fine as a porcelain doll's. Her white dressing gown made her seem ethereal.

"I hope you don't mind me coming to see you. My baby's having a nap and I fancied a little walk."

She spoke hesitatingly, her face beautifully sorrowful. "Nurse Hall told me your son's in the neonatal unit. That must be so awful for you. But it's the best one in East Anglia."

Immediately I had the measure of this frail girl-woman, from her pale skin and white-gold hair to the brightness of her personality. She was one of those optimistic, sunshine types who normally avoid women like me. But she was blinded by the hospital tag round my wrist, a match to her own, and the empty crib by my bed.

But maybe her instinct was right. We weren't the same, but we'd both given birth, had a child, both laboured. Although my child had been cut from me with a knife. Two babies, two little boys, one fighting for life in an incubator, one sleeping peacefully.

She sat at my side and asked about Joel. "My son was born yesterday. The labour was so sudden, I was lucky to get here in time. My husband drove like a maniac, it's a wonder we didn't crash!" She laughed as she said this. "But it was all fine in the end. We've got to stay in a few days, because I tore quite badly," she whispered this, a confession from one woman to another, "but I don't mind staying. Get my confidence a bit. It's not coming very naturally to me, all this. I had to be shown how to change a nappy!"

I listened and envied her those pathetic worries. I tried to keep my voice light. "Have you thought of a name for your son?"

"I haven't discussed it with my husband yet," she said, "but I want to call him Luke. Dominic will be visiting later, so we'll talk about it then. He won't admit it but he's worn out, what with working all day and then being up all last night with the excitement. I told him that he needn't come tonight, to go home and rest, but he wouldn't hear of it. It's so hard for the men, don't you think?"

"Mmm."

"They must feel so helpless during labour. He was supposed to take two weeks off after the baby was born, but he went in to work today. He doesn't see the point in using up his holiday just to sit around here. He's a deputy head at a boarding school, so it's hard for him to switch off. What does your husband do?"

"He's in catering."

"Dominic works so hard. He'll be here soon. I asked him to bring in some makeup. I just wish I had some decent clothes to wear, but nothing fits." She squeezes the spare flesh on her stomach. "I'm a dance teacher. I used to teach twenty lessons a week. You wouldn't think it to look at me now, would you?"

It all fell into place. The mention of dancing was the switch that sparked my memory. She was the young student dancer who you fell so hopelessly in love with. She was the woman in the photo you kept in your wallet. She was your ex-wife, Emma.

My pulse throbbed. Thoughts of you going to her, of the night you came home smelling of green apples, raced through my veins like poison.

I knew you mustn't see her. She mustn't know who I was. I had to keep you away from her.

If you were to see each other, all those months would have been for nothing.

"Dominic!"

"Hello, love. The nurse said you were here."

Her husband walked into the room, tall and imposing in a grey suit. I was struck by how much older he was than Emma.

"This is Rose," she told him, but Dominic barely glanced at me. He only had eyes for Emma.

30

Black Book Entry

The following morning I woke to the sound of the early shift changes, to the mumble of nurses discussing cases during handover while a cleaner listlessly pushed a broom under my bed. I was still in my own room, still segregated from the other women. Thoughts of Emma tormented me. Despite myself, I remembered her singsong voice, her guileless face. And she was just yards away. Just when it seemed I could have everything I wanted, when I'd finally won your love via Joel, all too easily I could lose it if you saw her. I couldn't let that happen and knew I had to keep you away.

I waited for my breakfast impatiently. Afterwards I could go and see Joel in his plastic crib. I wanted to ask if I could bath him. I looked at the clock – it was 8.15. Breakfast was late, but I could hear the trolley approaching. When it came into view I saw the smiling Nurse Hall, who greeted me with a yawn. "You look tired," I said.

"Yeah, it was a mate's birthday last night, so we went clubbing. I didn't get home till three. I've got a hangover from hell, but it was worth it."

Nurse Hall wasn't that much younger than me, I guessed she was about twenty-five, but her life seemed like a teenager's.

I couldn't ever go to a nightclub. It just wasn't my kind of thing, though you'd tried to persuade me to go a few times. I felt too old for dancing and besides I wasn't attractive enough to feel good in a club. I wondered what it would be like to get dressed up, to drink vodka, to dance on a podium to loud music until three in the morning. I wondered if it would be possible to forget my worries, envying Nurse Hall the dark shadows under her eyes and her pounding head.

"How's Joel?"

"He's put on three ounces in the last four days."

She beamed at me. "That's excellent, Rose. He'll soon be ready to go home. Have they said anything about that?"

I shook my head, concentrated on stirring my tea. I daren't think about us going home, it was too big a step. The thought terrified me. But something else terrified me more: you seeing Emma.

"I wondered if you'd do something for me." I said.

"What's that, Rose?"

"Will you phone Jason? Will you ask him to give me a bit of space, to stay away for a day or two?"

"That's a bit of a tough request."

"I just want to rest. It won't be for long. I don't want him to see me tired and teary."

Nurse Hall bit her lower lip. "If you're sure, Rose, then I'll call him."

"I'm positive," I said. "He needs to stay away from the ward. Just for a few days."

"Okay. I'll do it now." Nurse Hall touched my shoulder. "You've got a visitor."

I looked up and saw Emma. She was radiant in a powder blue smock, and cradled into the crook of her arm was her sleeping son.

"Hi, Emma," Nurse Hall said and I was disappointed that she used the same friendly tone of voice with her that she'd just used with me. "How are you? And how's little Luke?"

171

Emma beamed down at the baby, whispering so she didn't disturb him. "Both good, thanks. In fact, guess what? We're being discharged this morning." She said this to both Nurse Hall and me, sharing her news. "I'm nervous – it seems such a big responsibility. I wish I could stay here for a bit longer."

Nurse Hall gave her a reassuring smile. "It's just so special taking a baby home. You'll be just fine, Emma. A good mother always worries." She whispered my consolation prize, "It'll be you next, Rose."

As if embarrassed by her good fortune, Emma sat next to me on the bed. "Of course it will. Shall we go together to see Joel?" Her hand was warm on top of mine and I could smell her perfume, light and sweet like green apples.

Together we walked to the neonatal unit, Emma almost pulling me along despite the weight of Luke in her arms. She didn't support Luke's head too well, and it lolled about precariously. I was slow, measuring the fear with each step. I wondered if this would be the last time I would walk it. I tortured myself with the thought of an empty crib at the end of it.

When we arrived I saw Joel was in his incubator, and relief poured through me briefly before I saw how small he still was. He was awake, navy eyes focused on me as I bent over him.

"Can you see me, Joel? Or am I just a blur?" I whispered, offering him my finger to grip.

He was silent, but his mouth was open as if he would speak, if only he could. Now free from the machines and wires, I could touch him easily and I kissed his cheek, then the bridge of his nose. His hand held my arm, as if to cuddle it, and I kissed him again.

"He's a beautiful baby." The nurse behind spoke, making me jump. I turned around and smiled. But she wasn't talking to me. She was talking to Emma and looking at Luke. Emma was animated.

"Everyone here's been so wonderful, it'll be hard to go

home and be alone with him. It's a bit daunting, to think about having this new responsibility. Do you know what I mean?"

The nurse nodded, turned to me. "Joel is looking alert today. When Dr Cross comes round we'll ask when she thinks you'll be able to go home."

"Really?"

"He's gaining weight steadily, and feeds well from his bottle. In fact, you could try him at the breast, if you like. He's probably strong enough now."

The nurse was oblivious to my heart thumping in my chest, and came to my side, lifting Joel out of the crib. He lay in her arms like a doll, pale and serene. "Now then, young man. Would you like some milk? Shall we try without the bottle today?"

She gently handed him to me, and I weighed his light body. His mouth found the skin on my arm and lightly sucked; the nurse saw this. "I think he's hungry, Rose."

The nurse fussed around, pulling a chair closer. I sat, knowing I had no choice. "You've been expressing milk with a machine, so this will feel a little weird." With a casualness that comes from dealing daily with people's bodies, she lifted my top. My doughy breasts were knotted with milk, tattooed with blue veins. Emma was watching and I wished she would turn away. "Luke's bottle-fed," she told me. "So I won't be much use to you, I'm afraid."

Joel started to move his head from side to side, his mouth open like a tiny bird, and the nurse was pulling at me, trying to position me. Emma cuddled Luke, watching the performance, as the nurse pulled me this way and that, when all of a sudden it was too much. I couldn't handle it. "Get off me!" I shouted, pushing the nurse away, and she pulled back like I'd slapped her. Emma was there in an instant, her free hand around me. "Don't worry, Rose. It's okay. I couldn't get the hang of breastfeeding either."

Your lover was comforting me. Can you imagine how that felt?

It was quiet in the unit after that. Emma helped me to feed Joel from a bottle, and didn't mention me losing my temper. The nurse didn't approach me again, but stayed at the desk writing until the end of her shift when she scuttled off, leaving me with Emma. It was nearly visiting time, and she was expecting Dominic. She was coming round to the idea of leaving the hospital. "Dominic will be so pleased. He's hardly had a chance to get to know Luke yet. It's scary, but at least he'll be home to help for a while." She took a makeup pouch from her handbag. "Could you hold Luke, while I go to the toilet? I want to put some lippy on."

She left me with the two boys.

I'd never studied Luke closely before. His skin was a healthy pink, and his eyes were a navy grey. He wore a blue cap, which I pulled from his head. There was a thin covering of pale curls. I looked closer. Golden-red curls. I looked at his face anew, thinking how familiar it looked.

Looking around, I saw that the nurse had left the room and was talking to another nurse in the corridor. I went to Joel's crib and lay Luke next to him.

They could have been brothers, with Luke the stronger, fitter eldest. I had given birth to the runt.

Although Joel was smaller, the shape of the face was the same, and their almond eyes almost identical. And that beautiful gold-red hair. I saw what I should have seen straight away: his face was yours, Jason.

I picked Luke up, out of Joel's crib. It wasn't his fault that his mother was a whore, his father weak. But my fury with you scorched my face, made the blood rush inside me. Where was the justice? Emma had given you a beautiful son, when the one I had produced was sickly and pale. It was so wrong, so unfair and I felt hate take over my heart. Rita and Mum had both warned me to leave you, that pain would follow if a child was born.

The new nurse on duty arrived, and eyed me warily as she went to the desk. I could tell she'd been warned of my earlier outburst.

I returned to Joel, lying still in his crib. I looked down at my own baby, smiling, until I saw that his eyes were fixed. Fixed on me. Until I moved and his gaze didn't follow. His skin looked waxy and I stroked him, shocked that he was cooler than normal. I pinched his arm, and when he didn't respond, I put my head to his ribcage. There was no movement of his chest.

I panicked, throwing Luke into an empty crib, grabbing Joel by the chest and shaking him. "Joel! Joel!"

The nurse was straight over, snatching Joel from me and laying him back down, her ear to his mouth. She turned and ran for the alarm, a red button she punched with her fist before returning to Joel.

"Please," I whimpered, "tell me what's happening?"

The nurse wheeled a machine to his side, moving me away, focused only on Joel. I wanted to rush forward, to grab him and shake life into him. I heard running feet. I was moved aside, and all I could see was a doctor's back and the edge of the plastic crib. Luke was crying and I picked him up. Another nurse saw me, whispered to the doctor, then came over, guiding me from the room.

The door was shut, the blind pulled down, obscuring the window. But under the gap I saw the movement of white coats and hands, the pumping of arms as they tried to save my son. Our son.

I watched, holding Emma's baby.

31

It's Sunday, and as usual the atmosphere in the prison is tense. I try to keep my own feelings in check, whatever is happening elsewhere. There are no civilian staff in the prison on weekends, just officers and inmates. And the chaplain, of course, if religion is your drug. There are no education sessions, no offending behaviour courses, no shrinks to analyse us. We're as close to being free as prison gets, but this also brings boredom and the dreaded time to think. For some inmates it's too much, and the day will be splintered with catfights and tantrums.

Also, it's the day for canteen, when we collect our measly wages, or spend the money family or friends have sent us on the limited but still precious items which we will squirrel or barter, trying to make it last until next weekend. It's like a primary school tuckshop and we jostle like school kids, impatient to hold the chocolate bar in our hand, or pull the nicotine into our gasping lungs. We can also buy cheap shampoo or beauty products but some women moan about the lack of choice, longing to feel pretty, if only for one day, because Sunday afternoon is visiting time.

Convicted prisoners like me can be visited once a fortnight, and squabbles puncture the weekends between visits, as the women try to distract themselves from thinking of the husband or boyfriend they can't see, the son or daughter they can't hold. On visiting Sundays, the tension is different. Imagine waiting to see the face of someone not seen for far too long, or a child who has grown older and taller; the terrible silence as you search for something to say when your world is so grey. Then, the pain and loneliness and fear crashing down when the order comes for goodbyes to be said. The tears of the children are the worst, especially those too young to understand. Afterwards we return to our cells. Newer inmates, or those who have just been told about family events they have missed, that a boyfriend or husband has been unfaithful, that a son has cut his first tooth, cry into their thin pillows.

These things will be true for the other women, but for me today is just another step towards freedom. The parole board meet in two weeks and I'm wishing the hours away like a girl impatient for Christmas. I should be released. I've been a good inmate. I'm a hard worker, the screws like that. They don't think of me as a bully; they don't see me fight. I give fags to women who have run out, and don't demand two in return.

The officers are changing shift, and Officer Burgess is replacing Officer Callahan. In prison you learn to listen.

The thing about officers is that they can't keep their dicks in their pants or their tongues between their teeth. Especially the young ones, since they've got so much to prove. Arriving on duty Mark Burgess sprang along the corridor like he'd won the lottery, stopping at Janie's door to ask if she'd got anyone visiting her later. He likes Janie best because she doesn't scare him. When he goes past my open door he never stops.

Dave Callahan was on duty last night and he's in the office, feet on the desk, reading the *Sunday Sport*. Inmates aren't allowed any pornographic pictures, but the officers can bring them in anytime they like. I stand by my cell door and listen.

"Morning, Dave. Fancy a brew?"

"No, ta, mate. I'm off in five."

"Everything alright last night?"

"Yep. No trouble. I had a decent kip."

"I had a good weekend too."

"Yeah?" Dave sounds like he couldn't care less.

"Went to a party at Paul Chatham's."

"At the queer's house? Did you see his boyfriend?"

"He was alright, actually." Mark sounds uncomfortable.

"Were there other poofters there?" Now Dave is interested.

"No. Cate Austin was, though." I prick up my ears.

"She's a looker, but she's got a stick up her arse. Did she relax any?"

"She did. All the way, as it goes." There's innuendo in the way Mark speaks and a long silence follows.

"You lucky bastard."

"Yeah," Mark says, "all the way."

I'm as surprised as Dave. I need to fit this piece into the jigsaw picture I've been building of her, and I don't know where to put it.

I go to Janie's cell, where she's drawing a picture of a cat. It looks like a child's drawing.

"Hey, Rose. I got a letter from my dad yesterday." She takes it from under her pillow, already opened and creased even though she can't read the words. "Will you read it to me?"

"Of course I will, poppet. First, though, I want you to tell me what happened on Friday. On your little trip into Ipswich. Did you find the address I gave you?"

I'm making light of it, of course. I'm desperate to know. But like all accomplices Janie must be managed. She's not as brave as me. I can feel Mum and Rita watching over me, warning me to be steady.

"Oh, yes. It was easy. My teacher's so nice, she didn't even mind when I arrived late. She knows it's the only day I have on the out, and she likes it when I go to the park and bring her a daffodil. Last week I went into Boots and tried on all the tester perfumes. She said I smelled like a garden centre when I walked in the classroom."

I try not to be impatient, but sometimes it's hard with Janie. "Did you find the house?"

"Yes, that map you gave me was good. The house was just like you said. I had a little look through the windows, like you told me to, but I couldn't see anyone. Nice place, though. Great big lounge with a smart TV – worth a few bob – and one of those L-shaped sofas."

"What else?"

"There was a baby chair in the room."

"A baby chair? Are you sure?" I sense Mum is with me, warning me to leave it.

"Yeah, you know – one of those bouncy ones. It was pink with yellow stars on it. And a little bar with plastic rattles, just like for a new baby."

"Pink, you say? And new?" The spirits are noisy in my head, telling me to stop delving into things that can only hurt me.

"Which is funny," Janie scratches her head, "cos in that photo in her office her daughter looks way too old for a chair like that."

"Office?"

"In the probation officer's room. That photo of her daughter, Amelia. She isn't a baby anymore."

"No." I feel strange, a bit dizzy.

"You think Cate Austin's got another kid?"

"Janie," I say, carefully, "that house is not Cate Austin's."

She frowns. "Whose is it then?"

"A friend. She must have had another baby." I rub my temples, and take a few deep breaths. "You've done well, Janie."

Janie beams at me, always glad to be of service, and I stagger out of her cell, into my own, and collapse onto the bed.

Think, Rose, think. A new baby. Does she have red-gold hair?

Rita and Mum are with me, in the cell. Warning me.

32

Tick, tock, tick, tock. The minutes pass until the parole board meet.

Cate Austin's parole report is the key to my freedom. She must recommend my release or I won't get my parole. I need to show her I'm reformed.

I'm getting to know her better, thanks to Janie snooping in her office. I know her daughter is called Amelia, and she is four or five years old. I know there are no photos of any man. And now it sounds like she might have fucked Officer Burgess, if he's telling the truth about her going "all the way". She should've known better then to go with a schoolboy like him, who couldn't wait to start boasting. Why are women so weak when it comes to sex? She has to be all professional in the prison, but her personal life is a mess, just like Emma's was.

I'm putting the pieces together and forming a picture. So, she needs a man. And I know that Amelia had an accident. Cate having a child could be helpful. She'll understand how it would feel, to lose a baby. Two babies.

She seems so pulled in, so tight, that I can't imagine her blooming with pregnancy or nursing a baby. I didn't imagine there could be any softness there.

After Joel was born I was all soft flesh, all rounded and plump like some mediaeval wet nurse. But that soon changed. When he died, the fat melted off me, like my bones were hot irons. I never regained the weight, and even now my hips jut into the thin mattress in the night, my belly sunk in resignation. But it's my breasts that suffered the most. Once plump with milk, they hang limp and empty.

33

Black Book Entry

"We think his heart just gave way. I'm so sorry."

It was just one hour after Joel's death and Dr Cross was talking. The door to my room was closed, the blind down. Luke had been taken from me and returned to his mother. You'd been called straightaway, and had arrived from work flustered and scared. You were at my side, your sweaty hand gripped vice-like to mine. You couldn't make sense of it, refused to believe it. "But he was getting better," you kept saying. "He was out of danger."

Dr Cross paused to let what she was saying sink in. "We thought so, yes. It was looking positive. Before we get the post-mortem report it's difficult to say, but it's likely he had a congenital defect. A weak heart."

You were shaking your head in disbelief. "But he was in intensive care. He was being looked after. How could you have missed something like that?"

"We couldn't have detected it without invasive tests, and Joel was too weak for that. It's likely that his heart just gave way. The staff did all they could to resuscitate him. Of course, we will know more after the autopsy."

"No," you said, your voice breaking up. "For God's sake

his little body has been through enough."

But the doctor was adamant, her calm voice unequivocal. "It will mean we can establish the exact cause of death."

"What difference does it make?" You slumped onto the bed, anger giving way to grief, and began to sob. "We've still lost our son." You buried into me, your grief wracking my body and I wanted to push you away. This is your fault, I thought. As you leaned against me, sobbing, I couldn't feel anything for you but anger. Your unruly hair scratched my face; your tears dampened my neck. But my eyes were dry.

They left us like that for a long time, as you tried to make sense of our son's death.

"I'll never forgive myself," you said. I would never forgive you either.

There was a light tapping on the door and the door slowly opened. It was Nurse Hall. She came to us, putting her arm around us both.

"I'm so very, very sorry."

I could hear in her voice that she'd been crying, and in my surprise I looked at her face. Her eyes were red. She sat on the bed next to me, her hand on mine, your head on my shoulder. We sat like that, the three of us, listening to our own thoughts, none of us knowing what to say. Suddenly there was a buzz and Nurse Hall pulled apart from us to check her pager. She read it, switched it off. "They're ready for us." We slowly stood, and Nurse Hall held the door as we trudged into the corridor. She took my elbow, supporting me, and we began the terrible journey to see Joel.

They'd put Joel in a side room, in a crib. He was wrapped in a white fleecy blanket. His face was pale and slick, like a plastic doll. You held on to the side of the crib for support, your sobs rising again as you stared at our dead son. Nurse Hall stroked your back, in tears herself. You leaned in to kiss Joel. When your lips touched that impassive cheek, I thought you would collapse. Nurse Hall steadied you, helped you to the chair, and I too kissed Joel. His skin felt warm. I placed my cheek to his, desperate to feel breath.

Please, God, let it be a mistake. Let him wake up.

But there was no God to listen. No miracle. Just a chasm of nothingness. There was no meaning to anything. I wondered if my mum was watching.

We sat with Joel's body for about an hour, and I knew it was way past Nurse Hall's time to leave work but she didn't move to go. I appreciated that.

"I want to go home," I said.

Nurse Hall nodded. "Of course. Would you like me to go and pack your bags? I could complete the discharge paperwork."

"Yes. Yes, please."

When Nurse Hall returned she had packed all my belongings into a plastic bag. She led us out of the room, and back down the corridor. We passed the neonatal unit, but I didn't look in. We passed the maternity wards.

It slowly dawned on me that we were nearing Emma's room.

To my horror, I saw the door was open.

I couldn't cope with this, I needed to slow everything down, and my feet began to drag. I needed to make you stop.

We were getting closer, and I could see Emma, and her husband. He was holding Luke, showing him a small toy. Emma was smoothing a skirt out on the bed, carefully folding it, placing it into a suitcase. Her husband leaned over to her and said something, and she kissed Luke, smiling. She was preparing to leave as well, but she was taking her baby with her.

You hadn't seen her yet, but I knew that if you did, if you saw Luke, it would all be over for me. In just a few seconds my whole world would collapse, and still each step took us closer to danger.

She was picking up her bag now; in moments she would step into the corridor, just as we reached her room.

Like a sail crashing down, I dropped to the floor.

I crouched, doubled over my heart in agony. You cradled me, lifted my hair from my face, as you soothed and stroked.

It was moments. Only moments. But when I came to my feet I saw Emma's back, saw her husband hold the door open for her, as she left. I thanked whoever had been looking down on me that she hadn't looked back. I thanked Mum and Rita that you hadn't seen Luke.

34

When Jason Clark opened the door on Monday morning his hair was still wet from the shower and his shirt half unbuttoned. Cate checked her watch, wondering if she was early, but it was gone ten. He stood aside to let her enter, pointing upstairs. "You know where to go." The last time she had seen him he had been crying on the floor, but his face betrayed no memory of this.

He followed her to the lounge, which was neater than the last time she'd been here. The CDs were filed away and the table clear of clutter. "Do you want a drink?"

"Coffee, please."

"Black, one sugar, right?"

"Thanks."

He disappeared into the kitchen and she heard him moving around, the click of a boiled kettle. As she waited she took her notebook and pen from her bag and placed them on the table.

He appeared in the room, holding two steaming mugs. "Don't spill it this time."

"I won't. Sorry about that." Cate looked down at the carpet, where a dark stain showed. "You were pretty upset when I left."

"Yeah, well."

"You said I shouldn't try to open a can of worms. What did you mean?"

"Just what I said. Sometimes it's best to let sleeping dogs lie."

"I'm afraid that isn't possible. The parole board are meeting next week and I need to ask questions to write the report."

"And Rose needs a good report from you to get released."

"Yes." Cate blew the heat from her drink.

"Will it be good?" He fixed her with a hard stare.

"It wouldn't be appropriate for me to tell you that, even if I had made a decision yet." Cate used her coffee cup like smokers use cigarettes, sipping between sentences and using her mug as a barrier.

"See, that really pisses me off. You come into my home, ask all these questions, but you won't tell me anything. For God's sake, she's been locked up for four years. Isn't that enough?"

His voice was raised and his shoulders tense. Cate put her mug on the table.

"Rose was found guilty of manslaughter. I need to assess if she has sufficient insight into her offence to accept full responsibility, to be as sure as I can be that she'll never offend again."

"It was an accident," Jason's eyes welled and she remembered how last time he had swung from upset to anger. "She's suffered enough."

"I have to be certain that there is no risk of future offending."

"Of course there isn't any bloody risk!"

"Well, I need to be certain. That's why I have to ask these questions. I need to get a handle on what led her to stalk Emma. You said that losing Joel was the tragedy that triggered her obsession, but I also need to consider if Emma was just a trigger, if the seeds were sown in her childhood."

"Christ, you're even digging into that? Her mum committing suicide when she was a girl. Is that what you mean?"

"Yes, it is. Insight into her behaviour is crucial. If Rose understands why she did it, she can recognise the signs if they happen again. And seek help."

"You people!" He leaned towards her, his face so close she could smell his breath. He'd been drinking. "Why do you do it? I mean, what's in it for you? Power, is that it? I hate the prison. Can't stand visiting. But you…you've chosen it."

Cate leaned away. "I didn't exactly choose it. I think it's just something I have to do. And anyway, aren't you making a choice too?"

"What's that supposed to mean?"

"It means you're still with Rose. A lot of relationships don't survive prison."

His breathing was ragged and he looked at Cate with bitterness. "I've just been pulled along by events. When Rose was arrested it was a shock. I just got bogged down keeping journalists away and speaking with solicitors, keeping it together at work, that sort of thing. It never felt like a choice. Just like you, I think it's what I have to do."

"That would be hard for anyone."

He toyed with her pen lying on the table in front of them. "I didn't have time to think, which made it easier. The trial was the worst part. Speaking in the witness box knocked me for six. I don't know how Rose was so calm. I kept breaking out in a sweat. And when I saw Emma…poor Emma." His eyes welled with tears and he looked away.

Cate thought about Emma, her terrible loss. "It would have been worse for her than anyone."

He stood up, moved to the window so all she saw was the outline of his back, the rays of sun making it hard for her to look at him.

"I hadn't seen her in a while, and I was shocked. The last time I saw her was just before…before it happened. She had always been so beautiful. So – I don't know – vibrant. But in the courtroom she didn't seem to know who I was. She couldn't make it to the witness box without staggering. Her husband managed well enough, though, the bastard. He stared at Rose the whole time he was giving his evidence." Jason turned and the sun made him a silhouette.

"He was acting like Rose was a murderer. He said as much in the witness box. Thank God the jury didn't believe him."

"Did you never doubt her?"

His voice rose. "It was an accident." He reached out to her, grabbing her wrist with his hand. "I need to show you something."

Pulling her arm free, she stood up. "I think I'd better be going, you seem agitated..."

"If you want to know what's going on in Rose's head you need to see this!" Jason grabbed her wrist, led her down the hall, past the kitchen and bathroom, to the closed door at the end of the hall. She felt her heart hammering in her chest, and wondered where he was taking her but let herself be led to the closed door.

He slowly opened it.

The room beyond gave her a shock. It was a baby's nursery. A cherry wood cot, with all its bedding neatly folded. A rocking chair, a changing table. An unopened pack of nappies. Most heartbreaking of all was a row of baby clothes on tiny pastel hangers. The clothes still had their tags attached. In the corner was a pram with the distinctive beige and cream check of Burberry.

They both stood in silence, taking in the perfection of the room.

"I'll never forgive myself," he murmured, as if to himself.

"What do you mean?"

He snapped his head to her, as if remembering she was there. "She wouldn't let me redecorate. I wanted to get rid of all the baby stuff, but she wouldn't hear of it. Rose used to spend hours in here, just staring into space. She would sit in that chair, holding a toy, or looking at the clothes. I thought it comforted her. Now I think it made her worse. I shouldn't have let her dwell on it."

Cate searched for a response, knowing that whatever she said would be inadequate.

"Look at this room, how she's kept it so perfect. She wouldn't even let me get rid of the pram. How could a woman with this much love in her harm a baby?" Jason turned to Cate. "Rose loved Luke as much as she loved Joel." He looked her in the eye. "She would never harm him."

35

Black Book Entry

After Joel died we tried to pick up the pieces, but nothing made sense anymore. When the phone rang I ignored it, because the only words I wanted to hear could never be said. I didn't open any post, as the only news I wanted to hear was impossible – that Joel was alive. Each morning my first thought was that he was gone.

You were still doing occasional shifts at Auberge, but business was so quiet you'd taken on a part-time job in a record shop. You liked it, being surrounded by loud music that deafened your thoughts, and you would go to work each morning, leaving me in bed, and come home to find me still there. I didn't care. I had nothing to say to you. You had no idea how to cope with the stranger I'd become, so you left me for the world you understood, where music and chitchat were the order of the day.

I got into the habit of sitting in the nursery where Joel would have slept. The cot was made up with fitted blue sheets and baby blankets. I'd bought tiny blue and white Babygros, which still smelled of new cotton, not of warm skin and baby lotion like they should have. I couldn't throw any of it away. I took the blackbird nest from the back of my knicker drawer and carried it to the nursery, gently placing it in the cot, nestled against the jointed teddy bear.

I sat in that sterile room hour after hour until I heard your key in the door. I always pretended to be asleep but you came up and sat next to me, stroking my face. I knew you were trying, but I wouldn't let you reach me. It felt like a betrayal of Joel, to let anything in my heart but grief. What I remember most is the loneliness, as I sat through the long days nursing a blanket stolen from Joel's hospital cot. It still smelled of him, though less each day. I would never wash it.

I hadn't been out of the flat since the funeral. You gently commented on the mess and the lack of food in the fridge; we were living on takeaways and whatever could be foraged from the cupboards. But I couldn't eat. I couldn't do anything.

Three weeks after we buried Joel, I forced myself to get up, steeled myself to sit at the breakfast table despite the tiredness in my arms and legs. You were pleased to see me, and gripped my hand. Then you looked at my baggy pyjamas. I was still wearing maternity clothes, which now swamped me. It was all I could do to butter a piece of toast, which I had no desire to eat.

"Maybe, Rose," you said softly, "it would be an idea if you saw a doctor."

I occupied myself in scraping the butter on the toast. "I saw plenty at the hospital."

A beat of a pause. "Not that kind of doctor, pet. A psychiatrist. I think we need help."

But you didn't mean "we". You meant me. How could you think that I could ever see a psychiatrist? I wasn't afraid of the drugs – I'd had those in hospital and welcomed their temporary numbing effect. But an ordinary doctor could give me those. To see a shrink meant I would have to talk. And not just about Joel, but about other things, too. Things better left hidden. Things I had kept buried so deep all these years that I'd be damned before I'd let someone dig them out of me. I would have to talk about my childhood, about Mum. About Peter and Mrs Carron. About Auntie Rita.

I'd have to talk about the blackbirds.

Talking wouldn't do any good anyway. Joel was gone, and nothing could change that. Even in my dreams I was alone and empty. I never had my boy even when I was asleep.

You were worried, though, and I knew I had to show you I was getting better, on my own. So, after you kissed me goodbye and I heard the front door shut, I went to the cupboard with all the cleaning things. I hadn't opened it since the week before Joel was born when I'd polished and dusted the whole flat. The memory of this winded me.

I did just enough. Enough for the smell of bleach and beeswax to fool you into thinking the flat was clean. I should have stripped the bed, changed the sheets, but I couldn't face doing it. One step at a time. There should be a word for it. If I'd lost a husband, I would be a widow. But what is a woman who loses a baby? There is no word.

The only room in the house that was pristine was the nursery. I sat on the nursing chair and gazed at the cot, cuddling the "suitable from birth" teddy bear I'd bought in the posh shop, and cried. It was the most painful place to be, but the only place I wanted to be. I could remember putting up the too-long curtains, choosing the cherry wood cot. I gazed at the Burberry pram, and touched the handle, rocking it slightly.

After my caesarean the surgeon patched me up as best he could, but he couldn't save my womb. I'd lost a baby and any chance of having another.

And so I sat until the clock approached six when I knew you'd be home. I got dressed. I should have showered first, but didn't want to see myself naked. The scar on my abdomen reminded me that my body had betrayed my son. I pulled a jumper over the pyjama top and replaced the bottoms with maternity leggings. Too loose around my thin waist. Still, it was a step forward.

When you arrived home with the usual brown paper bag of Chinese takeaway you were delighted with me and kissed me on the mouth, taking me in your arms. "You look better."

"I went to the doctor," I said, pulling away. "She gave me some pills." It was a white lie, to make you happy. I sat with you while you ate, pushing the rice and chicken around my plate. You didn't mention me seeing a psychiatrist again.

The next morning I knew how a marathon runner must feel the day after a race. I was exhausted, but you didn't see that.

You were still pleased, still sure that my recovery had begun. I couldn't disillusion you, so when you put my dressing-gown on the bed I'd no choice but to put it on and follow downstairs.

"Why don't you go out today? You could go for a walk. Get some fresh air. Why not treat yourself to some new clothes?" You eyed my baggy nightwear.

Don't push me too fast, I thought. My stomach was a knotted rope at the prospect of going out and facing people whose lives carried on. But I had to force myself to do it if I was to keep you happy.

To keep you.

I drove to a large supermarket in Ipswich, where I'd never been before, so I wouldn't see anyone I'd recognise. But I did see someone. Or rather, she saw me. I was concentrating on buying food, dropping apples into a bag, reaching for vegetables. I'd already put some clothes in the trolley, picked on the basis of simplicity: indigo jeans, black leggings, a selection of T-shirts. Just as I was about to move into the next aisle I turned and saw her.

Emma.

I hardly recognised her, she looked so different. Tired and scruffy, her hair scraped back in a rough knot. And in the trolley, snug in his portable car seat, was Luke.

"Rose!"

Oh, Jason, you can't imagine how it felt to see Luke again. He was your son and my first thought was to grab him and run home. It was just too much, seeing him, dressed in a blue babysuit and hat, fast asleep. I felt dizzy, was hardly aware of what was going on.

Then I collapsed.

I only fainted for a few seconds, but when I came to Emma was cradling my head on her knee, fending off bystanders. I opened my eyes. She was still there. She helped me to my feet, steadying me with one arm.

"Rose, I think we should find somewhere for you to sit."

After helping me through checkout she said, "How do you feel?"

"Woozy. I don't think I can drive."

"We'll go back to my house. You can have a rest and I'll make you something to eat. I'll drive you back to get your car later."

As she drove I stared out of the window, trying to resist the urge to turn and peek a look at Luke. Her home wasn't far from the shop. It was a big house in the centre of a strip of Middle England. If I were to describe it in one word, it would be "safe". But of course you know that, Jason. You'd already been there, hadn't you?

I watched as she unfastened the baby car seat, adjusted his hat so it covered all his head. Luke was now awake and starting to mewl. Emma talked to him wearily, struggling with the straps and buckles on the seat.

Inside the front door the warmth enveloped me like the stifling heat of the hospital ward. Luke needed changing and she carried him hurriedly up the stairs. I wanted to follow, to see the bedroom where you had fucked her, but I didn't trust my emotions. I waited in the hall.

"Rose, go and sit in the back lounge," Emma called down.

The room was pleasant, a comfortable size, with pictures and tasteful pieces of china. By a glass door leading to a raised deck outside was a blue bouncy chair with red kites pictured on the fabric. I'd bought a similar one, which was still wrapped in its cellophane. This one was already stained with milk, sick, probably wee. It looked like it could do with a good wash.

When Emma returned, she was holding Luke. "What would you like to drink?"

"I'd love a cup of tea."

I could see her wondering if she should hand Luke to me. Was she asking herself if a grieving mother could cope with holding a baby? Instead, she fixed him into the chair and disappeared into the kitchen. He grizzled at being put down, hands clenching the air until a massive yawn overtook him and his eyelids dropped slowly. He was so much bigger than when I last saw him.

Once Emma had placed the cups on the table she sat on the sofa next to me. I braced myself for questions about how I was feeling, how I was coping, but she didn't ask them. Instead, she bowed her head to my shoulder and started to cry.

"I'm so sorry, Rose. So sorry about Joel."

My eyes stung, and I swept her hair out of my face.

Eventually she pulled away. "Before I left the hospital I went to your room to say goodbye. It was empty, but that nurse saw me standing there, the nice one, Nurse Hall. She was packing your bag and told me what had happened. Nurse Hall knew we'd become friends and, though she said she shouldn't, she gave me your telephone number. She thought I could help you. And I took your number, Rose." The tears came again.

Luke started to cry and Emma looked at him, exhausted and weepy. "Oh, shut up, please!" she begged. She heaved herself to her feet and picked him up from the chair, jiggling him awkwardly, not even looking. I ached to show her how to hold and soothe him. She stuffed a dummy in his mouth and flopped back down beside me.

"But I just couldn't do it. I was too scared to call you, scared that I wouldn't know what to say, Rose, or that you would hate me, with Luke being the same age as Joel. I didn't think I'd ever see you again, but I've thought of you every day."

We didn't say much more, just sat drinking tea, watching Luke fall asleep.

"Can I hold him?" I asked, longing to feel the weight of a baby again.

I saw her hesitate, then smile quickly. "Of course."

I remember it so clearly. His warm body felt surprisingly heavy. As I held him in my arms he stared at me like he knew everything. His head lolled to one side and Luke's eyes regarded me intently, with the wisdom of an old man. I would never have another child, would never have a baby like him. I pulled his hat from his head, and saw those red-gold curls. If I closed my eyes, I could have been holding Joel.

I didn't close my eyes.

36

The officer's canteen was getting busy; a line of uniformed staff and some teachers pushed wooden trays along a silver counter, taking plates of food from the inmates serving up the dish of the day. As Cate took her plate of meatballs and gravy she spied Rose working in the kitchen. Perhaps sensing her looking, Rose looked up. For a moment both women stared, then Cate nodded a greeting and moved towards the till where Paul was paying for his meal.

They sat at a table in the corner, next to a group of officers from D Wing who were just finishing. A few of them nudged each other and laughed. Paul waited until they had left. "Well, sweetheart, you've certainly got yourself noticed."

"Hey?" Cate speared a meatball and looked up at Paul.

"Word on the landings is that you and Mark Burgess are the new Posh and Becks of Bishop's Hill."

"Give me a break," Cate groaned, swallowing the meatball whole. It was warm and solid and she realised how hungry she was, having skipped breakfast.

Paul lifted his own spoon and tapped her wrist. "Tell me then! I saw you leave my party with Mark in tow, and you were both pretty drunk."

"Don't remind me."

"So?" He leaned forward eagerly. Cate sighed, wiped her mouth with a napkin and pushed her plate away.

"So. I couldn't drive home in that state so I went back to

his. He lives with his mum, by the way. When I got there I started to throw up, but that didn't stop him thinking he'd struck lucky. It ended up with him on the floor covered in puke."

"Yuck!" Paul raised his hands in horror.

Cate sipped her drink. "I'm an idiot. I'm not ready to be let lose on men again. I should join a nunnery."

"Frankly, sweetheart, I'm not sure they'd have you. Not after you vomited on that poor boy."

"Paul!"

"Sorry, love." He chewed thoughtfully. "Seriously, though. It doesn't matter. Prison gossip will soon move on to something juicier."

"I know. It's not just that."

"What then?" He reached forward and rubbed her hand. "You're doing okay, you know."

"Am I? God, Paul, I want to get things right but this morning I visited Jason Clark and it ended badly. Rose Wilks has got under my skin."

"I warned you…"

"I know. And I know you're trying to help but she was a mother and her child died. She can't ever have another." Cate looked around, to make sure no-one was listening. She could see Rose from where she was sitting. "She swears she never did anything to cause Luke's death and when she says it I believe her."

"But she was convicted and the jury is always right. You know that, babe."

"Even when it's wrong?"

"Even then."

37

We all feel vulnerable when naked. As if cotton and polyester can protect us like armour. Maybe it's because we're born that way, totally dependant. Whatever the reason, shower rooms in prison are feared by all the inmates. No-one spends longer than necessary, standing with other bare women, eyes averted, quickly washing their hair. It's like showers after PE at school. I remember dipping my arms and legs under the spray, hoping to fool the teacher that I was clean of pubescent sweat. But that trick wouldn't work in here, where the smell lingers in your pores. I fantasise about deep baths in warm bubbled water, and no-one watching.

I've been cooking in the officers' canteen and I'm back late on the landing. Everyone else is banged up. Officer Burgess is watching the wing. It's not shift-change time yet, and whoever else is on duty with him will be taking the food trolley back to the kitchens. He has his feet up on the desk, and is reading some men and motors mag, safe in the knowledge that the cons are locked away.

"Officer?"

He jumps, not expecting me. He swings round, feet on the floor, and tries to hide the magazine behind a stack of files. "Bang-up time, Wilks. Off you go."

"Could I have a shower, please? I had to work because the Governor's got guests from the Home Office, but I stink of garlic and onions. I haven't showered in two days."

I see him weighing up the hassle of having to fetch a female officer to supervise me, against the accusation of his ignoring my human rights. It's marked on our files when we inmates have showers, and he wouldn't want an inspector to see he'd refused a request.

"Make it snappy then." He goes to unlock the shower room as I fetch my shower gel and thin towel.

I can hear him outside the shower room door, clearing his throat. I quickly clean myself without thinking, a routine procedure, each part of my flesh soaped in the usual order, slowing slightly as I rub a hand over my caesarean scar. It's white now, and surprisingly smooth. The only sign that I'm a mother. I can't say this in the past tense; I will always be a mother.

I switch off the shower and grab my towel, too small and threadbare to dry myself properly. When I'm released from this place I've promised myself a bath sheet in thick Egyptian cotton like we used to have at The Grand. I rub my arms and legs, and then I notice that I can't hear Burgess shuffling and clinking his keys. The corridor is silent. I'm immediately wary and start to gather my clothes. Without a guard, I'm vulnerable and when I hear footsteps coming down the hall I freeze.

It's not Burgess's heavy shoes. It's a woman. I think of all the inmates who would risk a go at me – a child killer – for the kudos it would bring them. Like that woman at Highpoint. I grab my knickers, bending low to put them on. The steps come close, splashing on wet tiles. I see shiny boots. Navy trousers. A prison uniform.

"You still look dirty to me."

I right myself, and come face to face with Officer Deborah Holley. I know what she did to Susan Thomas in the shower room, how Susan looked afterwards.

"Switch the water back on." Her voice echoes off the hard tiles.

"I've already showered, miss."

I don't move. She could attack me and no-one would hear. She takes a step forward, threatening. I back away, the chrome tap against my spine.

"I said, switch the fucking water on."

It's slow, so slow how she speaks. Everything is half-speed. I daren't turn my back to her so I reach blindly for the tap and turn it once. The icy shot of water falls on my head, and Officer Holley steps back, her eyes mocking me.

"Haven't you forgotten something, Wilks?"

And with her hand she reaches forward, into the water, and grabs my knickers.

"Take them off."

I don't know if she means to humiliate me, or worse, but I've no option. Standing as upright as I'm able, I untangle my legs from my only layer of protection. I hold my knickers in my hand, standing naked in front of Officer Holley, who looks me up and down with such disdain.

She comes closer, watching the water on my face, the hair sodden on my cheeks.

"You are a filthy nonce, Wilks."

That word again. I can't have her saying that.

"I'm finished with my shower." I stand tall, and make to walk out of the room. She knocks me back with the heel of her palm.

"Are you disobeying me, nonce?"

I look at her, water dripping down my face, pooling around my bare feet. "Don't call me nonce." I'm surprised at the strength and assurance in my voice.

Her eyes narrow and a smile plays on her thin lips. "But that's what you are, Wilks. A nonce. And I'll call you whatever I like. What are you going to do about it?"

And reaching behind me to the tap, she swings it the other way, full-force, turning her back on me as the hot water scalds my skin. When she punches me my head collides with the tile wall. The pain is no more than I deserve.

38

Black Book Entry

I got into the habit of calling at Emma's home almost every day.

One time I visited her, Emma took a long time to open the door and once she had it unlatched, she started back up the stairs, calling over her shoulder, "Come up. I'm just doing some sorting out."

I followed her upstairs, then along the hall to her bedroom at the front of the house, where a black iron bed dominated a burgundy room, and a massive mahogany chest of drawers blocked half the window.

"Ghastly, isn't it? Dominic just loves antiques but they're damn heavy. And they make the room so dark."

On the bed was a mound of baby clothes. They were tiny – almost doll-size – and I reached for one, holding it up, reading the label. It said "newborn".

"He's been getting mad at me," she explained. "I'm useless at throwing stuff away. And every time he goes to dress Luke he pulls out something that's too small. So I'm putting away all the stuff he's outgrown. I can't believe how big he is. This used to swamp him."

I took the blue snowsuit from her, touching the teddy-like ears on the hood. It looked brand new.

"He wore this when we left hospital."

She was wistful until she saw my face, then flushed. I was still holding the newborn bodysuit, and I folded it, placed it in the bag where she had neatly stacked the items.

"Let me help you."

We folded the trousers and tops, tiny hats and scratch mitts into plastic bags.

"Are you keeping them for the next one, Emma?" I hardly . know how I managed to ask the question.

She had the grace to be bashful. "Well, most of it's blue, so it wouldn't be any good for a girl. But it would be a shame to get rid of it. Especially if I had another boy."

So, even though her cup of good fortune overflowed, she still wasn't satisfied. I was a sore wound, raw to her insensitivity.

"Are you pregnant?" I almost choked on the question. I thought she wouldn't answer me, that she would realise what it meant to someone who couldn't have any children. But I was wrong; she was only concerned with her own feelings.

"Not yet." She looked up, a shy smile, and confided in me. "But I am trying. Dominic thinks it'll be too much for me but I'm sure two can't be much harder than one. Besides, it'd be nice for the children to be close."

She sat on the bed, gazing out of the window. "To be honest, we haven't used any contraception since Luke was born, and nothing's happened."

There it was. She was trying for another baby, when Luke was just a few months old. I wondered what would become of me if she wanted the same man to father it.

We heard Luke cry out, ready for a feed. Emma looked at the final pile of clothes with a sigh. "I'll just go get him."

Luke's nursery was next door to Emma's room, and in seconds she was back with him in her arms. He was flushed from recent sleep, rubbing a fist against an eye, but he raised a smile for me.

"Oh no, Luke, you've got a really smelly bottom. You need a new nappy."

"Do you want me to do it, Emma? I don't mind."

She hesitated, and I knew she wanted to say yes but didn't have the cheek. "It's okay, Rose. I'll do it."

"If you're sure," I told her. "I'll finish folding this pile of washing."

"Thanks." She was pleased with me, with my kindness, and I heard her chatter to Luke in the bathroom, heard his gurgling reply.

Alone in the bedroom I saw it properly for the first time. The room where you had betrayed me, the bed where you fucked her.

It was a masculine room, dark red walls and heavy damask curtains. The second drawer in the mahogany chest was slightly open and I went towards it. I could hear Emma saying, "Oh Luke, it's gone everywhere. Hold still, will you?"

I slid my hand into the drawer. My fingers touched cotton and the firm arch of an underwired bra. Her underwear. The drawer was wide enough for my hand, my wrist, but not my forearm and I pulled at the drawer, heaving it wider, lifting it so it was silent, a trick I learned at The Grand. Inside was an assortment of cotton knickers in a rainbow of colours, and a couple of white bras. There was a box, the type used for expensive lingerie, and I lifted the lid. Sure enough, inside was something silky. I pulled at it, and saw a scarlet red camisole. Underneath were some matching French knickers. Touching them, I could feel the slip of silk, the rough lace, and then something underneath: something she had hidden.

It was a long glossy envelope, the kind you get photographs from the chemist in. I slid it out and opened the flap, thinking they would be photos of Luke. But they weren't.

The photos, Jason, were of you.

In the first photo you were young and nervous, wearing a

dark morning suit. And by your side, her willowy dancer's body lightly covered in white silk, was Emma. You made a beautiful couple. Emma was holding a simple posy of pink carnations, and you had one in your lapel, probably taken from her bunch. Your hand was around her tiny waist, your heads close together. You gazed at her with puppy-dog devotion and she looked beautiful. Younger, fresher, full of hope for the future. I wondered what her husband would say if he knew she still kept the photos of her first wedding day.

I heard Emma's steps on the landing, coming back to the room, and just a few feet away. I fumbled with the photos and dropped the envelope. One photo slipped out and disappeared under the chest. I frantically picked the rest up, tossing them back into the lingerie box. I didn't have time to close the drawer before darting to the window just as she walked in, Luke in her arms. She stopped when she saw me.

"Rose?"

She had found me out.

I started to cry; it was so hard, seeing those pictures of your wedding day, seeing you together. And her knowing that I had been snooping – how could we be friends now? I would have to admit that my lover was her ex-husband. And, worse of all, she would stop me from coming to see Luke. I couldn't bear that. My tears came freely.

She rushed over to me. "Oh God, Rose, how could I have been so stupid. It was callous of me, asking you to put away baby clothes. I didn't mean to hurt you. I wouldn't do that for the world." And then she put her arm around me, Luke snuggled in the other. We stood, a close trio, and I knew that it was okay. That I had been lucky. I had got away with it.

Later, when we were all downstairs, I pretended that I needed to use the loo. I went back to the bedroom and took the red camisole, slipping it into my pocket. I also took the photo from under the chest.

You and she were kissing under a snow of confetti.

39

Black Book Entry

"Oh, Rose. Thank God." When Emma opened the door with Luke in her arms she looked petrified. Her relief at seeing me gave way to tears.

"What's wrong with him?"

"He had his jabs an hour ago. Oh God, what if he's having a reaction? What about that doctor who said it caused autism? What if he was right?"

Emma became panicky, but that was nothing new. She often overreacted, saying she'd been pacing for hours in the night, trying to calm him with a dummy, which he would suck twice and spit out. She was often unable to deal with him, and would get hysterical, making him cry more. But this time he really was unwell. His cry was sharper, spiky with pain.

"Rose, he's got a temperature. Feel his head, he's burning."

I put my hand to Luke's cheek. It was fiery red. His head was clammy, hair slick with sweat. She was holding him tightly, afraid to let go.

I tried to calm her. "He's hot, Emma, but I don't think it's too much to worry about. I read somewhere that it's quite common after injections. He'll be fine. Why don't you give him some Calpol? Something to take his temperature down."

"I've run out!" She still looked desperate. "I'll go to the chemist now. I'll take him in the car."

I put my arm around her shoulders. "Leave him here, Emma. It'll be quicker that way. Give him to me."

She hesitated. She'd never left him before, not even for half an hour. Thinking that she might resist if I gave her the opportunity, I took him from her, holding him gently and rocking slightly to soothe him. In my more relaxed grip his crying abated, and Emma's panic to get to the chemist overrode her reluctance to leave him.

I was relieved when I heard her car speed away from the house. We were alone at last. All those weeks of coveting him, stealing kisses when she left the room, and now I had him to myself for at least twenty minutes. Can you imagine how wonderful that felt? And then the reason his crying had eased was clear; he was rooting. He had found out my secret, could smell my milk, and was snuffling into my shirt, making a wet circle of moisture where his mouth nuzzled. It was his need rather than mine that made me unbutton my shirt.

Although I had never suckled a baby, my breasts were heavy with milk. When Joel was born he was too sick to feed from anything other than a plastic tube and, on good days, a bottle of expressed milk.

After he died, when I was back at home, I still expressed my milk. I'd been given tablets to dry up my supply, but taking them would have been the final proof that I was no longer a mother. So I carried on siphoning off the bluish white milk, and tipping it down the drain. It became something I did without thinking, a secret part of my life. I hid Daisy Mark 2 in the nursery. I always slept in a bra, in case I leaked. Since leaving the hospital you'd tried to comfort me at night, but when I stopped you removing my top you didn't pressure me.

It was as though a wall had been built between us, down the middle of the bed, and I didn't have the energy or inclination to climb over it. When you reached for me I tried to respond, but I just couldn't do it. That was difficult for you, I know.

Breastfeeding wasn't as easy as I had thought it would be. I wasn't sure how to position him and he was still upset. He took some time to find my nipple, which was frustrating for us both. After a lot of fumbling, I felt the grip of his mouth and knew we were joined. The tug in my breast as he sucked the milk was uncomfortable at first, but delicious. I felt, finally, that I had a purpose. That my redundant body was able to comfort a child, even if it couldn't comfort a man. That I could heal Luke, as I'd never been able to heal Joel.

He fed for long, precious minutes and I stroked his golden hair, watching his half-closed eyes watching me. I will always remember the sight of his little fist resting on my exposed breast. It was so natural, so right. I didn't want it to end, but eventually his mouth slackened, eyes closed and he slept. He had never looked more like you, Jason, and I had never felt such love.

Emma found us like that, me in the armchair, Luke sound asleep in my arms. She was brandishing a bottle of Calpol, but his fever had already passed. She was relieved he was peaceful. Rousing him, she spooned the pink sticky syrup into Luke's mouth, but the real medicine had been my milk.

40

It took Cate a few moments to realise she was being talked about. She had just taken a seat in the canteen, her internal navigation directing her to the far corner, away from where a huddle of officers were guffawing and joking, when she noticed the hush.

Biting into the sandwich Rose had just prepared she looked up to see several pairs of eyes assessing her. Dave Callahan and Deborah Holley and a red-faced Mark Burgess. *Oh shit. He's told them about the party.* Cate glanced to the serving hatch, and saw Rose was also aware that something was going on. Mark looked away first but Callahan swaggered up from his chair, collecting a rolled-up newspaper from the table. *Oh no, he's coming this way.*

Cate swallowed her food. "Hello Dave."

"Hello yourself, sweetheart. How're you settling in?"

"Fine, thanks."

"Seems like you've settled in real *easy*." From the officer's table Holley sniggered.

Callahan tapped Cate on the arm with his newspaper. "Just remember to find a more mature fella next time, when you've had your fill of that kid." Laughing at his own humour Callahan left.

Officer Holley checked her watch, dabbed her lips and collected her tray. Walking out of the canteen she shot Cate a contemptuous glance. Mark was quickly stacking his empty wrappers on his tray, still red in the face, when Cate marched over to his table.

"What have you told Callahan?"

Mark's fingers slipped on his can of drink, sloshing it onto the tray. "Nothing."

"Didn't sound like nothing. Have you told them we slept together?"

He didn't answer. She was aware of Rose listening and lowered her voice.

"Mark, I know I shouldn't have come back to your house and I'm sorry I got sick. But telling people we slept together isn't fair. I'm new here and I don't want that rumour going round. You'll have to tell them the truth."

Mark looked directly into Cate's face. She was shocked by the anger she saw in his eyes.

"Tell you what isn't fair. It's you leading me on."

"I didn't mean to do that. I was drunk."

"Yeah, well, so was I. Or I'd never have looked twice at you."

He stood, knocking his chair back on the floor, and left the canteen in a hot hurry, leaving Cate alone at the table.

Rose came from behind the serving counter. Without saying a word she cleared up Mark's spilt drink and tray. She then fetched Cate's half-eaten sandwich from the other table and brought it to her.

"Eat that, miss. I'll get you a cup of tea to go with it." She brought the drink to Cate, spooning in two sugars.

Cate picked up her drink but couldn't swallow anything, her throat was so tight. Rose's kindness made her want to cry.

Cate barged into her tiny office to discover Janie trying to get a smear of peanut butter off the computer mouse. Hearing the door open, she jumped out of her skin. "Oh miss, you frightened me!"

"Hello, Janie. How did you get in here?"

"One of the officers let me in, miss. They do that if I need to clean a room and the person's not there. I didn't take nothing."

"I know that, Janie. It's okay. I just wasn't expecting anyone to be here."

She wiped the cloth over the mouse for a final time. "There. As good as new."

"Thank you. You've done a great job."

Expecting her to leave, Cate was surprised when Janie hesitated, twisting the cloth in her hand. "Miss? Can I ask you something? About Rose?"

"What about Rose?"

At her sharp tone Janie shrank back. "I know I shouldn't be saying nothing, it's just I don't know what I'll do if she leaves here. Rose looks out for me. I don't think I'd cope without her."

Cate saw Janie become the kid in the corner of the playground, the one with no friends who attracts bullies. She felt sorry for her. "Are you worried about Rose getting parole? You know I can't tell you anything confidential. Are you saying you don't want her to be released?"

"Oh no, miss. That wouldn't be fair. It's just…going to be hard without her." Janie forced a smile. "But Rose is my best friend. I want her to be happy. I want her to get her parole. She deserves it. It's just…"

"What?"

"No. Nothing."

"You'll be released soon yourself. Isn't that right?"

"Yes."

"What are your plans?"

"I'd like to live in Ipswich, miss. To be near Rose. And also carry on with my studies."

"Ah, yes, at the local college. How's that going?"

Janie's face warmed under her attention. "Really well. My teacher is a lovely lady."

"Well, that's great. I really hope it works out for you."

Ruth Dugdall

When Janie had gone and Cate was alone in her office, she tried to push all thoughts of Burgess from her mind as she opened Rose Wilks's case file. She was visiting Emma and Dominic Hatcher later, but first she would read their statements.

Statement of Emma Hatcher
Age – Over 18

On the night of the fire I had gone to bed at the usual time, checking that Luke was asleep. My husband had gone out. He's the deputy head at the local boarding school and does one sleeping duty week. I had deadlocked the front door. We'd had an argument earlier, and I was a bit upset so I took a sleeping tablet, and then went to bed. I awoke at 3 a.m. to the smell of smoke. Then I saw smoke coming from under the door of my bedroom. I always leave the door open, in case Luke wakes up, so I was shocked to find it closed.

I ran to open the door but the handle was so hot it burned my hand, so it took me several goes. When I opened it there was smoke everywhere in the hallway. I started coughing, trying to see my way to Luke's room. I just panicked and tried to get to him, but it was like a wall of fire in the hallway. I just couldn't get through, and the flames were forcing me back. I was coughing, and could hardly see for the smoke and I got badly burned but I'd have died before I gave up. I somehow got in and ran to the cot, lifting Luke up. The smoke was so thick, and I went to the window in his room, struggling but eventually opening it.

Someone had already called the fire brigade and a ladder was put up to the window. Very soon a fire officer appeared there. He took Luke first, and then came back for me. When I was on the ground I saw that they had placed Luke on some makeshift mattress on the floor, and that they were giving him mouth-to-mouth resuscitation, pressing his chest. I screamed. I couldn't stop.

An ambulance arrived, and they sat me in it, putting a

213

blanket over me and trying to calm me down, but I just couldn't stop shaking. They explained that Luke was already dead when I handed him to the fire officer. The smoke had killed my son, probably before I even woke up.

Statement of Dominic Hatcher
Age – Over 18

During the day, my wife, Emma, and I had been out. We left our son Luke with Rose Wilks. She has babysat for him several times before.

Our trip out was not a success, and we came home following an argument. I don't want to go into detail about what the argument was about, but I accused my wife of having an affair.

Because of the argument I packed a bag and spent the night at the school. I am the deputy head, and there are rooms for the staff on night duty, so I sometimes sleep there.

At around 5.30 a.m. I was woken by a police officer, who had arrived at the school to tell me that there had been a fire at my home. I was told that my wife and son were at the hospital, and was taken there.

At the hospital I was taken to a room where Emma was being comforted by nursing and police staff. Just looking at her face, I knew that Luke was dead.

41

Black Book Entry

In our flat the emptiness smothered me, and sitting in the nursery left me desolate. When I was home I longed to be with Luke, with the comfort of his baby smells, the sight and touch of new life. I had become Emma's best friend, and she was glad of my visits, glad to share the drudge of changing nappies, the messy feeding, the rocking to sleep, the general boredom of having a baby. She would tut when he pooed and groan when he posited. She found Luke to be a burden.

The best moments came when Emma was called to the phone or went to make lunch, and Luke and I were alone. Emma was always happy to leave the room and make herself busy elsewhere. He was always so peaceful in my arms. In those moments he was my little boy.

You saw that I was getting better, didn't you? I was recovering. You saw the clean flat and that I'd neatened myself up and thought I was back to normal again. You asked breezy questions about how I'd spent my day, who I'd seen. I said I'd become good friends with a woman I'd met in hospital. Of course I never said any more than that. I never told you her name.

That evening I put on the silky red camisole. It was tight

on my bust, and across my back, but the silk was smooth and sensual, and the faint aroma of a spring orchard made me feel nice. I closed my eyes and imagined I was pretty. I imagined that you loved me.

I wanted to know more about her, the woman who had been your wife and lover. Whose son lived when mine died. I wondered what my life would be like if she hadn't left you. If you were still together, a happy family with beautiful children. I would still be alone and unloved. The idea haunted me. All I wanted was what most people take for granted: a family.

Emma had everything I didn't, and she wasted it all. She would moan and say how tired she was, and even went to the doctor for sleeping tablets. It seemed wrong to me, her taking sleeping tablets when Luke might cry out, need her in the night. Sometimes she ran out of baby milk or nappies and had to dash to the local shops for more. And she fed Luke from jars. If he were mine I'd have bought the freshest vegetables to cook and mash.

Dominic cast a shadow over our friendship.

He was the kind of man who people say has "authority". He was a lot older than Emma, but I imagine that even when he was younger he commanded respect. Not exactly tall, he stood very upright, as if to attention. His hair was white and thick, a neat conservative style, cropped short over the ears, and his eyes were like two blue pools. I bet the kids at his school were terrified of him. But despite his austere good looks, it was when he spoke that I understood why Emma left you for him. It was never a choice I would have made, but I could see his appeal, especially to a woman like Emma. Every opinion was a fact; he was so sure of everything. And weak people admire arrogance. They think it's strength.

If he were at home when I visited he'd watch me as I held Luke, even though I came round most days and Luke always smiled to see me. I could tell Dominic was suspicious from his snide comments, his sneaky glances. I worried that he thought I visited too much, and although it was agony I did manage to stay away for a few days at a time. I tried to avoid being there when he was home, but it wasn't always easy, as he would pop home at odd hours.

He looked at me carefully, as if I was a puzzle he couldn't quite figure out. A crossword with one clue missing. He didn't see that we were the same. I never liked him, but I understood his jealousy. If he caught me there, I left quickly. I had to stay away until I was certain it was safe to go back.

Then I came up with the solution.

A way to love Luke, to keep an eye on Emma, and without any interference from Dominic Hatcher.

I'd been in Emma's house enough times to know that the back door key was kept on a tiny hook on the wall at the rear of the kitchen. I knew that the key wouldn't be missed if I were quick about returning it.

It was easy enough to take, a simple task of slipping it into my jeans pocket. For the first time I was eager to leave the house. I drove back to the supermarket where Emma had found me, and had a second key cut in the little shop there. I trembled as I watched the young assistant make my copy. Key rings were for sale on the counter and I chose one. It was inscribed: Home is where the heart is.

I needed to return the original key quickly. The longer I waited the more chance there was of it being missed, so early the next morning I rang Emma.

"Rose," she said when she heard my trembling voice, "you sound awful. What's wrong?"

"I want to ask you a favour. Just say if you don't want to..." I let the sentence trail off.

"You know I'll do anything I can."

I paused, and then said in a rush, "It's three months today since Joel died."

"Oh God, Rose, I'm so sorry." She sounded sincere. I also

heard her relief that it was my grief and not hers.

"I want to visit his grave, but I don't think I can face it alone." I let a second's silence pass. "Would you come with me?"

How could she refuse such a request? She couldn't. "What time shall I meet you?"

A quarter of an hour had passed since I made the telephone call, and I sat in my car at the end of her road, watching her pull out of her driveway. I planned to arrive at the cemetery after her, when I would explain how difficult it was for me to get into my car to make the journey. I would tell her I'd stood in my flat for ages, trying to muster enough strength.

Instead I moved, quickly as a cat, on a journey that took me out of my car, along the street, then down the side passage and to her back door. My heart raced as I held my key. I remember as a child I would build nests with my mum under the duvet, our den, our mini-home to feel safe in, a place to hide. Emma's home was now my nest. The feeling was so strange and powerful. My life had been out of my control since Joel died, but now I was taking it back.

I looked around, then slid the key in the lock and carefully turned it. The click of the lock being opened was like the approval of heaven, or some such place. I moved quickly inside, replacing the original key on its hook, and rubbed my copy between my right thumb and index finger. Emma shared her home with me now. I should have left for the cemetery, where Emma would be waiting, but I couldn't resist going further.

My pilgrimage began in the kitchen, through to the hall. Rather than climbing the stairs I went to a room I didn't know well. The front room. Emma had never taken me there. I noticed the absence of toys; this room was for adults only. The back wall was flanked by a massive bookshelf, weighed down by books of all sizes and colours. Ornaments and knick-knacks, some Russian dolls and an oriental fan decorated the spaces, but my eyes were drawn to the spines of books, mostly by writers I hadn't read. I wondered if Dominic read them for pleasure; they must be his books since he was the teacher. There were a few books on dancing. She was a dance student when she met you, Jason, when you worked behind the Arts College bar. My biggest achievement, after Joel, was making you want me, after having had her.

But then I spied something that did interest me: photo albums. A whole shelf of them, neatly labelled by year. I took the one at the end and read its label: Luke's first year. It was only half full; empty pages waiting for memories.

I turned the pages greedily. There were pictures of Emma, one of her heavily pregnant, wearing a party dress and holding a fluted glass of something. It must have been taken on New Year's Eve. On to the next page, and my heart was pumping fast. Here was Luke, just born, in a hospital crib. As I flicked the pages over he got bigger and fatter and then, at around six weeks old, a smile immortalised forever, his hair curled and golden. I took this photo from the album and slipped it into my pocket, careful not to crease it.

I remembered the photos of your wedding, hidden in her underwear drawer. What else had she kept of that day? I was like a dog following a scent.

I made my way upstairs and went immediately to the spare room.

This was the room where I'd helped her to store the outgrown baby clothes. As she'd regained her figure, I'd watched her fold her maternity clothes neatly and stow them away in this room, anticipating another baby at some future point. There was a cupboard over the narrow wardrobe, and I had to move a chair towards it to reach up. I was quick, knowing Emma would be at the cemetery, tussling Luke from the car seat into the buggy as she prepared to meet me.

The cupboard clicked open and I saw Christmas wrapping

paper, tinsel and a leather overnight bag. Further back was a long white box and I knew that I had found what I was looking for. I wanted to snatch at it but I needed to be careful not to mess up the neatly stacked cupboard. I eased my fingers beyond the glittering tinsel and pulled at the box until it slid free.

Once it was safe on the floor I lifted the lid, tearing the thin tissue in my excitement.

My hands caressed pure white silk, slippery smooth under my fingertips. The dress from the wedding photographs. Emma's wedding dress when she married you.

I removed my clothes, quickly, yanking my sweater over my head, pulling off my jeans, until I was just in my knickers and the red camisole. I lifted the dress, the weight of silk was heavy across my arm, and unzipped the back, stepping into the sea of white. The arms were tight, and I had to pull firmly to get the dress to my shoulder. It squashed me across the chest, and I couldn't do the zip, but at least it was on. I lifted the train and went to the bedroom, where there was a full-length mirror.

Walking along the hall I played with the thought of being a bride, stepping slowly, smiling left and right. The red camisole under the white dress, both made me feel pretty. Like a bride. I stopped in front of the mirror. I looked ghastly. The dress was too tight, too slim, and its colour drained me. I looked lumpy and pale, my eyes unnaturally dark, my hair thick and lanky. I looked like a freak, some horrific mockery of a bride. Yelling in anguish, I unzipped the dress, pulling it off, flinging it to the floor.

I took the key from my pocket and slashed the beautiful fabric. The silk frayed easily. Slash, slash, her past, my present – with the same man.

When the dress was in tatters, I carefully folded it, sleeve over sleeve, silk to silk. I wrapped it into the delicate tissue paper and put it into the box. Slowly, I carried the box back to the wardrobe, pushing it into place.

42

Black Book Entry

Joel's grave was in a modern plot, large and flat, and had a simple headstone. It still looked painfully new. The flowers on the grave were dead and brittle. I couldn't bear to come often.

Emma saw me approach, and stood up from Luke's pushchair, walking towards me. Her face was puffy and she wiped her eyes with a tissue. She cradled me in her arms. I prayed that she wouldn't start crying and I could feel my anger boiling. She had no right to tears.

My heart had not stopped racing since I'd torn her wedding dress, and she seemed to recognise something hectic in my eyes. "Oh, Rose." I felt her lips on my cheek and smelled her mint-fresh breath. "I'd do anything to take your pain away."

Not knowing that by giving me her home she already had. "Looking after Luke helps me," I said. "Just let me babysit sometimes."

We stood silently together by Joel's grave for about ten minutes, but it felt longer. She didn't know what to say to me, or whether to speak at all. She fidgeted with Luke, adjusting his hat, giving him a dummy. I moved forward, towards the white headstone. I knelt on the fresh soil and traced the inscription with my finger.

Joel Clark
Taken by the Angels

"Oh!" she said, surprised. "My surname used to be Clark, before I remarried."

"It's a common name," I said.

It had been important to me that Joel carried your name. It tied us together.

"It's a lovely inscription, Rose. Upon Angel's wings – it's just beautiful."

"He's with my mum," I said, "and my Aunt Rita. He's safe."

I didn't know if I would call the place where he now was heaven, but I knew he was somewhere, watching me. I could feel him sometimes, especially at night when I was alone.

I kissed the stone where his name was etched. The sun had warmed it. Behind me I heard Emma sob, interrupting my peaceful meditation.

She was searching for a tissue among the nappies and baby wipes.

Luke was asleep, his cheeks rosy as he snuggled with his blanket. She didn't deserve him.

43

Dominic Hatcher watched as his wife, zombie-like, led the probation officer to the lounge and mumbled an offer of a drink, an offer that he knew she would forget to carry out.

Anticipating Emma's inability to perform even this simple task, he had already boiled the kettle and set out three mugs. He lingered just long enough to hear the probation officer say, "Coffee, please. Black, no sugar," and disappeared to make it.

Stirring the drinks Dominic tried to still his brain, knowing the main guest at the table of his sorrow was anger, which he must control. Anger at Rose Wilks, that she was found not guilty of murder. But he was also angry with Emma. Angry that she had invited Rose into their home, that she had failed to see what that woman was, and the monster she would become.

Dominic and Emma's marriage was cold and businesslike, with no arguments, no passion. Emma lacked the energy for anything and Dominic feared that if he started to show any emotion he would not be able to staunch the volcano of his feelings, which would consume them both.

He was quick making the drinks, but not quick enough, and when he entered the lounge a strained silence had already been established. He saw by the way the probation officer was leaning forward, pen poised, that she was waiting for an answer to a question she had asked Emma, which he knew would never come. Emma was teetering on the sofa, staring into the middle-distance. The thought entered his mind that he would like to slap her, just to get some reaction.

He placed a mug in front of the probation officer, who was young, barely out of university by the look of her. She had a serious face, though, and was frowning. She put her pen down and took the mug into two hands, held it tight, and told him to call her Cate, beginning once more to explain why she was there. Dominic heard the words – "parole report", "impartial", "your views" – but they barely penetrated. It was just jargon. There was only one thing he needed to know.

"So when will that woman be let out?"

He watched Cate sip her coffee, and then hold the cup from her mouth. "That depends on what the parole board decide when they meet next week."

His breath caught. "When do you think it will be?"

She pursed her lips before she answered. "If she doesn't win parole she'll be in prison for another two years."

"Only two years? That's an insult!"

"But if she's successful, she'll be released in September."

Emma looked up, surprised. "But that's next month."

Cate put down her cup. "She would be out on licence and have to report to a probation officer working in the town. We'd require her to complete some offending behaviour courses. She wouldn't be able to get a job without our permission, and we would have to approve the address she lives at. It's not an easy ride for a released prisoner."

"You just don't get it, do you?" Dominic's heart thumped in his ribcage. "She'd be free. That's the point." He wished there was something to slam his anger into.

Emma mused to herself, speaking softly and slowly as she shook her head in disbelief. "I could see her in the street, at the supermarket. She could walk past this house."

"No," said Cate, "we wouldn't allow that. If she's released there would be a condition of no contact."

Dominic stared at her earnest face, heard the certainty

in her voice, and despised her for it. "She killed our child. Do you really think anything you say would stop her doing whatever she wants?"

"If she broke any parole conditions she'd be sent straight back to prison."

He sat down heavily on the sofa, feeling the weight of his own fury bearing down on him. "So how much will our views really count when you write this parole report?"

He could see by her face, sympathetic yet professional, that she was trying to manage him, trying to diffuse his anger, but it was futile. He had been angry for four years, and nothing she could say would change that.

"Well, I'd like to know of any conditions you would like imposed. For example, we could have one to stop her from entering this neighbourhood. If Rose Wilks is assessed as worthy of release, your views are unlikely to influence that, but they would influence the nature of the licence."

"In other words, this is a waste of fucking time." Anger gave way to something more painful, the hopelessness of defeat. Emma, at his side, stared at the floor.

"Mr Hatcher, I want my report to represent your views too. I haven't made a decision on whether to recommend release or not, and I'd really like to know how Rose became so involved with your family. Can I ask you about the case? I've read your witness statements, but if you feel able to talk, I'd like to listen."

He had been waiting for this. Another stranger wanting to delve into their pain, to pull around with the whys and wherefores when none of it would change the fact that Luke was dead. He was about to say as much when Emma surprised him by speaking first. Her voice was a monotone.

"I felt sorry for her. I wanted to help, to be her friend. She was a bit odd, but then who wouldn't be, after losing a baby?" She gave a sound like a sob, and her pain punctuated the words as she struggled to finish her sentence.

Dominic dutifully moved closer to Emma on the sofa, placing an arm around her waist, but she didn't respond. It was like embracing a statue. She was silent; her body slumped as if whatever energy she had was spent.

"Did you notice she was becoming obsessed with Luke?" asked Cate.

Emma took a long time to answer, her head shaking slowly before the words followed. "No. Not really. But then I was wrapped up in being a new mum. And she was always there. I got used to her. I was grateful for the extra help. I was finding it hard."

Dominic made a guttural noise, like a suppressed roar, forcing down his desire to shout. He was sick of hearing that Emma had found it hard to be a mother, that Rose had seemed to be helping her. Luke had been a perfect baby, and they had a nice home. She'd had a supportive husband, and yet she still said it was hard.

"Tell her about your dreams," he commanded. "Go on, tell her."

Emma was mute, studying the pattern on the carpet.

Cate leaned forward, saying gently, "Is there something else you think I should know?"

Dominic tightened his arm around Emma's waist, urging her to speak.

"When Luke was about two months old, I started having these strange dreams. Just when Dominic was away. Not really nightmares, but they were frightening. I dreamed that somebody was in the house, in Luke's room, and sometimes that there was someone in bed with me. It was so real – I felt that they were touching me, kissing me. It was strange, but the next day everything seemed back to normal so I assumed the sleeping tablets were to blame. One morning I found something. A torch, on Dominic's side of the bed." She gasped, as if realising once again that she had been touched, invaded, in her own bed. That even sleep was not safe.

"Was the torch Rose's?" Cate asked.

"At the time I thought it must have been Dominic's, and I just put it in the kitchen drawer and forgot about it. But afterwards – after the fire – I remembered it and showed him. It wasn't his after all. So then I began to think about my dreams. Maybe they weren't dreams at all. If she really had…"

"You think she touched you while you slept?"

"She's a freak! I'm going to show you something…" Dominic dashed from the room, collecting a carrier bag from the cupboard and returning to the room. He emptied the bag onto the floor. It looked like a bundle of fabric scraps, all frayed and in strips. All white.

"It's my wedding dress," Emma whispered, reaching to touch one of the silk pieces. "She did this."

Unable to stop himself any longer, Dominic erupted. "The twisted bitch! She was in our home, creeping around when we were asleep. Setting fire to the house. She burned our child to death – he hadn't even seen his first Christmas. And you think that sick woman deserves to be released?"

Emma began to sob, reaching for him, and buried herself into him. He held her tight against himself if only to stop the urge to throw her to the floor. From above came the baby's cry.

Dominic disentangled himself but Emma wiped her tears away, her lips pursed tightly together. "I'll go to her, Dominic."

Upstairs, the crying was replaced by the low sound of a mother soothing her baby.

"That's our daughter," said Dominic.

Cate looked surprised, "I didn't know you had another child. How old is she?"

"Eight months. You can't imagine how that little girl has made us feel – she can't take the pain away, nothing can. But, my God, at least she gives us a reason to live."

Cate nodded slightly.

"After we lost Luke we were heading for divorce. There

was nothing to keep us together, but then Emma fell pregnant and that changed everything. It saved us."

"Has it helped your wife to move on?"

Dominic ran a hand through his hair. "She's had a reason to get up in the morning. A reason to go out each day. And she never complains about being tired or any of that other crap that used to get her down with Luke. We both count our blessings. So, yes, since our daughter was born she has seemed better. She's still on sleeping tablets, of course."

They both listened to the mewling baby overhead.

"After Luke died," Dominic said, "she couldn't bear to be alone in the house. I had to give up my job at the boarding school, she just couldn't cope with me being away. She had nightmares, and heard noises in the night. It was better for the first few months, after the birth, but just recently…" He felt himself wavering.

"Yes?"

"Look, I don't want to make out that my wife is mentally unstable, but I want you to know how much damage that Wilks woman has done. Maybe it's knowing the parole date was looming, but over the last few weeks Emma's nightmares have returned."

Dominic scrubbed a mark on his trousers, and then looked up at Cate.

"Emma says she's seen someone hanging around the house. A woman, or maybe a girl. Last week she said she saw her looking in through the window. Then Emma got it in her head that the back door key was missing. She called me and I came straight home, drove like an idiot. But when I got here I found the key, just where it should be, on a hook by the back door."

"Have you reported this?"

Dominic looked incredulous, and his lip curled. "What for? There was no-one looking in the window, no key was taken. The only person who would want to do that is Rose, and she's behind bars. It's Emma's brain playing tricks. That's what I'm saying to you. That even a new baby can't cure her of the fear. She'll never feel safe again."

Just then footsteps came down the stairs, and Emma appeared in the doorway, speaking low and evenly to the child in her arms. The little girl was in a pink Babygro, and she had wisps of golden curls.

"She's lovely," Cate said, "what's her name?"

Emma gave her daughter a kiss on the cheek and then turned to Cate. "Hope," she said. "Our daughter's name is Hope." Emma sat on the L-shaped sofa, leaned forward, and strapped her daughter into the bouncy chair. It was pink with yellow stars.

Cate couldn't start her car, her hands were shaking so much. Tears blurred her eyes. It was useless to fight, so she let go of the tentative hold she'd kept throughout the awful interview, finally allowing herself to be a mother again, rather than a probation officer.

As she cried she thought of Emma and Dominic Hatcher.

Emma was a woman defined by her terrible loss and she must live with the fact that she allowed Rose into her home. Luke could even now be running around on podgy infant legs, clumsily kicking a football and rushing into her embrace.

Cate thought how easily life could be taken. If anything happened to Amelia, she knew she would never survive.

And Rose Wilks dared to hope that she would be released after four years, but Emma and Dominic Hatcher would never be free, never be released from grief. If Rose hadn't been in the house, hadn't lit that cigarette…Murder or manslaughter, intentional or a terrible accident, it was still Rose who caused the fire that killed Luke.

It was Cate the mother, not the professional, who placed the key in the ignition and drove to the prison. What a waste. What a senseless waste.

44

Black Book Entry

Emma had no family close by so she used me more and more to babysit while she popped to the post office or the shops. I'd always try to persuade her not to rush back and she never did. She even began to arrange lunch dates, sending and receiving texts on her phone and saying there was someone she wanted to meet with, would I be able to babysit for a few hours? She enjoyed her time away from Luke and would return flushed and happy.

Finally I was asked to babysit for a whole day. It was Emma and Dominic's first wedding anniversary. If it was me I would have wanted to celebrate as a family, go on a day trip somewhere, but they didn't want to take Luke. I was glad that they wouldn't be back until the evening. Luke and I would have our own celebration.

When I arrived at the house Dominic was full of himself, boasting about how he'd managed to get tickets for the owners' enclosure at Newmarket, through one of his pupils' fathers who was some business hotshot and owned a racehorse. I tried to look impressed. His white hair was smoothed with Brylcreem and he wore a pink shirt, too trendy for a man his age. As I made all the right noises about how smart he looked

I was thinking how pathetic he was. He was impatient to be off; having finished admiring himself in the hall mirror, he called upstairs for Emma to hurry.

She appeared at the top of the stairs with Luke in her arms. I called his name, and he smiled at me, gurgling as she handed him over, and I couldn't resist kissing the top of his head, where his golden hair was growing unruly. I could have cuddled him all morning, but I forced myself to look at Emma. She was dressed in a ridiculously short pink dress and hat. The skirt was too tight on her stomach, as she hadn't yet lost all the weight she'd put on in pregnancy.

"You look lovely, Emma."

She kept pulling at her skirt and fiddling with her straps.

"Oh, Rose, it's so long since I've been to anything like this. Dominic's colleagues are mainly women, and I feel like my brain's turned to mush since having Luke. And I don't know anything about horseracing."

"You'll be fine, Emma. Just choose the horses with the best names. Have a few glasses of wine and you'll soon relax."

"You think so?"

"They'll love you."

Dominic was standing at the open door but Emma hesitated by the hall mirror, fussing with her hair. It took all my patience not to scream at her. I bit my tongue as she told me which toys Luke preferred, what time he had his milk. "There's a bottle made up ready in the fridge."

We stood at the window, watching the car pull out.

I held up his arm, so he was waving goodbye.

It was a fresh spring day and I wanted to push the pram. Not Emma's pram, but the one I'd bought for Joel. I lifted it out from the boot of my car. It was immaculate. I'd refused to get rid of it. I'd known that one day it would come in useful. I left it in the porch and fetched Luke from his blue bouncy chair.

"Look," I said, "this is your new pram. Do you like it?"

He gurgled at my excited voice, kicking legs in joy. As I lowered him onto the mattress I thought of how this simple pleasure should have been mine a million times over.

I walked into town slowly, pushing the pram, taking in the world. I talked constantly, pointing out dogs and birds and motorcars. A new baby attracts attention, and several women looked in the pram to admire my boy. I wasn't selfish; I stopped and indulged them.

"He's three months old. Yes, he's a good baby – he was poorly when he was born but now he's thriving."

But after a while he became fretful, so I decided to take him to our home.

As I pushed the pram over the doorstep to our flat I knew what a newly married man must feel, lifting his bride over the threshold. It was a new beginning. I carried Luke up the stairs and along the hall into the nursery. Like the pram, his room was immaculate. I showed him the cherry wood cot, the jointed teddy bear in its pristine waistcoat that had never had a child's love. I showed him the tiny birds nest, and told him how the babies in it had died.

It was Luke's room now; everything in it belonged to him.

When Emma returned it was just after five. She walked with a wobble and when she snatched Luke from my arms I could smell alcohol on her breath. Dominic followed, looking sulky.

"You're back early," I said, as Dominic shrugged off his jacket.

"Emma totally overdid it. Downed a bottle of champagne before we'd even eaten the main course."

He went to the kitchen and I heard the click of a beer bottle being opened. Emma was swaying too much to notice, and I took Luke from her, afraid she would drop him.

Dominic walked back in, drinking from the bottle. He seemed to have forgotten that I was still there. "I've never been so embarrassed."

"Oh, sod off! When did I last have a chance to drink? And why didn't you warn me how stuck-up your friends are?"

"They're my pupils' parents. They pay my wages."

"Well, they were boring. All that talk about jockeys and trainers and handicaps – not one of them asked me about my life. Not one!"

"Well, what do you expect them to say? You were slurring your words and spilling your wine on them."

Emma shot her husband a reproachful glare. "I was bored, Dominic. And I'm still young, remember? Not like you. I just want to have some fun for a change. God, I'm so sick of this house and nappies and bottles and being tired. I just wanted to have one night when I could just be me."

"For God's sake, Emma! What the hell's wrong with you? You're talking like you're in prison. You've got a beautiful home, a healthy son. Me. Stop being such an ungrateful bitch."

She swung round, staggering forward. "Don't you speak to me like that!"

Dominic was furious. "You ruined our day. What a waste of a ticket. There's a concert on at six. I've a good mind to go back on my own."

"Well, go then. I'm not stopping you."

"Fine."

Emma sat heavily on the sofa. "You piss off and enjoy yourself. Don't worry about me."

Dominic grabbed his coat and stalked out of the house.

When the door slammed Emma stared at it, fury on her face.

"Luke's just been fed," I told her. I'd already tipped the formula milk down the sink. "And I've given him his bath."

"God, I'm sick of this." She closed her eyes and leaned back into the sofa.

"You look shattered. Why don't I put Luke to bed for you?"

I took him upstairs. He looked so perfect in the cot, so cosy and soft and drifting into sleep that I just wanted to climb in and lie down next to him. As I kissed him I said I'd come back later. I looked at him, and touched his cheek to seal my promise.

When I got back downstairs to Emma I saw that she hadn't moved.

"Was your day out that bad?" I asked, sitting on the floor near her feet, collecting the scattered toys and putting them in a pile.

"Fucking awful," she cried.

"What is it, Emma?" I sat down next to her and put an arm around her shoulders. "Is it just too much drink?"

"What?" she sniffed, wiping her nose with her hand. "No – not that. It's Dominic. Sometimes I feel like one of his bloody pupils. He treats me like a fucking child. I just wish he could talk to me like a normal person. You know, like two equals."

"Maybe it's because he's so much older than you?"

"He's not that much older. He just likes lording it over me. A marriage shouldn't be like this. It should be fun."

"Like your first marriage?" I don't know how I managed to say it. I held my breath.

She thought about it, biting a torn nail. "My first husband was totally different to Dominic. I didn't see how easy he was to be with until now."

"Do you ever see your ex-husband?"

I held my breath waiting for her answer.

"I've bumped into him a few times." She twisted the gold band that was loose on her finger. "They say you don't appreciate things till they've gone. Life's so bloody unfair."

My throat constricted, and I couldn't say anything. I pushed her away, no longer able to stand her self-pity. The bitch already had Luke, and now she wanted you back.

By 11 p.m. the house was in total darkness, except for the landing light, which I knew she kept on until morning.

You were working shifts at Auberge and didn't get home

before midnight, so it was easy for me to spend evenings in my car parked across the road from Emma's house, watching. I knew what time the house was hushed, when the nursery light was switched on for Luke's late-night feed. But I'd never left the safety of my car before.

Great care was needed. I'd waited patiently, knowing I would never have the courage to do this if Dominic was at home. Thanks to his selfishness he was back in Newmarket. I'd already planned what I would wear: light shoes, trainers. Nothing likely to rustle, just black leggings and a black top. I looked like a cat burglar, sleek and silent, a creature of the night. Searching through our hall cupboard I had found several torches and chose the smallest. I collected what I needed, laying it out on the bed, feeling like Cinderella before the ball, my heartbeat outstepping the clock, which slowly ticked towards the time when the dance would begin. I was giddy, full of fearless love. It would be a brief, glorious dance but I must leave before the clock struck midnight.

Parking my car in the street next to Emma's, I skirted hedges and climbed fences until I was there, tiptoeing up the side to the back door. I put my key in the lock, eased down the handle and opened the door very quietly, leaving it slightly ajar.

The house was still, the darkness only broken by the streetlights outside. My torch was a spotlight as I padded through the hall, my trainers squeaking as I climbed the stairs, the carpet at least dulling the sound. I switched off my torch, allowing the light from the street to guide me.

I trod carefully to my first destination: Emma's bedroom. Inside the room it was silent, her mobile phone was on the bedside cabinet, switched on.

I'd never seen Emma asleep. She looked more beautiful than when awake. Sleep smoothed her face, the lines of worry gone, her lips softened into a near smile, some happy dream transporting her away from the dangers of this world. I envied her. Even asleep I was plagued with the loss of Joel.

Half-drunk with my recklessness, I put down my torch and lay next to her, where Dominic would normally be. Where you had lain, Jason, when you betrayed me. It was a warm night and the duvet was pushed low below her bare breasts. I gently pulled it down further to reveal more of her. She was naked and her skin was luminous. Her breathing was so deep and steady that I knew she wouldn't wake.

Intoxicated with my daring, I touched her shoulder, my hand cupping its soft contour. She rolled towards me, and my hand stroked her bare breast. I was hot, on fire. The rise and fall of her chest mocked my unsteady breathing. It was as though she controlled me, despite being unconsciousness. I inched closer until my body mirrored hers, and pressed my lips to the graceful curve of her neck and then, on the pillow next to her, I saw a long golden-red hair.

Too golden to come from Emma's scalp, not silver enough for Dominic's, too long to belong to Luke, although it was the same colour.

I lifted the hair, stared at it in the moonlight, wondering if I was losing my mind. Then I had another thought: her mobile phone. I picked it up and walked into the hall. I went to her messages and looked down the list. There were messages from Dominic, from me, from her hairdresser, then…my heart thumped when I saw your number. I retrieved the message:

I'll come 2 U. Usual time?

In her sleep Emma moaned softly, beginning to stir, and I switched the phone off, placing it back on the cabinet. Breathless, I inched away from the bed and out of the room.

It was only when I tucked the key back into my pocket that I realised I'd left my torch behind.

45

When Rose appeared in the classroom Cate could see that she had been asleep from the pillow crease on her cheek. Callahan had told her that a lot of inmates slept over lunch, which was a lengthy two hours. There was not much else to do in a cell, especially when the weather was warm. Rose sat on the chair opposite, and began to take a cigarette from her lapel pocket, then, looking at her, replaced it.

"It's too hot in here," Cate said, feeling sweat itch her neck. She thought about removing her jacket but rejected the idea.

"Always hot in here. Except when it's freezing, that is. They never can get it right."

When Rose turned her face, Cate saw the purple bruise on her brow and cheek. "What happened?"

Rose touched her cheek, as if she had forgotten the injury. "The usual. Someone called me a nonce."

"Did you tell one of the officers?"

"Oh yes," Rose smiled slightly. "They know all about it."

Cate focused on her notepad. "I understand that you've already seen Officer Callahan's parole report. It says you get on well on the unit. That you're popular."

Rose sneered. "Well, there isn't much choice for company on the inside. And I come in handy, I suppose. I like to look after the new girls. I feel sorry for them, especially the ones with kids. At least I know where my boy is, and he's safe."

"In heaven, do you mean?"

"Maybe. I believe in something like that, anyway. Don't you?"

"No," said Cate. "I'm afraid I don't."

"I thought you do-gooders always had some kind of faith."

"Not this one." Cate took a breath, watching Rose, her impassive face beyond reading. "I wanted to speak to you about Emma Hatcher. I visited her yesterday."

As soon as she heard this, Rose's face crumpled into lines of concern. She leaned forward as if to pull the information from Cate. "How is she?"

The words came in a rush and Cate decided not to spare her after all. It would be a test, another hurdle that Rose could never adequately clear. "Terrible. She's very fragile."

Rose rubbed her fingers on the bridge of her nose and lowered her head. "And her husband?" This was said with less intensity.

Cate cast her mind back to the interview, and remembered how angry Dominic Hatcher had been, but also how he had put his arm around his wife to support her. "I should think he's coping a bit better. But the future won't be easy for either of them."

She didn't mention the new baby. Rose had no right to know of Hope's existence.

Rose looked up, crystal clarity in her eyes. "They need to learn to accept it," she advised, "to see it as something greater than themselves. That's how I manage. Joel and Luke are in a better place now, in the sprit world. That's what gets me through. Have you ever lost anyone?"

"No. I've had no bereavements."

"It doesn't have to be through death, any loss is the same. You have to adapt, to change the way you feel about things. My father is still alive but he's more lost to me than my dead mother."

"That must be hard."

"And my brother, Peter, is the same. Mind you, we were

never close. Do you have any siblings?"

"A sister."

"And are you close?"

"Used to be, when we were kids. There's only fifteen months between us."

"What about now?"

"I haven't spoken to her in a long time. "

Cate felt Rose had taken over the interview. It was time to shift the focus back. "Now, I think we should talk about you instead of me. That's why we're here."

"What do you want to know?"

The truth, thought Cate. "You stalked Emma to get control over her life. That's the link between your childhood and what happened with Luke." Rose frowned, but was listening. "When you lost your mother it was a devastating blow, and then you felt Mrs Carron was trying to replace her. You couldn't control that, you were only a child. But the peephole, watching her like you did, gave you a secret power. It made you feel better."

"I don't like where this is going."

"And then when Rita died, that was hard. You had to fend for yourself when you were still quite young. But you did the best you could, worked hard, met Jason. But then you lost Joel, another loss, your third. You felt that things were out of your control again, you were scared. So then, by chance, you meet Emma and begin stalking her. Was it sexual?"

"What do you mean?"

"When you entered her house at night, did you touch her?"

Rose hesitated. "Yes, but not how you mean. I didn't fancy her. I mean, I've never fancied a woman like that. But I did think she was beautiful. I've always wondered what it would be like."

"So the stalking was your way of trying to regain a hold on a situation, to feel that in some things at least you were making decisions?"

"You've been analysing me."

Cate dismissed Rose's taunting tone. "The important thing is, Rose, am I right? Does my theory hold water? Does it have psychological truth?"

Rose leaned back in her chair and closed her eyes. "All of what you said – the stalking, the need to keep a hold of things – it's true; I am guilty." She looked at Cate now, tears welling. "But none of that means that I wanted Luke to die. I admit the rest, all of it. But I never started that fire."

Cate watched Rose cry without pity.

When she left the prison Cate saw a figure standing by her car, at the far side of the staff car park. She realised with a jolt who it was. Emma Hatcher. And she was waiting for her. Immediately Cate felt dread. *I really don't know how to comfort her. I don't know how to make her heartbreak, and now Rose Wilks's possible release, bearable.*

Emma's hunched demeanour indicated she'd been waiting a long time. She was very still, with her head low and hands deep in the pockets of a faded sweatshirt. She looked like a little girl and an old woman at the same time.

"Hello, Emma. Are you here to see me?" Cate's throat was tight.

Emma looked up, unruly hair scattered around her face, which was as pale as porcelain. But she wasn't looking at Cate; she was looking over her shoulder to the prison. "Rose is in there somewhere." It was a statement. "How is she?" Emma asked, with a note of concern.

Cate hid her surprise. "She copes. She seems to have adapted to prison and she's regarded as trustworthy."

Emma said bitterly, "I trusted her."

Cate heard her pain, like barbed wire, tangled in the words. She wanted so much to help this woman. "Anybody would have, Emma. The way she pretended to be your friend – you couldn't have known her real motives. No-one would have suspected."

But Cate also knew that any mother would feel terrible guilt. After all, Emma had let Rose into her life, her house. She had trusted her with her son. Christ, Cate still felt guilty about Amelia having that accident at the park, and her injury was fairly superficial. Guilt was just part of being a mother, and if your child was hurt or ill you carried the wound yourself.

Emma was still looking at the prison, still silent. All Cate's experience, all her training, counted for nothing as she struggled to find something to say.

It was Emma who broke the silence. "I want to ask you to do something for me."

And, of course, Cate knew it would be about Rose's parole. About her report. "Okay."

But it was not okay. Cate held her breath, knowing what Emma would ask. Knowing what she would ask in Emma's shoes.

"I want to ask you to recommend release."

There was a moment's pause as Cate struggled to make sense of what Emma had just said.

"That wasn't what I thought you'd ask."

"I don't want my husband to know about this."

"So you feel differently from him? Even after what you said, about Rose touching you while you slept? Destroying your wedding dress?"

"She's served her time."

"That shows an unusual amount of compassion. How did you find the strength?"

Emma's face hardened. "I want you to recommend release. Will you?"

Cate's inner voice was screaming that of course she wouldn't recommend release. Rose should never again be free after what she did. A child had died and she should pay forever for her culpability. How could Emma be so bloody saintly? But Cate stood outside her workplace, wearing her smart suit, the prison badge on her lapel, and tried to forget that she was a mother.

"I never thought you'd be asking for Rose's freedom."

"She was my friend," said Emma, still staring up at the prison.

46

Black Book Entry

With Emma and Luke in my life I was able to cope with losing Joel. I was able to function. It was the part of my life that made sense, which gave me the missing piece of the puzzle. Luke was my surrogate son, and I could keep a close watch on Emma. But it was my love for you, Jason, that made me long to be with them.

Loving you was like riding the sea on a life raft, hanging on through the storms, praying for calm. Waiting for safety, a light in the distance, when I could capsize with the next wave. I knew that you didn't love me, and you were drifting further away. Maybe it was of my doing, I was angry and jealous. I kept looking at the hair I'd stolen from Emma's bed, now on black velvet in the bottom drawer of my jewellery box. I was sure it was yours, but never held it against your head, which I could easily have done. And then there was the text message.

In a straight fight with Emma I would be certain to lose. My one advantage was that I was sure she wouldn't leave Dominic. She was just using you to bolster her ego and for sex, maybe to have another child.

I needed to give you something more: I would give you a family.

Business was better at Auberge, and by that time they'd taken you on full-time. You didn't mind me turning up at the end of your shift as long as I was smartly dressed. I liked to watch you swagger between the tables of rich, ugly businessmen and seduce them into purchasing the oldest whisky, the finest champagne. You had a way with people, of serving them, that made them want the best.

It was risky to take Luke to see you that first time; I didn't know how you'd react. If you would see what I saw in his face. If it would reawaken your love for Emma. But if we were to be a family I had to take the risk.

Emma was at the hairdressers having highlights, so I had a couple of hours. It was late afternoon and I knew Auberge would be quiet. You would be surprised to see me, as I'd told you I was visiting the friend I made in hospital. I thought it was time that you discovered who my friend really was.

The Burberry check pram clonked up the wide steps awkwardly, and I hoped that you wouldn't see our ungraceful arrival. A dapper man in a navy blazer with brass buttons walked ahead and held the door open. In the reception area I neatened my hair in the mirror, straightened my top, which was a replica of Emma's. Luke was looking around, pulling at the ears of his white rabbit as he ravenously sucked a dummy. I leaned into the pram and kissed his rosy cheek, adjusting his hat, which Emma always insisted he wore.

The bar was quiet and you had your back to me, standing by a corner table talking to the dapper man, chuckling with him over some shared joke and then refilling his glass with wine. I saw him gesture for you to have one, but you shook your head, so instead he slid a folded note into the crease of your hand. You earned more from tips than wages, said it was like taking sweets from children.

You saw me and came over to where I sat, my hand on the pram handle, pushing it gently.

"Hello, Rose. I didn't expect you to drop by today." Your

tone was formal, your working voice.

"We thought we'd surprise you. This is Luke."

You glanced at the pram, and I wondered if you recognised it. If you knew it was Joel's.

"So you're babysitting, are you, for your mate?"

"That's right. For Emma."

You didn't even register the name, too busy scanning the room for any customers who needed service, for any tipping opportunities. Satisfied there were none, you sat down. A ray of sun caught the gold name badge on your waistcoat, making it shine.

"Jason, I want to tell you about my friend. About Emma."

Your fingers fidgeted with your waistcoat, pulling it smoothly down. You were distracted.

"I've found out that you know her." I looked for recognition, or even interest, but found none. I had to say it plainly. My palm slipped on the pram handle. "She's your Emma."

"My Emma?"

You saw me then, alright, for the first time since I arrived. I nodded like a dumb mule, suddenly petrified I'd gone too far. That just mentioning her would send you into despair. I gabbled, rocking the pram vigorously. "I had no idea, Jason. Not until she started talking about her ex-husband. And then I saw this."

I took the folded photo from my handbag, the one I had stolen from her drawer.

You snatched it from me, glaring at the frozen image of your wedding day.

"She doesn't know. I never told her."

You were silent, watching my mouth form words. You looked back at the photo.

"And this is Luke. Her son."

You turned your head to the pram, eyes taking in the blue blanket, travelling higher until they fixed on Luke. You peered in, looking down at his face. Your mouth slackened, your hand still clutched the photo. I wanted to tell you not to crumple it, but daren't.

"He's beautiful, isn't he?" I said. I reached forward and removed his hat, revealing his golden-red curls.

Gingerly you placed your hand in the pram and stroked his cheek, touched his hair, your face a mixture of wonder and pain.

"Emma's not expecting us back for a couple hours. She's given me her membership card for the swanky tennis club in town. We could all go. Luke could play while we have a drink…"

Your jaw had tightened again, and still you stared at Luke. Tearing your gaze away from him, you said dryly, "I don't think so, Rose. I've got too much to do. This isn't a place for children. Please don't bring him here again."

Dismissing me, you stood up and left us. As I walked away I realised that you were still holding the photo in your fist.

47

Black Book Entry

You worked late for the next two evenings, or so you said, coming home in the small hours and sleeping late into the mornings. Our conversations were those of people who pass daily in the street, polite but of no consequence. I imagined your conversations with Emma, saw your bodies together, driving myself mad with envy. I wondered if you confronted her with the knowledge that Luke was your son. Maybe you already knew, had known all along. So many questions which I would never know the answers to. I longed for my heart to become stone.

It was three days later that everything changed. I was looking after Luke again. Emma was on a refresher course that she had to take so she could return to teaching dance, and wouldn't be back until five. I didn't understand why she wanted to go back to work when she had a baby to care for, and it wasn't as if she needed the money. She said it was to do with status, or identity, something like that. It sounded like bullshit to me.

I told you that I was taking Luke to the tennis club. I liked it there. It had a large area with sofas and magazines and a soft play area, which was always quiet. I could get a coffee, Luke could safely explore while I watched the play on the indoor courts through large glass windows. It was exclusive – I'd sneaked a look at the price and the monthly charge was as much as our rent. I knew Dominic didn't pay a penny, though, since the membership had been a Christmas gift from one of his pupils' parents. I liked watching the impossibly tanned ladies in white mini-skirts, the men in white shorts, and wondered what they did for a living that allowed them to play sport in the middle of the day.

I was an impostor there, but you, Jason, have always been a chameleon. I knew you'd be tempted when I said I had the membership card again, plus money for food that Emma had given me. I didn't know how you felt about Luke being there, but I lured you in with descriptions of the smart cars and the sports bar. Don't think I didn't see that you wanted to find out what Dominic was able to offer Emma. You wanted to see what her life was like without you.

It was your day off, so you were at a loose end, and quickly swapped your jeans for navy jogging pants. When we arrived at the tennis club you acted like a member, smiling confidently, swaggering in Nike trainers and a white polo shirt. All you lacked was a racquet.

We went to the sofas, and I lifted Luke from the pram, secretly watching you for any recognition as I pulled off the baby hat. But you were too busy looking around. "I'll get us a drink," you said, taking the money from my purse and disappearing to the upstairs bar. You were gone before I could say that all I wanted was a cup of tea.

Later, when it was nearly time to go, I carried Luke up the stairs to the bar. You were perched on a stool, chatting to a slender man dressed in citrus colours. Between you was a bottle of cognac, and I watched you swirl the bulb of the glass, your other hand motioning with a slim cigar. You looked magnificent. To the manner born. To interrupt would have embarrassed us both. I returned downstairs and waited patiently.

I didn't mind waiting. I'd achieved my goal; you had met your son.

We had been a family.

48

Janie was emptying out the probation officer's bin, marvelling at the number of sweet wrappers, her mouth watering at the thought of milk chocolate and sweet caramel. Miss Austin stood to let Janie get to the bin, and they moved around each other like awkward dancers. Janie eyed the sweets on the desk.

"Would you like one?" Miss Austin asked, offering the packet.

Janie unwrapped the sweet, thinking what a mess the office was. Piles of scrunched-up paper, pens without lids, and the computer keyboard smeared with greasy fingerprints. "I'll just wipe this for you, miss."

"I'm sorry, Janie. It's a bit grubby."

"Don't say sorry to me, miss. It's my job." Janie thought it was funny how some of the staff seemed to feel bad about letting her clean up their mess; maybe that was why they pretended she wasn't there. But most staff took it as their right, and would tell her to dust the photos of their families with extra care.

The Governor was very particular about her polishing his desk with beeswax – no spray polish for him. She had to make sure she put the photo of his missus back just so, at the right corner of his leather blotter pad. It drove her nuts.

Miss Austin never made demands, but Janie wouldn't have minded if she did. She was alright, and always asked Janie how she was doing when everyone else looked right through her.

Janie polished the keyboard, and then started to work on the desk, spying a pile of notes to her side. On its own in the out tray she recognised her friend's name and sounded out the words in her head:

ROSE WILKS – PAROLE REPORT.

Janie started to cough and moved her hands to her throat. "My sweet!" she wheezed.

Miss Austin speedily banged her on the back, dislodging it, and Janie gasped, then coughed again. "I need a drink, miss."

"Of course – I'll go get some." Miss Austin dashed out of the room, rushing to the nearest drinks machine two locked doors away.

And, as cannily as that, Janie was alone in the room. Her reading lessons at the college were going okay, and she carefully mouthed the words, saying them as she read, until she'd got to the conclusion in Rose's report.

Miss Austin wanted Rose's parole application to be refused.

49

Black Book Entry

Something was wrong between Dominic and Emma. Dark thoughts kept coming to me, whispering that you were the cause. The text message I had found from you on Emma's phone made me certain that you and she were lovers again. *I've bumped into him from time to time*, she'd said. It was months since she'd told me that she and Dominic were trying for a baby, nothing had yet happened. Had she decided to use your seed? I thought about the hair on her pillow, I knew it was yours.

Dominic was working long days at the school as it was examination time, so I only saw him occasionally. If he arrived home when I was still there I would make a swift exit, and I never called at weekends if his car was in the drive. Once he said, "Here again, Rose? I should start charging you rent."

He would look at Emma with longing, but she never returned the gaze. Even though I disliked Dominic, I understood him. His possessive love for Emma, his jealousy of Luke. The way he wanted to take her out without their son, have her to himself. Emma was desperate to go out too, to be free of a crying, smelly, demanding baby, and was pleased when he came home with theatre tickets or suggested they try a new restaurant in town. I was always happy to babysit. Looking after Luke was what I lived for, and the further away Dominic took Emma the better.

It was in the hours when I had Luke to myself that I was happiest. But it made me complacent and in the end it was my undoing.

Dominic had taken Emma to Southwold, even though it was a drizzly day. Southwold is a seaside town, but not like Felixstowe or Lowestoft. It's a mix of expensive galleries and quaint teashops, really posh. Not my idea of the seaside, or a child's; there are no donkey rides or ice cream stands.

As usual, I took my pushchair from the car and strapped Luke in it. I'd brought a couple of toys to attach to the pushchair and he clapped his hands when he saw them. I strode into Ipswich town centre. I was braver now, and had started to enter the main precinct. I didn't know many people in the area; even working in the hotel in Felixstowe, I'd never tried to make friends. Once I met you, Jason, friends didn't matter. We had only been together a short time when I fell pregnant and then, after Joel died, any neighbours who might have been friendly stayed away. So I'd stopped worrying that someone would see me and, even if they did, I would simply say I was babysitting for a friend.

I enjoyed being alone with Luke, being a mother again. I pushed the pram happily around shops, talking to him constantly, stopping to show him a toy or to hold an item of clothing against his small frame, checking for size. If I bought anything I'd use cash, as I didn't want you to see children's shops on our bank statement and become suspicious. I had learned this after buying two nursing bras.

"What did you buy at Mothercare for £50?" you asked me one day.

I spoke quickly, turning away to hide my face. "Oh, a gift for Luke's christening."

You said that it was a lot of money to spend, what with me still not working, but carried on watching TV. I knew that I'd got away with it but I'd have to be more careful in future. As for the items I bought, I kept them in the nursery, a room that you never entered.

Luke and I whiled away a few hours, but then the rain began to fall, a fierce summer shower, and we took shelter in a cafe. He was getting restless, and I knew he was hungry, so I ordered myself a drink and took a seat in the corner where I could get some privacy. I kissed his head and settled him down to feed, a blanket discreetly draped over my shoulder. I glowed with the pride of motherhood.

I was happy. Despite losing Joel, despite feeling lonely in my own home, despite my fear of you betraying me, in that moment I was happy. Luke belonged to me. I fantasised about Emma and Dominic having some tragic but mercifully quick accident, so I could be with him always. So that we could be a family. After all, a boy needs his father.

The waitress, a bouncy girl with a pink headband and peroxide hair, fussed over him. "Aw, he's gorgeous. What a handsome boy." She slid her pen behind her ear and chucked him under the chin with her finger. "What's his name?"

"Joel," I said.

"He's a beauty. Hello, Joel."

He opened his mouth, looking around and mewling, as I began to unhook my nursing bra, she looked on admiringly. "Nothing like mother's milk to settle them, is there? Now then, what can I get you?"

She was back in moments with my tea, cooed a little more, and then went to serve other customers.

If life has taught me one thing it is this: happiness is fleeting. If a moment arrives when you find joy, then don't blink.

I didn't even recognise her immediately. The hospital was so far away from my thoughts that I hadn't even registered that I was near it. The bell over the door announced her arrival but I didn't know it was Nurse Hall until I heard her voice, placing her order with the waitress. She was in uniform, and had a magazine, which she opened and began to read. Her hair was shorter, and a brighter red, but the purple eyeliner was the same. I remembered how she'd told me about Joel's condition, how she'd taken us to see him that final time. She had always been so caring to me, and when Joel died she had held me, comforted me.

"Ah, bless him. He's a hungry boy! Would you like anything else?" Damn that waitress, with her loud voice, taking my empty cup away so soon. I couldn't risk speaking in case Nurse Hall heard me, so I shook my head. "I'll just get you the bill then, shall I?"

It was now lunchtime, and all the seats were taken, yet people were still coming in from the rain, standing at the doorway and waiting. A few had spied my empty table, seeing that I would soon be ready to leave and were looking at me expectantly. I wondered if I could get out without being recognised. Luke was still feeding so I pulled my nipple away, and he cried out in protest.

Nurse Hall, primed for the cries of children, looked up. She saw me and the recognition was instant. Even in a job where sickness and death are not unusual, she hadn't forgotten me. She immediately came over. "Rose!"

By the time she was at my side a dummy had pacified Luke, and my T-shirt had been quickly pulled down.

"Hi, Rose. It's so good to see you. How are you?"

She put her hand lightly on my shoulder, her eyes intent on mine. There was genuine feeling in her voice that brought tightness to my throat.

"Doing okay, thanks." Minimal words, minimal contact. I just wanted to be out from there.

"You look well." Her eyes fell on Luke. "Hello, there. Is it a boy?"

I nodded. "His mother will be expecting us. We should be heading back." I bundled him quickly into the pram, taking £10 from my purse, the only money I had, and putting it on the table. The dummy fell from his mouth and he began to cry. "Hush. Good boy." I adjusted his hat, and it slipped, revealing his distinctive golden curls.

Her eyes widened as the penny dropped. "Isn't that Emma Hatcher's son?"

What could I say but yes?

She looked closer now, a professional interest for a baby she had seen being born. "He's looking really well. Can I hold him?"

She gently lifted him away from me, examining his face with assessing eyes. She spoke to herself rather than me. "Hello, my lovely. Oh yes, you're thriving, aren't you? Good boy. What a beautiful smile." As he gurgled he posited white-blue milk, thinner than formula, down his chin and down the front of her uniform. She laughed, picked up a napkin and wiped his face.

I was agitated. "I really should go, Nurse Hall. It's nice to see you but Emma will be waiting."

She handed Luke back, smiling. "I'm glad you look so happy, Rose. And it's nice you've stayed friends with Mrs Hatcher. Please say hello from me."

I tried to make it to the exit quickly, but chairs had to be moved and the waitress insisted on coming after me. "Your change!"

"Keep it," I said.

As I pushed past, the waitress put her head into the pram. "Are you happy now you've had some of mummy's milk? Bless." We were almost out of the shop as she called, "Bye bye, Joel!"

The waitress's words knocked the wind out of me, and I stumbled as I stepped into the street. The rain was torrential but I was too distracted to think of shelter. I pushed the pram quickly down wet streets and back to Emma's house, trying to calm myself. After all, what had happened that could not be explained away? I was babysitting, that was all. I was worrying about nothing. Nurse Hall had not seen anything that could arouse suspicion, and probably hadn't even heard what the waitress said.

But the day was not on my side. When I returned I saw Dominic's car in the drive. Emma would be wondering where I was, without her pram, which was still in the hall. Without the car seat, which was still under the stairs. But worst of all, the bottle of formula milk was still in the fridge where she had placed it five hours ago. How would I explain that?

50

Black Book Entry

I stood outside their front door, and heard the rumbling thunder of Dominic's anger. He was arguing with Emma. It must be about me. They would have seen the pram standing in the hall, the formula milk untouched in the fridge.

Leaving the pram in my car, I knocked on the door with a fist forced against itself; my instinct was to flee. Dominic opened it.

"Where the hell have you been?"

He was red in the face, and his voice was booming. My heart palpitated, my chest too tight and I couldn't speak as I carried Luke into the hallway. I busied myself in taking his jacket off.

"He was restless, so I took him for a short walk."

Dominic looked at the pram in the hallway.

"I carried him – we didn't go far. I hope that's okay. I think he needs changing."

I wanted to escape from his scrutiny and started to head for the stairs but Dominic snatched the boy from me and took him up. I was left standing in the hall, wondering where Emma was.

I had to get rid of the bottle of formula milk in the fridge, or they would wonder why Luke wasn't screaming with hunger. I could hear Dominic in the nursery, forced baby talk, and then the downstairs toilet flushed.

The door opened, and Emma came out. Her eyes were red from crying.

"Rose! We've been back ages. Where's Luke?"

Hearing her, Dominic yelled, "Up here having his nappy changed."

She hurried past me and up the stairs.

They began to bicker.

"I'll do it, Dominic."

"Gently, Emma. For God's sake!"

There was a muffled sound and then Emma said, "You'll upset Luke. There's no need..."

"Isn't there? I think I've got every right to shout if I fucking well..."

My heart was racing, every muscle made me ready to run. I went to the kitchen, opened the fridge and took the bottle out. I quickly unscrewed the teat and tipped the milk away down the sink. A quick rinse and into the dishwasher.

I heard Emma's voice. Louder now, frustrated. "You've got it all wrong."

Luke started to cry and his parents' voices rose.

"Well, I'm upset too, Emma. What do you expect?"

"You've got the wrong idea. I would never be unfaithful..."

I stumbled, reaching the doorjamb for support. So that was the argument – it wasn't about me at all. An opened bottle of red wine stood on the work-top and I poured the wine into a tumbler, knocking it back, and refilling it to the brim, listening to the conversation above me.

"So what about those messages on your mobile? How do you explain that?"

"He just keeps calling me, but I've told him I'm not interested. He just won't take no for an answer."

I froze. She was talking about you.

I went to the hall to listen to the conversation going on above my head.

Emma was pleading with Dominic. "Please, you don't need to…please, Dominic…"

I heard footsteps along the hall and Dominic's voice was unsteady with controlled anger. "I'm going to stay at the school for a few days."

I could hear Emma getting hysterical, her voice shrill above Luke's crying. "Why? You don't need to stay away. I haven't done anything, Dominic. I'd never be unfaithful to you."

I knew it was a lie. I stuffed my fingers in my mouth to stop a yell and walked upstairs, stepping slowly and listening carefully.

And then Dominic boomed, "I'm not a fucking idiot, Emma. Don't you think I know what's going on? Those texts, you being secretive. You smelling of cigarettes. When I come home after a night away I can *tell* someone's been in my house!"

I dropped my glass and wine flew everywhere, red stains bloomed on the cream carpet. Dominic shouted, "Rose, what the hell are you still doing here?"

He came downstairs holding an overnight bag and stormed out of the house. I went to find Emma.

Emma was hunched on the bathroom floor, cradling Luke, both crying.

"What's happened?"

She tried to compose herself, but failed, and didn't resist when I took my boy from her, passing her some toilet tissue to wipe her cheeks. Her words were punctuated by sobs.

"Something Dominic's got in his head. Some stupid idea that I'm seeing someone."

I looked at her suspiciously. "Why does he think that?"

Emma's mouth quivered. "He got hold of my mobile and checked my messages. He had no right to do that! And he's got this idea that I've had someone here while he's been doing nightshifts at the school. Says he's noticed things..."

I looked at her hard, thinking what a convincing act she put on.

"He's paranoid. I need to talk to him." And she tried to stand, steadying herself with the wall, but legs buckling under the weight of Dominic's accusation.

"I'll take Luke downstairs while you wash your face."

I picked up Luke and took him downstairs. I heard the tune of Emma's mobile ringing, and Emma dashing down the corridor to grab it from her room. I stood in the hallway and listened.

"Hello? Yes, this is Emma Hatcher. Nurse Hall...Oh, yes, how are you...Oh, he's fine..."

I opened the front door, still listening to the phone call upstairs. There was a long silence then Emma said, "Well, yes, Rose is very fond of him..."

I stepped outside, Luke in my arms, and ran.

51

Cate pumped the brake pedal as a group of students ambled across the road, clutching folders and linking arms, chatting in the sun. She put the car back into gear and parked up outside the flats on Coronation Road. The steering wheel slid in her wet palms. Last time she had been here Jason Clark had shown her Joel's nursery, and the time before she had left him fighting tears on the floor. And this interview was certain to be worse.

The parole board was sitting at 10 a.m. and she wanted to be back at the prison by then. It was just after nine when she pressed the buzzer and the door opened immediately. Jason stood before her, bedraggled hair and rumpled shirt, like he'd just leapt from bed.

"Not too early I hope?"

"Come in. I'll make us some coffee."

The flat was back to the mess it had been on her first visit. In the lounge crumpled cans of Stella and cigarette butts ground into ashtrays littered the table. Jason came into the room with two mugs of steaming coffee, pushing aside the debris and sitting down. "So, today's the day."

Cate's stomach tightened, and she felt her professional mask slip into place. Her mouth became tight and her eyes serious. "It certainly is. The parole board will meet this morning and they already have my report, along with those of the prison staff and others who have met Rose."

"But your report carries the most weight?"

She shifted slightly. "Not necessarily. But it would be unusual for someone to get parole if the probation report was strongly opposed."

"So put me out of my misery, then." He sipped his coffee casually but she heard the anger under the surface.

She took a quick breath. "I don't think Rose should get parole, Jason. I've recommended she stay in prison."

He slammed his mug down on the table and coffee sloshed over the sides. "What?"

"I know it's not what you want to hear."

"But why, for God's sake?"

Cate leaned back in the sofa; let some space settle between them. "I don't think that Rose has any remorse for Luke's death. She has never fully accepted the part she played in it."

Jason erupted, "Because she didn't mean to start the fire! Jesus, how many more times?"

"But it was her cigarette…"

"You people! Hasn't she done enough? Four years of her life for nothing."

"For stalking and starting a fire that caused a death."

"No!" Jason's eyes were bulging and he moved closer to her. "Don't you dare do that! I've told you she's innocent. Oh, God…"

Cate put her coffee down. "Whether or not she gets parole is up to the board. But I wanted you to know my conclusion."

"Just get out."

"Jason, I…"

"Go now!"

Cate stood and walked swiftly from the room, turning when she heard the sound of shattered glass to see that Jason had punched his fist through the photograph frame with the picture of his dead son. There was blood on his fist and he was crying, muttering to himself those same words she had heard before. "What have you done? Oh, God, what have you done?"

52

Black Book Entry

10 a.m: the parole board will be sitting around a table, piles of reports in front of them. Talking about me. They'll have Callahan's report, which I've read, and Cate's, which I haven't.

I'm watching from the window as seagulls perch. Where do they nest? I'd like to see, like to watch them care for their chicks. I would like a chick. A new baby. A girl this time, sitting in a baby chair, pink with yellow stars.

I hold my nest, my precious nest. The twigs are old and brittle, but still entwined in that perfect shape of a home.

Rita and Mum come to me often now. Tell me there is a new baby, a little girl. I know she's yours, Jason, and soon she'll be mine; I'm just like a magpie, stealing from another's nest. Oh, my head hurts so much. It hurts from watching the clock and waiting.

I need to be released. I need to be free to find a nest.

Natalie Reynolds pushed a handmade card under my cell door earlier. *Good Luck*, it says, with a black cat on the front made with sequins and pipe cleaners. Funny how black cats are associated with luck when they're such sly, aloof creatures. I've been like a cat, dressed in black, padding softly through

Emma's home. Cats can have lots of homes; they'll feed from several people, each one thinking they are its master when all along it has mastered them.

I'm lying on my bed, watching the ceiling and making out shapes, as a free person would watch clouds. Every wall has stains or marks that can be beautiful if you squint. It's after lunch and I'm sleepy, dreaming away the time before I get my news.

Heavy boots coming. Stopping outside my cell. The key turns in the lock. It's the only notice we get, as the officers never knock.

The door heaves open and Officer Burgess stands in front of me. His skin looks sore and he has purple bruises under his eyes. He's too young to look so haggard, so defeated. A boy like him has no business working in a prison.

"Alright, Wilks?"

He doesn't look me in the eye. I make him nervous. He wouldn't unlock my cell without a good reason.

"Get your shoes on. We're going for a walk."

"Where?" I ask.

"To see the Governor."

This is the moment I've been longing for and dreading, in equal measure. I close my eyes, my hands clasped together as if in prayer, and think of freedom.

I follow Burgess off the landing and across the prison to the administration block, trying to control my breathing, knowing I'm about to hear my fate.

The Governor's office is large and dominated by a massive desk. On it is a blotting pad, a wooden desk-tidy, and a picture of a smiling woman with burgundy lips. Sitting behind the desk is the massive bulk of the Governor poised like King Canute before the sea. My stomach folds in waves, which only he has the power to stop.

Burgess is in awe of the imposing figure, and swallows

hard as he speaks. "Here's prisoner Wilks, sir." He pushes me forward, and I step to the front of the desk, head slightly bowed.

"Thank you, Burgess. Are you her Personal Officer?"

"No, sir. Officer Callahan is. He's on nights this week, sir."

The Governor eyes me up and down with undisguised fatigue. "Do you know why you're here, Wilks?"

"Because of my parole decision, sir."

"That's right, Wilks." He lifts a piece of paper from his desk, and I crane my neck but it's too far away to read. He looks at it, as if reading it for the first time. Like he has all the time in the world. And then his head snaps up, relish on his lips.

"Bad news, Wilks. *You didn't get it.*"

It must be wrong. There must be some sort of misunderstanding. "What?"

"You heard."

"But I told her everything!" My brain is confused: she has a child. I told her I didn't hurt Luke. "The probation report…"

The Governor doesn't let me finish, his voice rising above mine.

"She said you don't deserve parole. The board weren't going to release you after that."

My head hurts. The tension inside me breaks, shattering into a million parts. All that time, hoping and praying and for nothing. *You didn't get it.*

"You can go now," he says, both the Governor and Burgess watching me. All those hours, waiting. All those words wasted.

My knees give way, and I collapse to the floor, sobs wracking me for the first time in four years, tears salting my mouth.

53

Black Book Entry

I was sitting on the sofa, catching my breath. Waiting.

Emma ran into the tennis club, nearly throwing herself at me. "Where the fuck is he, you witch? What have you done with my son?"

She was close, too close, and I thought about slapping her hard, but I saw that with any movement she would go for me, like a dog. Her face was contorted with misery and anger. I slowly looked to the large windows, to the empty tennis court beyond the glass.

I'd called you, and you'd come readily. You were walking with Luke, holding him, and pacing the outer edge of the court. Did you think I was stupid, Jason? I knew all along that you were fucking Emma. It was time to stop pretending.

"He's over there," I said to Emma. I watched as she saw her son with her ex-husband. "With Jason."

"Oh, Jesus," she whispered, forgetting me. "How the fuck?"

"I want it to stop, Emma."

Her voice curled up like a snake ready to bite. "What twisted game is this, Rose?"

"Jason's mine. You had him, and you left him. He's mine now."

She was still looking through the window. "Who are you, Rose? Who the fuck are you? I know about the breastfeeding, you sick bitch...I'm going to get my son."

She was backing away from me, seeing me for the monster I am, and I grabbed her arm, held her fast. She was terrified.

I pulled her close, and she flinched in my grip.

I spoke quietly but shot every word through with force. "I want you to stop fucking Jason. Or I'll tell Dominic who Luke's real father is."

Emma's face collapsed, her mouth dropped open.

"Did you think I didn't know, Emma? I can see the likeness even if your stupid husband can't. He wouldn't want you if he knew, would he? If he knew you were still fucking your ex. And I will tell him, Emma. I promise you I will."

She was mute, looking from me to where you were still pacing with Luke, ignorant of what was happening just yards away. Ignorant that I'd discovered your secret.

"You're mad," she said, quietly. "Luke is Dominic's."

"Don't lie to me! I'm not an idiot."

"You're crazy." Her eyes were wide with fear and she was pulling away.

"I won't tell Dominic anything. It'll be our secret." I pulled her close, brought my lips to her ear, my teeth grazing her lobe. "But please stop seeing Jason. Please."

She wrestled out of my grip. "I want my son. Now."

I held her, a hand on each arm, thinking how fragile she felt. "I'll get him."

I went into the tennis courts, where you were holding Luke, telling him the rules of tennis as he gazed up at you, mesmerised.

You didn't want to see her, did you? Not while I was around. You thought I had no clue that Emma was still your lover. You quickly placed Luke in my arms, holding him just a beat longer than necessary, pausing to stroke his chin. "See you again, little man."

I told you nothing about my argument with Emma. I told you that I would see you at home later. I tried to smile, and you kissed me. Dry lips on my cheek.

I returned to Emma, handing Luke back to her. She snatched him from me. I thought she was pathetic, holding him away from me as if he was in danger.

She had made her mind up, and her voice was firm. "I'll never see Jason again. I promise."

The relief was immense, like my heart bursting open. "Thank you."

"But you are never, ever to see Luke or me, do you understand? We never want to see you again. Do you understand?"

I did understand. It was all over. Emma would give me you, but losing Luke was the price. I agreed.

And with that, gripping onto her son, Emma left.

I started the car, realised I was shaking. I'd lost him. For the second time a baby was being taken from me.

All the loss and grief of losing Joel snowballed into the pain of losing Luke and I hardly know how I managed to drive. There was only one place I could go to think, one place where it might make sense: Joel's grave.

The flowers had died, and I tried to arrange the dry buds as best I could. I hadn't been to Joel's grave since that day with Emma. I'd been too wrapped up in my worries about your infidelity, too much in love with your living son to care for my dead one. But Joel was out of harm. No-one could ever take him from me again.

Comforted, I knelt on the earth, kissing the sun-warmed headstone, tracing his name with my finger. "Oh, Joel. My boy. My darling."

I spoke as softly as if he were only sleeping, and felt calmer. The worst had already happened. Nothing could touch me now. I could survive anything. I put a hand in my pocket for a tissue and came upon the key to Emma's back door.

Taking it out I pressed it to my throat, feeling how the heat of my skin was soothed by the cold metal. I may no longer be welcome by the front door but I always had this.

But even as I thought it, I knew that secretive night visits would never be enough. I wouldn't be able to play with Luke but just sit quietly by his cot and watch him sleep. No more trips out in the pram or the car; I would never be able to take him to see Father Christmas, or to the toyshop or to play in the park.

I couldn't bear the thought. This shadow of motherhood was worse than no motherhood at all.

I couldn't bear to think of Luke growing up without me, but I knew I had no choice.

I would never see him again, but I would have you.

That night I went to say goodbye.

The house was in darkness, and Dominic's car was gone. I let myself in for the final time.

54

Janie stood alone in her cell, holding the present Rose had given her. Janie loved presents, especially when they came from Rose. The special gift was folded, wrapped up in yellow tissue paper. In her cell Janie slowly, very slowly, opened the present and unfolded the dress until it was flat on her bed.

It was lovely. Pink with tiny white flowers stitched around the hem. No sleeves, so she'd be nice and cool. It was so hot this summer. She'd need help with the zip, which was all the way up the back, but Rose would help her later, when she'd pulled herself together. Poor Rose. She really thought she'd get parole.

Janie pulled off her leggings and T-shirt, and stood only in her faded knickers. She doesn't wear a bra, doesn't need to since she's flat as a pancake, as her dad would say. The dress was a little loose, but so pretty and light that she loved it anyway. Standing on tiptoe, she twisted around to see herself in the tiny mirror above the sink.

Rose had chosen this dress from a catalogue. She'd had it sent in for her and gave it to Janie before she'd got her bad news. Rose liked it when Janie dressed up. And a new dress was a good trade for a bit of snooping. A bit of stealing. All she had to do was get her the key from the big house in Chantry Drive. The one with the pink baby chair with yellow stars.

At first Janie had thought it was Cate Austin's house but after a few visits she saw that another woman lived there. A

271

pretty, pale woman with a little baby girl. The little girl had golden hair.

Officer Burgess had told Janie that Rose hadn't got parole. He let her talk to Rose through the viewing window of her locked cell door. "Just for a few minutes," he told her, "she's in a bit of a state." He walked away from her, to the office at the end of the corridor.

"I'll come and visit you, Rose, after I'm released," Janie promised, trying to comfort her friend.

Rose didn't look up from where she lay. "They won't let you do that." Her voice was muffled.

"Then I'll write – I'm quite good now. I'll be waiting for you, on the day you come out. I'll find us a nice flat in Ipswich."

"There's no point. Not now."

"Don't say that, Rose. It's makes me frightened you're gonna do something stupid."

Officer Burgess was getting up from his chair in the office. He looked her way and tapped his watch. Time was nearly up.

"I just wish it had helped," whispered Janie, "me doing all that snooping."

"Nothing helped." Rose was crying. "I won't ever be free of the past."

"Rose, who is that woman who lives in that big house in Chantry Drive?"

"Someone who used to be a friend. My best friend. I don't think I'll see her again."

Officer Burgess was walking towards her, jangling his keys. In a few moments she would be locked up too. "Isn't there anything I can do, Rose? If you want me to snoop in the house, I will. I'll do anything you want me to."

Officer Burgess shut the flap covering the viewing window and led Janie away. She twitched her head like a faithful pet, ready to run in a wheel that could keep spinning for two more years.

55

Cate picked up the phone on its second ring.

"It's Callahan. I wanna talk to you."

"Hi Dave."

"Funny thing, love. Wilks didn't get her parole."

Cate leaned back in her chair. "Is she okay?"

"Hardly. I can't work it out, see. She's a model prisoner, and I said so in my report."

Cate breathed deep, knowing what was to come. Despite his jocular tone she knew that Dave was angry. "I didn't recommend release."

"Why?"

"I don't think she's ready." She wasn't going to go into detail with him on the phone.

"I work with that woman day in, day out and I think she's ready." Dave's voice rose. "You meet her for a few hours, say she isn't, and they listen to *you*? The day shift, you don't know nothing."

"Apparently the parole board don't agree."

"You patronising bitch!"

Cate sat up, knocking her knee on her desk. "Dave, we are both professionals. We both gave our opinions and…"

"Professionals, my arse. You weren't so fucking professional when you were opening your legs for Burgess, were you?"

Cate gasped. "That never happened."

"You would say that, wouldn't you? But he says different."

273

"Come on, Dave! He's just a kid."

Suddenly the line went quiet and Cate was aware of other noises, other voices in the background.

"You hear that, Burgess? She said you're just a kid and you don't have enough dick to satisfy her."

"Dave! Dave?"

But he wasn't talking to her anymore. Hearing the poisonous laughter coming down the receiver Cate realised that Callahan didn't care about Rose; he had set her up.

56

When Cate arrived at D Wing the landing was quiet. The inmates would be at their work or in lessons, and Mark Burgess was in the office with his feet on the desk and his eyes closed. She did not disturb him but continued to the far end of the corridor and stopped in front of Rose Wilks's cell door.

Cate knew that the Governor had told Rose that she would not be released. She would still be reeling from the news. Opening the viewing flap, she could see the shape of her on the bed, covered with a blanket. She selected the key from the chain at her waist and opened the door.

Rose didn't move. It occurred to Cate that she could be dead and she reached her hand for the place that looked like a shoulder. "Rose?"

The blanket was flung back and Rose was staring at her; her face was puffy and red but her eyes were dark. "I don't want you here."

"Rose, I know you're upset. I know you're angry with me."

Rose closed her eyes and pulled the blanket back over her head. She began rocking, the whole grey bundle shuddering on the narrow bed. A muffled sound came from her, which Cate couldn't make out.

"Rose?" Touching her shoulder again, she tentatively lifted the blanket. "Rose?"

She was curled around an object, and Cate saw her hands were cupping something. It looked like a pile of twigs. "Rose, are you okay?"

"I don't like fire," she said, whispering with her eyes still closed. "It scares me."

"Yes," said Cate, soothing her.

"I've always hated fire. When I was twelve I burned down a disused beach hut with a group of kids from school. They ran while I stood rooted to the spot, hooked by the leaping flames. It terrified me."

"Okay, Rose." She was rambling and dazed. Cate thought about calling for Mark, asking him to send for Officer Todd from the hospital unit.

"I've always smoked. Even when I was pregnant. It calmed me down, I'd peel back the fold of silver foil, releasing the smell of the cigs. Even holding the white and purple box relaxed me."

Silk Cut. The brand of cigarettes that had started the fire in the Hatcher family home. Was Rose about to finally admit her guilt? She continued to rock herself, eyes closed, as Cate stroked her back.

"Luke was so still in my arms, head nestled to my chest. And then I heard her."

"Who? Emma?"

"I heard her. Having sex."

Cate thought back to the witness statements. "But Emma was sleeping alone."

Rose muffled her face into the thin pillow, howling. "Luke, your beautiful boy. Oh Jason…"

"What is it, Rose? Tell me."

"With Luke still in my arms I went into the hall. I could hear the noises coming from Emma. Loud and noisy, and then I heard him."

"Dominic?"

"I heard Jason. My Jason. Saying her name."

Cate stopped moving her hand, stunned. "Jason was with Emma that night?"

"I stood and listened. She'd promised me she'd stay away from him; we'd made a bargain. I'd gone to say goodbye. But she'd lied when she said she wouldn't see Jason. He was there."

"So is that why you started the fire?"

"Oh Luke! How wonderful, to never wake. To never again feel pain or loss or grief."

"Rose?"

"I put Luke back into his cot. I left the house, I felt like burning the place down, but I didn't."

"So the fire started after you left? It was Emma or Jason who dropped the cigarette. Why didn't you tell the police that?"

Rose's rocking intensified.

Cate sat back on the cell floor, slowly realising what had happened. She had assessed Rose as dangerous because she had never accepted responsibility, but this was because she was innocent. The fire was started after she left, by Emma or Jason, and they had both let Rose take the blame.

Cate recalled Jason's anger and his sobbing, his repeated mantra, *What have you done*? Emma coming to the prison: *I want you to recommend release.*

Rose's voice was whiny and weak, her rocking erratic. "He was so peaceful. Wherever he went, Joel is there too. My two boys, side by side. With Mum, with Rita. Safe. I'm too tired for this."

This was suicidal talk. Cate propelled herself up and out of the cell.

In the office Mark was still snoozing. She knocked his feet off the table.

"Cate! What are…"

"Rose needs medical help. She's having some kind of breakdown."

But Mark wasn't listening. He was staring at Cate with a look of contempt. "You made me look like an idiot."

"Oh shit, Mark, not now. I'm worried about Rose."

"After what you said I've been the laughing stock round here."

"Mark, I'm sorry…but can we talk about this later, we really need to help Rose."

"You made a fool of me."

"And I regret it. But you've got to let it go. We'll be working together for a good while, so we need to get over it."

"Easy for you to say. You don't have Callahan and Holley on your back. Making out I'm not man enough to do it…"

"For Christ's sake, that's just bullshit. Come on, Mark, you're better than that!"

"Am I?" He looked up, shyly. *He's just a kid.*

"I want us to be friends, Mark. Let's work together. Because right now I need you. Rose needs you."

Mark sat straight, as if called to attention.

"She's not well. I think she might be psychotic."

"She's always been strange. Maybe not getting parole pushed her over the edge?"

"We need to act fast, Mark, before she does something stupid to herself or someone else. Call Officer Todd. Get her to come over from the hospital unit."

Turning on her heels, Cate returned to Rose's cell.

Rose was on her back, swaying from side to side, her eyes were open. She was talking as if to some vision in front of her.

"Oh, Joel, Joel. Forgive me. It was only you I wanted. If only I'd been able to keep you, if only you were alive."

Cate put an arm around Rose. "I've just asked for some help to come. I think you need a doctor."

"Tears and the heat. The dead boy in my arms."

"Rose, what are you talking about? You said you'd already left the house when Luke died?"

"Here," Rose looked at Cate and pulled something from under her body. It was a black notebook. "You have this. You read it. It's no use to me now."

Mark appeared at the cell door with Officer Todd by his side. He nodded to Cate, and took over.

"Help is here, Rose, you'll be okay now."

57

Cate opened the small black book and read:

Dear Jason, didn't you wonder why I took the blame for your crime?

This letter, this final letter in my Black Book will break your heart. It breaks mine.

You kept silent all these years, and let me take the blame for Luke's death. I heard you together. I saw the cigarettes on the table in the kitchen. I'll never know which of you lit that cigarette, but it wasn't me. I accepted the punishment because of Luke. Knowledge is a burden, which you'll have to carry now. I can't protect you from the truth.

In my cell, Luke and Joel visit me. They've been alive in my arms and safe from harm, my sweet boys, safe from harm.

The blackbirds are nesting, and no magpie can hurt them now.

I only have seagulls, but where is the nest? They don't seem to have any home.

I'd just discovered that Luke was your son. I was holding him, seeing him closely for the first time. His golden-red hair, just like yours. I knew then that you'd betrayed me, not just once, but many times. I was angry. I was hurt.

You never loved me, but you loved Joel. And I didn't know what to do with my anger. Lying there in his incubator, he was so small, so vulnerable. His tiny limbs, purple against the white of the over-large nametag bearing his name – Baby Wilks. The tag was to stop another woman taking him, to stop confusion over whether he was really mine. In those moments, looking into the incubator, he seemed so far from me. You loved him, I had seen how much. You didn't love me. You had betrayed me.

My love for Joel wasn't the fleeting love most mothers have for their sons, quickly forgotten when they come home muddy or truant from school. My own mother's love wasn't strong. She was so weak, so ill, that she barely noticed Peter or me. She took her own life, leaving us in the dark. I would never do that to my baby.

As I watched Joel I knew that at that moment, in that instance, my poorly, vulnerable son was loved as much as he ever could be. He was dependent on me in a way he never would be again. It was a moment of perfect love, of total devotion. If you had the choice, wouldn't you end your life at a point when you were loved so totally, so truly, that it could not be surpassed? Wouldn't it be the most perfect moment to die?

What a gift I gave my precious boy, he wouldn't suffer anymore. My hand went into the incubator and found his soft flesh, his bones visible under the thin skin. I stroked him, he opened his eyes and saw me, he knew. No pain, no tears, no grief.

And you, Jason.

I placed my palm, larger than his face, over his mouth and nose and cupped his delicate features. Snuffed out, like a candle. So quickly, so peacefully. When I started to cry and yell, the nurse ran from where she had been chatting in the corridor. She pushed me aside and I started to shake. This would teach you, *I thought.* This is your fault.

The nurses shouted, the doctors ran, and in the chaos my little boy was punctured with needles and pressed hard on the chest, his tiny face covered with a mask.

I walked out of the room. I wanted to remember his stillness, not their futile attempts at resuscitation.

It was hard afterwards, and I never stopped hating you for what you made me do, even when I had no choice but to love you. Then came the doubt. Those were the bad days.

When I saw Luke, I thought he could save me. A chance to love your son, to heal the pain I felt.

I killed Joel to hurt you. Just for one moment to be in control, for you to be the one who had a broken heart.

That's why I had to serve the sentence for your crime.

Cate heard a wailing noise coming from outside and looked out of the cell window to the courtyard where Rose was being led to the medical centre flanked by Mark and Officer Todd. She was bent double like a newly bereaved mother, finally giving in to her grief and guilt. Locked up for four years already and two more to come for a crime she hadn't committed, and forever haunted by the crime she had.

Cate closed the book. As she took a step something snapped under her foot and, bending down, she saw it was a tiny birds nest, crushed on the floor. She gently collected the twigs together, holding it in the palm of her hands, realising that this was what Rose had been holding.

She pushed the twigs carefully back into place, restoring its perfect symmetry. A home once again.